DEEP WATERS

Patricia Hall

This first world edition published 2016
in Great Britain and the USA by
SEVERN HOUSE PUBLISHERS LTD of
19 Cedar Road, Sutton, Surrey, England, SM2 5DA.
Trade paperback edition first published
in Great Britain and the USA 2016 by
SEVERN HOUSE PUBLISHERS LTD

British Library Cataloguing in Publication Data
A CIP catalogue record for this title is available from the British Library.

ISBN-13: 978-0-7278-8605-7 (cased)
ISBN-13: 978-1-84751-707-4 (trade paper)
ISBN-13: 978-1-78010-768-4 (e-book)

Typeset by Palimpsest Book Production Ltd.,
Falkirk, Stirlingshire, Scotland.

DEEP WATERS

ONE

Detective Sergeant Harry Barnard lounged on one of the plush banquettes which lined the embossed walls of the Delilah Club. His sodden raincoat lay on the seat beside him, with his trilby on top looking sadly diminished by the rain. On the table in front of him the ice in a generous Scotch was slowly melting, and the ash on his cigarette drooped precariously, threatening to drop on to the carpet at any moment. But his gaze was fixed on the young man in dark trousers and a crumpled white shirt sitting opposite him, his face pale and his eyes anxious as he twirled his own cigarette between his fingers nervously. The air in the dimly lit room was still thick with smoke and alcohol fumes from the previous night's activities. A couple of cleaners were desultorily emptying ash trays and wiping rings off the glass-topped tables.

'You must know how long it is since you saw your boss,' Barnard said irritably, thinking that the hair of the dog was failing to produce its usual magic this morning. 'How does he pay you? In cash? Have you seen him since your last payday?'

'He usually comes in Thursdays to do the books,' the young barman, who had only reluctantly admitted to the name Spike, muttered. 'But the manager brought our pay packets round last Thursday. Late, as it happened. About nine in the evening, after the place had begun to fill up. The cleaners were still hanging around wondering where the hell their money was. No one was best pleased.' He glanced around the bar anxiously. 'I was busy already. We had a gang of Americans in and they generally start early. I was shaking bizarre cocktails and looking for extra bottles of Bourbon. Wondered if I'd actually get paid that night at all. Or if any of us would.'

'And the manager is?'

Barnard had known Ray Robertson's managers at the Delilah for years, as the club established itself as a West End institution, part of Barnard's manor as a Vice Squad detective and part of

Robertson's dubious empire of clubs, sporting management and worse that stretched from the East End – where they had both grown up – to West London, where Ray had got a bloody nose in the process of trying to expand his empire into West Indian territory. But Barnard knew there had been changes very lately, and wondered if he had slipped up in not making himself known to the new man in charge at the Delilah and not finding out exactly what was keeping Ray Robertson occupied. Ray was not a man to take holidays if there was any chance of making any sort of a profit, legal or illegal.

In happier times he would have seen Ray himself over the last couple of weeks, maintaining the uneasy relationship that raised eyebrows in CID but which went back far too far into their wartime boyhood in East London to be lightly cast aside now they had taken their places on opposite side of the legal fence. But Barnard knew Ray had been deeply shaken by an attempt on his life by his own brother and might understandably be licking his wounds, physical and mental, well away from his usual haunts and his formidable mother who blamed him with Biblical intransigence for the fact that brother Georgie was awaiting trial for murder. On the other hand, Ray was just as likely be up to his eyes in new mischief of his own. But now Barnard's own boss wanted to talk to Ray and would not take no for an answer. One way or another, DS Barnard knew he had to deliver.

'What time does he come in, this manager? New, isn't he?'

'Yeah,' Spike said reluctantly. 'Been here a couple of months. Name of Stan Clarke.' He glanced at his watch. 'Should be in soon.'

'Well, get me another of these,' Barnard said, knocking back his drink and waving the glass in the barman's direction. 'I'll wait. Stan Clarke must know where Ray is.'

'Maybe,' Spike said noncommittally.

Barnard sipped his second drink more slowly, well aware he had best not breathe too many alcohol fumes over DCI Keith Jackson, a deeply puritanical Scot who had been appointed to root out corruption in CID only to be floored, temporarily at least, by the discovery of corruption at much higher reaches of the Met than the Vice Squad. He had not told Barnard precisely why he wanted to talk to Ray Robertson, and Barnard had not been able to pick up any inkling of his motive on the canteen grapevine. But in the light of recent scandals he knew it was politic to do as he was told without any argument. If he had ever been able to protect Ray, that time was past. The debt he owed him for protection from bullies and worse when as boys they were East End neighbours and went to the same school, and then became confused evacuees together on a farm, must by now have been well and truly settled. They had taken different roads and there was no going back. They both had other fish to fry.

It was another half hour before Stan Clarke turned up and Spike pointed him in Barnard's direction. The manager glanced across the dimly lit room then wove between the tables and a cleaner wielding a Hoover, with manic enthusiasm now the boss was here. Barnard could see that his expression was far from friendly. He was a bulky man, his blue suit too tight around his broad shoulders, his dark hair greasy and straggling over his collar. This was Ray's flagship venue, the place where he had always pursued his social ambitions with lavish parties and galas for a clientele that reached deep into the social and political establishment. Clarke looked as if he would be hard pushed to organize a piss-up in a brewery, and Barnard wondered if recent scandals had finally put paid to Ray's playboy ambitions among those who were no more than fair-weather friends out to get what they could from Robertson while able to associate with him safely. That time, he thought, might be almost over.

'Spike says you want to talk to me,' Clarke said before sitting down heavily across the table from Barnard. 'And you are?' Barnard flicked his warrant card in Clarke's direction and the manager's face darkened.

'I was looking for Ray Robertson,' Barnard said, his voice as uncompromising as his expression. 'My guv'nor wants a word. Your barman says he hasn't been in for a while. Do you know where he is?' Clarke shrugged, his eyes blank.

'No idea,' he said. 'Said he needed a break and would be away for a couple of weeks.

He left me in charge here and I've not heard from him since. Left the cash for the wages in a special account.'

'I don't think he's taken a holiday in living memory,' Barnard objected. 'He didn't give you a clue where he was headed? Was he going abroad?'

'He just said he needed a break,' Clarke said. 'Could have been Clacton. Could have been the so-called Costa Brava for all I know.'

'Did he say he was going to Spain?'

'He didn't say where he was going,' Clarke said. 'I told you. But it's not as if he's short of a bob, is it? They tell me Spain's getting to be all the rage these days. Can't say I fancy it. All that oily food and no decent beer.' Clarke's face twisted with a resentment that had Barnard's antennae twitching. He wondered how this unprepossessing specimen had persuaded Ray to give him a job.

'And you've not heard from him since when?' he snapped.

'Ten days maybe. I didn't expect an effing postcard. He told me to carry on as normal and left the wages in the bank for me to sign for.' Barnard sighed. He was puzzled and slightly alarmed, but he didn't think Clarke was going to tell him anything useful. He picked up his coat and hat and put them on, grimacing slightly at their sodden state.

'If Mr Robertson gets in touch, you can get me at the nick,' he said. 'In the meantime, I'll get the Essex police to see if he's at home.'

'Yeah, he told me he had a house out in the sticks somewhere,' Clarke said. 'Says he's thinking of putting in a swimming pool.' The sneer was implicit in Clarke's expression.

'Keep in touch,' Barnard said sharply. 'My guv'nor doesn't like being thwarted. If I don't hear from you, I'll be back.'

Outside the rain had eased. As he made his way towards Regent Street and the bustling crowds of shoppers he hesitated for a moment as a woman approached him, moving towards the Delilah with a determined look on her face. Smartly dressed in a fur-collared coat and a matching hat fashionably angled across her forehead supporting a wispy veil over startlingly red hair, she seemed to hesitate as she met Barnard's eyes. Then she swerved and moved quickly away, leaving the detective with a feeling that he should have recognized her. But he was unsure and, anyway, preoccupied. He had long ago lost count of the number of women he knew around the streets of Soho, very few of them a man could take home to meet mother. This one was no doubt no different if she was avoiding him, even if she was doing rather better for herself than most of the girls on the streets.

He glanced at his watch and decided he could reasonably stop for lunch before making his way back to the nick and could possibly pick up Kate O'Donnell from her office if she was free.

Before turning on his heel he glanced at the early billboards for the evening papers, which were following the first stages of the train robbers' trial out in Buckinghamshire. That eleven of them were in court less than six months after the robbery in the summer of '63 was, he supposed, something of a triumph for the police, but the way the papers were following the trial so avidly was more to do with the fact that the public had a sneaking admiration for the gang than with a desire to see justice done. It was the same with Ray Robertson. People knew he was a crook but they still admired his cheek.

He swung out of Regent Street and wove his way quickly into the labyrinth of narrow streets that had become his natural habitat since he joined Vice, a jungle of cafés and clubs, brothels and studios, where legitimate business and crime rubbed shoulders on narrow staircases and in elderly houses converted from homes into offices and the smartly dressed young women on the streets could be models or actresses, prostitutes or waitresses, and their men artists or poets or pimps. In Kate's case, she had improbably talked her way into a job as a photographer. And he had no less improbably talked a convent girl from Liverpool into his bed, although how long she would stay there he was never very sure. Nor was he sure whether that was what he wanted, if it was going to mean giving up on his freewheeling former life.

He clambered up the rickety wooden stairs to the Ken Fellows Agency in Frith Street and poked his head round the door without moving inside. Kate was sitting with her back to him, her unruly dark hair falling forward over her face as she concentrated on the jumble of photographs on her desk. He walked across the cluttered office, empty as usual when the photographers were out on assignment. The only light showing was in the glass cubicle where a shadow of the boss appeared to be on the phone.

'Isn't it lunchtime, Katie?' he said quietly and was flattered to see the smile she turned towards him.

'I thought you were busy this morning,' she said.

'I was, but got nowhere. I was looking for Ray Robertson but he seems to have abandoned the Delilah. I'll have to check out the gym later, but I've time for a coffee and a sandwich at the Blue Lagoon if you don't want to go to the pub.' He stood behind her while she shuffled the black-and-white prints she had been looking at into some sort of order.

'What are you working on?' he asked, realizing that some of the images looked familiar.

'The East Coast floods,' Kate said. 'Ken says they're opening some new housing development on Canvey Island in the summer and we should do a look-back at what happened in '53. I remember reading about it in the papers, but it didn't really register on our side of the country. No one had a television then, so not much film exists. But we should be able to sell something to one of the magazines, using still pictures. I'm going to trace some of the people who were there that night, see if I can do before-and-after pictures.' To her surprise, Barnard shuddered slightly as he flicked through the pictures.

'I was there,' he said quietly. 'I was in the army, doing my National Service, and we got drafted in to help. The awful thing was that I had an aunt living on Canvey, my mother's oldest sister. It turned out she drowned in her bungalow. The water filled the place up to the ceiling. She didn't have a chance, it happened so quickly and she wasn't very nimble.' Kate turned to him looking devastated.

'That's awful,' she said. 'And you were there? You saw it? Canvey Island was one of the worst places, wasn't it?' He nodded.

'I'll tell you about it later,' he said. 'Bring some of your pictures home tonight and I'll fill you in on stuff that never got into the papers. It was too grim to show. Come on. Get your coat and let's think about something more cheerful. I've got to gear myself up to talk to the DCI this afternoon. He reckons my contacts with the Robertson family are deeply suspect and he won't be too pleased with what I've got to report, which is exactly nothing. He probably won't believe a word I tell him.'

They walked up Frith Street together towards the Blue Lagoon, which had been one of their regular places ever since they first met. Back then, Kate's flatmate Marie Best had been working there with only half an eye on the coffee bar job and both eyes on her prospects of making it as an actress in the big city. Today something of Marie's final disillusion before she went back home seemed to hang in the steamy air as they ordered their cappuccinos and sandwiches and squeezed into the last remaining table.

'Don't let all that flood stuff get you down,' Barnard said. 'It's taken the sparkle out of your eyes. It happened a long time ago.'

'Not that long,' Kate said soberly. 'Not if you can remember it so clearly.'

'I had a personal reason to be upset,' Barnard said. 'It took a long time to recover all the bodies. My mother was going spare. Don't forget it wasn't long after the war. Parts of East London were still in ruins and there was a desperate shortage of houses. Why else would people have moved out to Canvey Island to live in what were not much more than summer beach houses? They were so flimsy that a lot of them were just washed away. People didn't stand a chance, especially if they were a bit old and infirm. They got washed away too.'

Kate looked at Barnard curiously. She had not often heard him make this sort of complaint, the sort of complaint she had heard often enough growing up in the slum housing of Liverpool's Scotland Road where German bombs had also fallen and it was not unusual to hear older people whisper that Hitler had done a few Scousers a favour by demolishing their rotting, bug-infested homes.

'I didn't know you felt so strongly,' she said quietly.

'The politicians keep on telling us the good times are coming back, but they were coming back pretty slowly then in the East End,' Barnard said. 'But come on, there's no reason why you should let all that history depress you. It was bad, but it is history now. If they're rebuilding something better on Canvey Island that's a good thing, isn't it? Cheer up, Kate. It wasn't the end of the world then and it's certainly not now. Tonight I'll see what I can remember that might help you and then we'll do something entirely different. OK?'

'OK,' Kate said. 'Is that a promise?'

'It certainly is,' Barnard said, getting to his feet reluctantly and kissing her on the cheek. 'You can bank on it.'

* * *

The rain had eased slightly by the time Barnard headed back to the nick. To his surprise, as he was waiting to cross at the traffic lights in Regent Street he noticed the smartly dressed woman he had seen heading towards the Delilah Club. This time she slowed down and took a place beside him on the kerb, waiting for the stream of cars to stop.

'Don't you recognize me, Harry?' she asked. 'I remember you from years ago.' She pushed the flimsy mesh of her veil up and gave him a knowing smile. With a slight shock of recognition he realized that he did know her, although it must have been ten or fifteen years since he'd last seen her.

'Loretta?' he said tentatively. 'Loretta Robertson? Where have you been hiding yourself all this time?'

'Not Robertson any more, darling,' she said, putting a proprietorial hand on his arm. 'But you know all that. You were around when Ray and me had our big bust-up, weren't you?'

'On and off,' Barnard said, taking her arm firmly off his sleeve and steering her across the road with a hand on her back. 'I'd just joined the Met and was a probationer out in the sticks, in South London. Ray wasn't best pleased with me either at the time. He took it as a personal insult when I joined the force after my two years in the army. But I had a pretty good idea where I'd end up if I hung around with Ray and Georgie.'

'He took everything as a personal insult if it didn't go his way,' Loretta said. 'You don't have to tell me that. I lived with it for a good few years before we split up. And Georgie was a complete psycho. I was scared to death of him. He reckoned that the fact that I was his sister-in-law was a challenge rather than a deterrent. Bastard.'

'So what are you doing in the West End?' Barnard asked, with an appreciative glance at her obviously pricey clothes and carefully made-up face. 'You're looking pretty good.' Loretta flashed him another smile, as much encouraging as affectionate, and pulled her veil down again, concealing her eyes.

'I was looking for Ray as it happens,' she said. 'I thought I'd catch him at the Delilah but they said he hasn't been in there this week. Does he still have the house out Epping way? He bought that house for me, you know. Said he wanted me to be somewhere away from the East End.'

'As far as I know he's still got it,' Barnard said, not too surprised that Ray had wanted to keep his beautiful new wife well away from his growing criminal empire. In fact that house was something he had intended to check up on before he talked to the DCI. If Ray Robertson had decided to lie low for a while, that would be as good a place as any to do it. Maybe he could fit in a trip to Epping later in the day.

'It's a long way out,' Loretta said, looking sulky. 'I thought I might catch him here, up West.' Barnard slowed down as they approached the nick.

'Well, as it happens I want to talk to Ray too. Why don't you give me a call at the nick on Monday and I'll let you know whether I've tracked him down or not. What's your surname now?' He scribbled the number on a Blue Lagoon receipt he found in his pocket. Loretta looked at it dubiously for a moment and then put it in her bag. She did not, he noted, make any attempt to give him her current surname.

'Is it anything I can help you with?' he asked, pausing just round the corner from the station. He was not confident that Loretta was someone who he wanted to be seen with until he knew a bit more about why she wanted to find her former husband so urgently and, it seemed, anonymously.

'No thanks, Harry. I don't think so. But it's good to see you again. I'll call you Monday to see if you've tracked that old bastard of mine down.' Barnard shrugged and planted a chaste kiss on her cheek, rewarded by a waft of perfume which was obviously not cheap. Barnard stood and watched as Loretta spun on her heel and made her way back towards Regent Street, her hips swaying provocatively above her stiletto heels, her skirt fashionably short and tight, and her hair a definite red where it had once been dark. Fashion, he thought, was a whole new world in 1964 and would give puritans like his boss a whole new raft of worries as they convinced themselves that the younger generation was heading to perdition.

Loretta had worn well and could just about carry off the mini-skirt. But she was an enigma and if she was being as well looked after as she appeared to be he wondered exactly why she wanted to talk so urgently to a man who had not been her husband for at least six or seven years. To his surprise, she did not disappear into the crowd of shoppers but got into a car parked close to the entrance to the Delilah and drove away smartly, heading towards Piccadilly Circus. He couldn't see the number plate as she immediately overtook a bus.

She looks as if she has fallen on her feet, he thought, and wondered what she wanted with her ex. It didn't seem there was much Ray Robertson could offer her that was not already being provided by someone else.

DCI Keith Jackson did not seem to be in a happy mood when Barnard reported back to him that afternoon. He steepled his hands under his chin and glared at Barnard as he listened to him outlining Robertson's unusually prolonged absence from the Delilah Club.

'But he's got this house in Epping, you say?'

'The local nick tells me he still owns it but they don't reckon he uses it very often, guv. They gave me a phone number but I got no reply,' Barnard said. 'They obviously don't treat him as a local villain. As far as I can remember, he bought the place for his wife. I don't think he used it much himself and I was surprised he'd kept the place on so long after his marriage broke up.'

'Keep trying, and ask the local nick to send a car up there, see if there's any sign of life. I'm surprised you don't know where he actually lives. I thought he was some sort of friend of yours.'

'Not a friend, guv,' Barnard said firmly. 'Not now. Not since we were kids and certainly not since I joined the force. He didn't think much of that move.'

'So you say,' Jackson said sharply, with a chilly disbelief in his eyes that Barnard had totally failed to eliminate since Jackson arrived to run Vice in the wake of a seriously dubious DCI.

'Ray's been a useful contact over the years,' Barnard shot back.

'So long as you're always clear who's paying who, and you're the one who benefits from the arrangement,' Jackson snapped. 'Have you been out to this house of Robertson's recently?'

'Not for years, guv. I've usually seen him at the club, or at his gym in Whitechapel. I could check that out later if you like, but it's not a place he'd be holed up in. He likes his creature comforts, does Ray. He'd be more likely to be at the Ritz than at the gym. You could keep a low profile in a smart hotel for months if you were able to afford it. And there doesn't seem to be much that Ray Robertson can't afford.'

'The Yard's worried that friends of his brother might still try to nobble him before the trial,' Jackson said, his eyes cold. 'It goes against the grain to offer protection to the likes of Robertson, but apparently that's what the Yard thinks we may have to do.'

'I should think Ray's quite capable of looking after himself,' Barnard said. 'He's been around for a long time.' He hesitated for a moment, wondering just how much he should pass on about the alluring Loretta. He decided he had better come clean. Reticence was not a quality DCI Jackson much appreciated.

'I bumped into his ex-wife coming away from the Delilah Club this morning,' he said at length. 'I hadn't seen her for years, but apparently she's looking for him too.'

'Did she say why?' Jackson snapped.

'No, she was being very cagey,' Barnard said. 'I asked her to contact me if she got anywhere.'

'When was the divorce?' Jackson asked, his distaste for the very idea easily readable in his eyes, the Scots Calvinist never far below the surface. Barnard often wondered if his boss had been given the Soho job because he was so unlikely to be seduced by its raffish charms.

'The divorce? Years ago, guv,' Barnard said. 'It didn't sound as if she'd been in contact with him much since then. And it certainly didn't look as if she was short of a bob or three.'

'And what about Robertson's mother? Have you spoken to her?'

'Not yet,' Barnard said. 'But I will, though I don't think she and Ray are on speaking terms any more. Not since Georgie.'

'Check her out,' Jackson said. 'And keep me up to date. The brass want to wrap him up in cotton wool until the trial, so we'll have to go along with it. With your history you have to be well placed to find him, so get on with it.'

'Guv,' Barnard said, ignoring the sinking feeling in his stomach. But he knew that however this assignment turned out it would do his future in the Met no good at all. He would get the blame if Ray Robertson was in deep trouble, and get little in the way of credit if he tracked him down successfully. He would simply be thought to be covering his own back. And not for the first time, the words 'poisoned chalice' sprang to mind.

TWO

Kate O'Donnell let herself into Harry Barnard's flat after standing on the crowded Northern Line to Archway station and then walking slowly up Highgate Hill and off into the steep streets to the right, carrying an increasingly heavy briefcase full of pictures and Press cuttings. She envied Harry the ease with which he swooped up and down these hills in his red Capri. She wondered vaguely if he would teach her to drive if she asked him nicely, or whether he was as prejudiced about women drivers as many men she knew. She sighed, paused to hitch her case into the other hand, and plodded on.

She had been surprised to discover that Harry had actually witnessed the floods she was researching. If he talked at all about his earlier life, which was rarely, it had been mainly about growing up as a small child in the teeming streets of the pre-war East End and then, during the war, witnessing the havoc caused by Hitler's bombs. He always looked slightly surprised when she told him that her native Liverpool had lived through similar harsh times. Londoners, she had thought more than once, seemed oblivious to the toll the war had taken anywhere else.

Back then, Barnard had spent a couple of years as an evacuee on a farm in the country where he and the Robertson brothers had been thrown together, sent to the country for safety as the bombs rained down on the docks and factories and huddled homes of East London. Later he must, she knew, have served his two years in the forces – compulsory National Service, which had continued for years after the war ended and had only recently been phased out. But he had never mentioned it. There was, she suspected, a great deal Harry Barnard never chose to talk about.

The flat was chilly and she switched on the heating before taking off her coat. Central heating was something she had not yet come to terms with. Back home it was still smoky coal fires or nothing and she had gone to sleep many a time as a child under a pile of coats. She made herself a cup of tea in Barnard's shiny modern kitchen and sat down to drink it in his favourite revolving chair. As far as the rest of the world was concerned she still shared a flat in Shepherd's Bush with Tess Farrell, the other old friend she had come from Liverpool to London with, all of them eager to try their luck in the capital. Her mother and Catholic family in Liverpool could not have coped with the truth of where she was really living. She smiled to herself. It wasn't so easy to ask the parish priest to talk to young women who strayed when the young woman was two hundred miles away.

Marie had gone back home eventually, her hopes of an acting career dashed after endless rounds of auditions left her disillusioned. But Kate and Tess had settled down together amicably enough until Kate, despite many doubts, had let herself be persuaded to move in with Barnard, who had a comfortable flat in Highgate which Kate wondered whether he could afford. She still had her doubts about her future with the sergeant and still paid her share of the rent for the West London flat, popping in now and again to see Tess and pick up her meagre post.

She suspected she was becoming too comfortable with Harry Barnard, who was unfailingly generous but still showed no inclination to buy her the ring that her family at home would certainly have expected if they'd known how she was living. But they were a long way away and for the most part she put them out of her mind, only taking the precaution of swearing Tess to secrecy if she happened to go north for a visit. For the moment she had no intention of doing that herself and in the dark reaches of the night, awake in Harry Barnard's warm bed, she persuaded herself that the long train journey would continue to insulate her from Merseyside and her family's traditionally moral expectations.

She sighed and finished her tea and got up to spread out her photographs on the shiny beech dining table. Many of them were dark and grainy, taken by amateurs long before the rest of the country learned of the massive storm surge that had swept south down the North Sea and overwhelmed low-lying coastal areas inexorably one after the other. Canvey Island was one of the last places to be engulfed and most of the population were already asleep in bed on that Saturday night when the water swept in. By the time the alarm could be raised, the damage had been done and more than fifty had drowned. When more professional photo-graphs had been taken later the next day the devastation became clear in the wintry light of a blustery Sunday morning, the sea still rough although the tide had receded and allowed the flood levels to drop.

Stunned survivors turned weary eyes on the rescuers who for so many had come far too late. Canvey Island itself, which had access by a single bridge to the mainland, had been completely evacuated later that day and the next, leaving behind a landscape of mud and water, floating rubbish and dead animals amongst the remnants of small often flimsy homes to which many East Londoners had retired to be close to the sea. What no one had realized before was that Canvey was so low-lying that in spite of its sea walls a combination of a very high tide and a very high wind from the North Sea could overwhelm it entirely.

Kate sighed again and pushed the photographs into a heap as she heard Barnard's key in the lock. She turned in her chair and gave him a slight smile.

'This is all very depressing,' she said. 'I'm not sure I should have brought the pictures back. It must have been dreadful to be there.' When he had hung up his coat and hat, Barnard stood behind her and held her shoulders.

'You mustn't make yourself miserable about something that happened ten years ago,' he said. 'I'll have a look at what you've got and tell you what happened when I was drafted down there, and then we'll go out for something to eat. That little Italian place in Hampstead? Will that do?'

He put the Kinks on the radiogram, newcomers to the charts and their newest passion, and turned the volume down from loud to moderate, before sitting at the table beside her and beginning to sort through the pictures she had collected. But Kate could see that looking at these graphic reminders of what for him must have been a traumatic few days was having its effect on him too.

'We got drafted there on the Sunday evening,' he said quietly. 'By that time they'd decided to evacuate the whole island, because the sea walls had been breached and although the water went down at low tide it was going to rise again every high tide. Anyway, very few of the buildings were habitable. Only brick or stone-built structures were usable, at least upstairs. Like the pub.

What was it called? The Red Cow, I think. There was no power, no phone lines, and sewage and debris everywhere.

'At first the rescue effort was just local volunteers, the Sally Army, St John Ambulance, people like that, and anyone who had a boat. When we got there we were supposed to be filling sandbags to keep the sea out, but even that was slow to get started. I managed to hitch a ride on a boat that was going to where my aunt lived, just under the sea wall. But the wall had been more or less washed away at that point. She had just a little holiday house really, very flimsy, which they'd used since before the war, but it had gone. After my uncle died, she went to live there permanently. Some of the houses had been lifted up by the water and dumped down again, but hers had disappeared completely and her with it.

'Later I trawled through the lists of survivors in case she'd got out in time, but I couldn't find her name. They found her body on the Monday, when they were evacuating, and did a thorough search to see if anyone was still trapped anywhere. But I don't think they found anyone alive. If they hadn't drowned, they would have died of exposure by then. Some people were standing up to their chests in the water for hours and small children died of the cold. That first day I waded back to where my platoon was working and got a bollocking for going off on my own. But I had to make sure. I needed to tell my mother I'd done the best I could. I couldn't get even a day's leave to go and tell her. She had no phone. I had to ring the police station and ask them to go round. She never really got over it. A lot of people affected never did.'

'It must have been dreadful,' Kate said, putting her hand over his.

'You've no idea. People's whole lives were just floating around in a sea of mud and sewage – dead animals, furniture, the wreckage of those flimsy holiday houses. No one could have stayed there. They evacuated more than ten thousand people in the end. And I think one of the worst things for the people was that no one knew what was going on. Phone lines were down, the civil defence teams that were there during the war had been more or less disbanded, the police were overwhelmed, they had to call in the army. Even the Americans GIs stationed in Essex came in to help. In the end they requisitioned every bus and car and lorry in the area to get the people out. A lot of them had lost everything.'

'Were you there long?'

'Two or three weeks. Sandbags became the priority because there was another very high tide due a couple of weeks after the flood and the sea defences were smashed to buggery. I'm not sure how many I filled but it seemed to go on and on from dawn till dark. Then we fell into bed and started again as soon as it was light enough. It's not something you ever forget. It was a shambles. Repair teams couldn't get in to restore the phones or the power. No one knew who was alive and who was dead, sometimes for days. I got sent over to Foulness Island a few days later on a small boat. Foulness is right at the end of the peninsula, very remote at the best of times. It's used by the forces for firing practice, but there are civilians there too, a village, farms, even a church and a pub. No one had heard a word from the four hundred people there, and RAF planes had gone over and seen no sign of life. They assumed they'd all drowned. But when we finally got out there by boat all but two were OK. They just hadn't been able to make contact with anyone.'

Kate sighed and shuffled her pictures into a rough-and-ready heap.

'I'll have to go down there tomorrow to talk to the people who went back for my captions,' she said. 'See what they think about the rebuilding. See if they feel safe now.'

'A lot never went back,' Barnard said. He smiled slightly. 'The National Service intake before mine got sent to Korea and we thought we were lucky to be stationed at home. But we got the East Coast floods instead. I'm not sure I wouldn't rather have been fighting the commies. People say they dreamed about the things they saw in the Blitz for years afterwards. I sometimes still dream about what I saw that weekend. You wouldn't believe water could be so quick and so deadly.'

Kate stuffed the pictures back into her case.

'Shall we go and eat? I'll go to Canvey Island tomorrow morning.'

'Southend train to Benfleet,' Barnard said. 'You can walk over the famous bridge from there. Tomorrow I've got to track down Ray Robertson, who seems to have gone AWOL just when the

DCI wants to see him urgently though he won't tell me exactly why. He just flannels about him needing protection but I've no idea from what. So let's eat and talk about something more cheerful, shall we, sweetie? Eat, drink and be merry, my dad used to say, for tomorrow we die. You never know when the sea is going to come through the window and drown you.'

'We mustn't forget to watch the new music programme that's on TV this week,' she said as they got into the car. 'What's it called? "Top of the Pops"? Maybe the Kinks will be on.'

'Maybe even the Beatles if they're back from the States.' Kate laughed delightedly.

'Who'd have thought it when we were at art college together, me and John Lennon. He's a funny lad is John. Maybe it'll cheer the Yanks up after what happened last year. My mam was made up when they elected one of our own for president. Half of Liverpool was looking for connections to the Kennedys in the old country, and the other half where dead jealous. My sister said my mam cried for a week after he was shot.'

'As I said,' Barnard said quietly. 'You never know when the sea will break through the windows.'

'And isn't that the truth?' Kate said.

Harry Barnard left early the following morning, flinging Kate a kiss before he went out. She lay in bed listening to his car door slam, and the growl of the engine as he accelerated down the hill towards Archway with his usual verve.

Before she set off to catch the train she planned to take from Fenchurch Street to Benfleet, she called Ken Fellows to confirm that he still wanted her to follow up the picture research she'd done the day before. By then Barnard was already in Whitechapel, where the traffic was still light. He knew that Ray Robertson's gym opened early to cater for anyone who wanted to spend time training before going to work and he reckoned that even if Ray was not there himself – which was only too likely – someone might know where he had gone to ground. It was not like Ray, he thought, to drop out of sight. His whole *modus operandi* was to make himself conspicuous in his legitimate and illegitimate activities, both his extravagant social events for boxing aficionados and his upfront and apparently untouchable dodgy schemes that dominated Soho and parts of the East End. In spite of all his troubles, Ray still regarded himself as the king of Soho and the fact that he had apparently not been seen for at least a week filled Barnard with anxiety.

He parked outside the gym and was even more alarmed to see that the street door was closed and that there didn't seem to be any lights inside. But when he tried the door he found it unlocked. Cautiously he pushed it open and listened to the echoing silence before feeling for the light switch. Even then, at first he could neither see nor hear anything wrong. The boxing ring in the centre of the room lay empty and undisturbed, the punchbags hung unmoving on their chains, the benches and skipping ropes and gloves were tidily put away, Ray's glassed-off office was unlit, and the usual odour of leather and old sweat hit his nostrils with its familiar tang. But there was something else, something familiar and sweetly menacing from which he physically flinched.

He pushed his trilby to the back of his head and, breathing hard, headed towards the office. Beyond a curtained alcove that housed a sink, he glanced through the half-open door of the bathroom and found what he more than half expected to find, though it still came as a shock like a blow to the stomach, something you never got used to. Lying in a pool of blood on the bathroom floor was the body not of Ray Robertson, as he had feared, but of his trainer, Rod Miller, who had worked for Robertson ever since he opened his gym fifteen years ago or more. This was the man who had bullied and cajoled a young Barnard to push himself further and further at a time when Robertson had convinced both himself and the seventeen-year-old Harry that he had serious talent with his fists.

The sergeant took a deep breath, which only confirmed that Miller had been dead for some time. He turned away, leaving the body untouched, and kicked the bathroom door closed before he doused his face in cold water from the tap at the sink in the alcove, drying himself on a grubby towel as years of training and experience slowly kicked in.

'Jesus wept!' he muttered as he walked back across the gym, closing the street door behind him, and slumped into the driving seat of his red Capri. He took several deep breaths before he

picked up the radio and called the nick and asked to be put through
to DCI Jackson.

'We've got a problem, guv,' he said when he was connected.
'I'm at Ray Robertson's gym. He's not there, but his trainer is
and he's dead. Looks like a single shot to the head, although
there's a lot of blood. He's soaked in it. It looks like an execu-
tion, but why the hell anyone would want to execute Rod Miller
I haven't the faintest idea. I'll wait here in case anyone else turns
up and tries to get in.'

'Don't move,' Jackson snapped. 'If anyone turns up, ask them to
wait. And if they argue, arrest them. I'll talk to the Yard and then
be on my way.'

Barnard slumped back into the car, lit a cigarette, and turned
the radio on. From where he had parked, he could see the whole
of the narrow thoroughfare in both directions and he was careful
not to allow himself to close his eyes. He needed to tackle anyone
who arrived at the door to the gym and in the end his patience
was rewarded when a burly man in the stained clothes of a market
porter strolled up the street from Whitechapel Road, his rolling
gait weary or possibly inebriated. Barnard knew the pubs opened
early for the market men. The porter stopped beside the red car,
clearly admiring it.

Barnard opened his door and got out.

'Nice motor, isn't it?' he said.

'I thought for a minute it was Ray Robertson's latest toy,' the
man said. 'He doesn't stint himself, does he?'

'Have you seen him lately?' Barnard asked. 'I was waiting
for him.'

'Nah,' the man said. 'I don't often see him. I go to bed when
I get home and start work at four in the effing morning.'

'Anyone else you've seen around lately?' Barnard persisted.
'The place is empty at the moment.'

'It's been quiet,' the man said. 'Though I did see a woman
trying the door last week. Dolled up like Lady Muck, she was.
When she saw I'd noticed her she scarpered. Got into a car
sharpish and drove away.'

'Did you notice what sort of car?' The man looked at Barnard
suspiciously.

'You the old bill or somethink?' he asked.

'I am, as it goes,' Barnard admitted. 'Looks like there's been some trouble here. Can you describe this woman?'

'Mutton dressed as lamb. Had a hat on, but that's about all I remember. I didn't take that much notice.'

'And the car?'

'Green, I think. You don't see many cars round here, do you? Not as smart as yours, but not a banger either.' The man hesitated and then pointed to one of the terraced houses across the street.

'Number eighty-two,' he said reluctantly. 'Name of Bradley.'

'We may need to talk to you again, Mr Bradley,' Barnard said. 'Thanks for your help.'

'Don't wake me up, son,' Bradley said. 'I need my beauty sleep.'

DCI Keith Jackson arrived with a convoy of marked cars, which also brought uniformed officers, the police doctor and forensic specialists with it. Barnard got out of his own car and was greeted with an icy glare from his boss, who opened the door of the gym and beckoned him inside ahead of the pack.

'Show me,' he said and Barnard guided him past the dim alcove to the bathroom where Miller lay. He switched on the light and let the DCI into the narrow space ahead of him. Jackson stood for a moment looking at the body with an expression of deep distaste.

'Right,' he said. 'We'll let the doctor do what he has to do. You can come with me, out of the way, and tell me all you know about the victim and his relationship with Ray Robertson.' He marched Barnard to some chairs close to the door and waved him into one. 'Everything,' he said.

'Rod Miller's worked for Ray Robertson for years, guv,' he said. 'Ever since the gym opened in these premises, I think. Though I went away to do my National Service soon after Ray decided to give boxing a serious go and began to look for somewhere to set up a gym. So I'm not entirely sure when they got together. Anyway, Ray must have opened up here in 1952, or maybe 1953. Before that, he did a bit of training in a church hall in Bethnal Green that had a boys' club running. That's where he tried to get me up to scratch as a fighter, before I went into the army. Rod Miller turned up before I went away. He was a damned good trainer, though in the end he told Ray I wasn't as good as he thought I was. I can't say I was very surprised.'

Jackson raised a sceptical eyebrow but said nothing. Barnard shrugged and carried on.

'Anyway, by all accounts the gym flourished from the start. I should think every lad who was keen on the fight game would have known Rod Miller as well as he knew Ray Robertson. And Ray – or more likely Rod – seemed to find the knack of producing winners. I think Robertson's been losing interest recently. He's more interested in his boxing galas and his posh friends than contenders. But Rod is – was – a fixture.'

'What was he like, this Miller?' the DCI asked. Barnard thought for a moment. It was unusual to be faced with a murder victim he knew as well as he had known Rod Miller and it threw him slightly.

'As far as I was concerned he was a quiet bloke, unassuming, devoted to Ray but determined that the kids who came here did well. He didn't let them get away with much. I guess it was the first time a lot of them had found something they might succeed at. Rod pushed them hard but I don't think many of them ever complained.'

'So he's not likely to have been knocked off by one of the lads who's got a grudge?'

'God no! I wouldn't think so, guv. You never know what the kids get up to round here, but Rod didn't seem the sort of person to make enemies.'

'Did he have form?' Jackson asked, but Barnard shrugged again.

'Not that I'm aware of,' he said. 'I've never worked this manor. I've never heard that he did time, though. The local nick should know.'

'Or the Yard,' Jackson said. 'We're only here, in another division, on their say-so. They're the ones who want to offer Robertson some protection, though it may be that this will make them think twice about that. I always thought it was a damn silly idea.'

'You don't think Robertson could have killed Rod Miller do you?' Barnard asked, trying hard to hide the fact that he was appalled at the suggestion.

'In the light of the Yard's worries, I think we need to look at two possibilities,' Jackson said flatly. 'Either Robertson is missing because he shot Miller, or Miller was shot by someone trying to find Robertson to do him some harm. Either way, it makes tracking down your friend Robertson more urgent than ever. We either nick him for murder or we offer him protection. Let's see what the doctor has to say about what's happened here and then you can step up your efforts.'

They went back to where the police surgeon was still crouching awkwardly over the body. He looked up as the two officers approached.

'If you want the time of death, you'll be more likely to get it from the post-mortem than here. He could have been lying here for days. It's very chilly on the tiles, so the body temperature isn't much help. The cause of death is obvious – a bullet to the head that blew his brains out. But there is more, which the pathologist will no doubt expand on. He'd been severely beaten up before he was shot.' The doctor turned Miller's head into the light.

'You can see there's severe bruising on the face and his hands have been smashed. And no doubt there'll be more bruising on the rest of the body when they get his clothes off. I'd say he might even have been dead or dying before he was shot. You're looking for an extremely violent man – or men – here. There's absolutely no doubt about that.'

'That doesn't sound much like Ray Robertson, guv. He's not like his brother, if that's what you're thinking,' Barnard said as they made their way back into the main part of the gym.

'He didn't have to pull the trigger himself if he wanted Miller dead for some reason,' Jackson snapped and stopped by the empty ring as a uniformed officer approached.

'There are lads outside wanting to come in and train, sir,' he said.

'Right, that's good,' Jackson said. 'We'll take witness statements from all of them, see if we can find out exactly what's been going on here in the last few days, shall we? Sergeant, wait until the body's been taken to the morgue and then set yourself up in the office and question them all. I'll get uniform to take names and addresses if they don't want to wait. We need to know everyone who uses this place. I want to know when Robertson was last here, what was going on between him and Miller, and whether anyone has any idea of where he might be now. You can see if there's anything of interest in the paperwork in there, while you're about it. Anything else I need to know?'

'There's a market porter, an old bloke called Bradley I spoke to briefly on his way home to bed. Lives at number eighty-two. He reckons he saw a woman trying to get in here last week when the place was locked up. Dolled up, he said. Mutton dressed as lamb, as he put it. He'd be worth a visit. It could be Ray Robertson's wife again. She seemed very keen to find him when I saw her at the Delilah.'

'Right,' Jackson said. 'I'll put someone on to that.'

'And do you still want me to talk to Robertson's mother?'

'Yes, I do,' Jackson said. 'I'll send you a DC from the nick who can take over the witnesses, and then you can talk to Mrs Robertson. I know there's no love lost between her and Ray, but she may have some idea where he would hide out. She might even be pleased to tell you.'

'Unlikely,' Barnard muttered under his breath.

'OK, guv,' he said aloud. 'I'll wait for reinforcements here and then chase up Ma Robertson. See what she has to say.' The DCI nodded and turned on his heel to brief the uniformed officers who were managing a small crowd of people who had gathered outside the door of the gym. Barnard watched him go and then went into Robertson's office and closed the door on the rest of the murder team, who were beginning to search the premises. He sat at Ray's desk for a minute before beginning to open the drawers and flick through the paperwork, but he could see nothing but details of gym sessions and boxing tournaments and the hopeful contenders who had trained here. He noticed that there were two distinct sets of handwriting on the documents and by far the most usual belonged to Rod Miller rather than Ray Robertson. As far as he could tell, the trainer had been virtually running the gym single-handed for the last few months. That fact did not surprise him. Increasingly Ray had been preoccupied with other problems in Soho and elsewhere as his hold on his more illicit empire had begun to slip. For that reason alone, Barnard thought Jackson was mistaken to think that Robertson could or would have killed Miller. It was much more likely that Miller had died at the hand of one of Robertson's rivals. But why that might be remained a mystery.

THREE

Kate O'Donnell pushed open the door to the lounge bar of the Red Cow on Canvey Island and peered inside. The air reeked of beer and cigarette smoke but at least it was warm. Outside, as she had been frustrated to discover when she got off the train and walked slowly over the bridge on to the island, a chilly clinging mist from the Thames estuary wreathed the island, making the task of taking photographs difficult if not impossible. She persevered for a while, knowing that whatever was printed might show little more than Dickensian gloom rather than the tidy streets of restored homes which here and there even ten years after the flood revealed gaps like missing teeth. In the clinging mist, turning now and again to drizzle, there were few people about and even fewer who had been willing to talk to her and fewer still who thought that having their picture taken was a good idea.

As the fruitless morning wore on, she was encouraged to see that a faint hint of the sun was beginning to lighten the sky in the south where the renewed sea-defence wall protected the low-lying roads from the waters of the estuary. She gazed out at the sea, which merged seamlessly into the grey sky, and marvelled at the fact that France and England were, the governments had just announced, to be joined by a tunnel. It seemed an unlikely prospect to someone who had regarded the tunnel under the Mersey as an engineering miracle and who stood at a spot where engineering had so spectacularly failed to protect innocent people from the sea on a stormy night. She glanced again at the fitful sunshine and was persuaded that perhaps she should hang around a bit longer in the hope of better conditions later on. But her stomach told her she was hungry, and the only place she could see where she might get something to eat was the pub, a solid two-storey building which had been able to stand up to the worst of the floodwater that fatal January night.

Kate went in and dumped her bag and camera on one of the

tables, closely watched by the handful of men already in the bar. She was being assessed but she was used to that when she ventured into a pub by herself. She loosened the toggles on her duffel coat before approaching the counter, where a heavily built man leaned silently on his elbows with a copy of the *Daily Express* spread out in front of him. He did not speak but raised a questioning eyebrow as she glanced at the pumps in front of him and the shelves behind.

'I'd like a half of shandy, please,' she said. 'And do you have anything to eat?' The barman waved towards a plastic cover which she had not noticed at the far end of the counter, before pulling her half glass of beer and turning for a bottle of lemonade from the shelf behind him.

'There's pickled eggs, sweetheart,' he said grudgingly. 'Pork pie or a sandwich. Cheese and pickle.' Kate took a closer look at the dry-looking offerings under the plastic dome.

'I'll have a cheese sandwich, please,' she said, not sure how long the pork pies might have been festering there and repelled by the greyish eggs in their jar of indeterminate liquor. She paid and carried her lunch back to the table where she had left her equipment, conscious of the eyes still watching her from nearby tables, not hostile exactly but full of a sort of avid, neutral curiosity. As she began to eat and drink, the silence lengthened though she knew that sooner or later it would be broken. Women still did not often venture into pubs alone. Where she'd been brought up in Liverpool it was strictly frowned on and even in this tight little community in the south, cut off from the outside world, she guessed that she was still a rare sight.

In the end the patience of one of the drinkers broke and a tall, thin middle-aged man with an almost military haircut, wearing nondescript green slacks and a tweed jacket, got up with empty glasses in hand and took a detour to Kate's table on his way to the bar. He glanced at the camera visible on the top of her bag.

'Not a very good day for taking pictures, is it dear?' he said, his tone avuncular although possibly hiding a multitude of sins that would spark the interest of a confessor.

'Not yet, anyway,' Kate agreed. 'I'm hoping the sun will come out a bit more.' The man's eyes widened slightly.

'Blimey,' he said. 'You're not a native round here, are you? Glasgow is it, that accent?'

Kate gritted her teeth. She should have got used to this reaction by now but sometimes it still stung. She didn't reckon most Londoners had ever been north of Watford and as for the inhabitants of Essex, from what she had seen this morning, she suspected they might as well live on another planet for all the contact they had with the big cities of the north.

'Liverpool,' she said. 'You know? Big river, lots of boats, just like London really.'

'Oh yes,' the man said, unabashed. 'Liverpool? So what's a girl from Liverpool doing taking pictures on Canvey Island? What's that all about?' He glanced at her camera. 'That looks like a nice bit of gear. You want to be careful it doesn't get nicked.'

'I'm working for a magazine,' she said, taking a cautious bite out of her sandwich but wishing she hadn't and putting one proprietorial hand on her camera just in case. 'They're opening some new flats here next month and the magazine's doing an article about how Canvey has recovered since the flood.' She could see that his two companions at his table were getting impatient waiting for their glasses to be refilled.

'Were you here back then?' she asked quickly, not wanting to lose his attention just yet. The man glanced at his friends as if to ask permission before confiding in Kate, but they remained stony-faced and he evidently decided to go ahead anyway.

'We were all here back then, duck,' he said, his face clouding over. 'More than fifty people drowned that night. It's not something you're ever going to forget, is it?' His hands tightened round the glasses he was holding, the knuckles white. 'Just let me fill these up and you can tell us what you're doing and we'll fill you in on how the place has changed, if you like. All right? Would that help?' Kate nodded. This, she thought, might be the best lead she would get. In the middle of a miserable weekday, the island was not so full of residents on the streets that she felt she had much choice. 'Can I get you another?' the man asked, almost as an afterthought.

'Half of shandy, ta,' she said trying to look cheerful.

Kate's new acquaintance went to buy his round and took the glasses back to his two friends whose eyes swivelled sharply in her direction as he spoke. She could see he was having some difficulty in persuading the oldest of the trio, a grey-haired man who could have been already drawing his pension, his face deeply creviced by some experience she could only guess at. But in the end even he shrugged a reluctant assent and the man who had approached her waved her to their table and they shuffled up on their chairs to allow a fourth person space to sit down and even put a beer mat down for her shandy. From the bar, the landlord glanced in the direction of the group in feigned surprise before turning back to his paper.

'I'm Tom,' the first man said. 'This is Reg and this . . .' He waved at the older man. 'This is Ken. We've all lived on Canvey since before the war – when most of it was just a holiday village for East Enders, a chance to get out of the slums for a while in the summer. But not many stayed in the chalets full time except a few retired folk. Then we all went into the forces, of course, and when we came back we found there was such a shortage of houses after the bombing and more people were staying all year round, making the best of it, families with kids even. At least it was a roof over their heads.'

'That was the root of the trouble,' Ken said, his pale eyes angry. 'It shouldn't have been allowed. Those houses were just standing on top of concrete bases. They had no proper foundations. Some had no power or sewage. When the flood came they just floated away or got smashed to buggery, taking people with them.'

'Or they filled up so quickly with water that people didn't even have time to get out. Anything with only one storey was a likely death trap if the water rushed in,' Tom said.

'If you were all here then, how did you all escape?' Kate asked.

'We'd all been here a long time and lived in brick houses with two floors,' Reg put in. 'We were away from the sea wall, just that little bit higher. I was asleep and when I woke up the water was halfway up the stairs. But it didn't get any further.'

'So you got away more lightly?' Ken took a deep breath and the other two men flinched slightly, embarrassed, and Kate realized she had said the wrong thing. Ken took a deep draft of his beer and shook his head.

'My lad had been to Southend that night and was on his way back when the surge came. He never got home. He couldn't swim. They found his body two days later. So I wouldn't say lightly, no.' There was a silence for a moment as if no one dared speak.

'I'm sorry,' Kate said quietly. The reality of the tragedy hit home, she thought, when you heard it from people who had actually been there. 'That's terrible.'

'It was all terrible,' Tom said. 'We were neighbours and Reg here had a dinghy, and when we could get out we took the boat to see who we could help. We were out all that night and half the next day bringing people to dry land – whole families, grannies, tiny children – all freezing cold and wet, with only the clothes they stood up in.' He turned away from Kate and she suspected there were tears in his eyes. 'Help was slow coming,' he said. 'Too late for some.' Kate glanced at her camera and then at the three sombre-faced men.

'I'll have access to a lot of the pictures taken at the time. But the reason I'm down here today,' she said hesitantly, 'is that I'd like to take pictures of people who are still here. Of you, for instance, if that's all right, as survivors of that night.' The three men glanced at each other and then nodded slightly warily.

'And it would be good, if you could help me,' Kate went on quickly. 'If one of you could show me round. I'd like to take pictures of what was there in '53 and what's been built since. To give people an idea of what's changed and whether people who live here feel safe now, more than ten years on. Building flats seems like a good idea—'

'If you're not on the ground floor,' Ken said bitterly.

'To be honest,' Tom said. 'I don't think anyone who was here that night will ever feel safe again. But I'll give you a walk round if you like, show you the sights such as they are, maybe find someone else you can talk to. Will that help?'

'It will,' Kate said. 'It really will. Thank you.'

DS Harry Barnard was not often taken by surprise, but the message DCI Keith Jackson had just delivered had shaken him. He worked on the premise that things were generally bad and could always get worse, but what Jackson had just said floored him.

'Off the case, guv? Why the hell would they think that was a good idea?'

Barnard had come back to the nick from the East End feeling understandably frustrated. When he'd been relieved at the gym, he had driven east to the narrow street of small Victorian houses where Ray Robertson's mother had lived for as long as he had known the family. But when he parked outside he was surprised to find it in darkness, and when he knocked there was no reply. He had stood on the pavement for a moment looking up at the bedroom windows before he realized he was being watched by someone standing in a doorway on the opposite side of the street.

'You won't find her this afternoon, dear,' the elderly woman said with what sounded like satisfaction. 'She's gone to the town hall, hasn't she?'

'The town hall?'

'Don't you know nuffink?' the old woman went on. 'It's the protest, ain't it? Ma Robertson's like me, lived here all her life. Came through the Blitz together, didn't we? The ruddy bombs missed this street, we was the lucky ones. And now they're going to pull it down.'

Nonplussed Barnard stared at her, taking in the grey hair scraped back from the wrinkled face, the hearing aid and the flowered pinafore. They dated her as a survivor of the worst Hitler had thrown at the East End, but she now looked defeated by the new threat that had arrived from much closer to home.

'The council's going to do that?' he asked.

'Redevelopment, they call it,' the old woman said. 'They're going to pull down twenty streets between here and the City and put us all into flats, like they've done already down Poplar way. Ma Robertson says we're not going to put up with it. She's gone to talk to the mayor and the councillors. Lots of us have gone to protest. I'd be down there meself if my hip wasn't so bad. It's a bleeding liberty. These houses came through the war. We don't want to be redeveloped to finish off what Hitler started.'

Barnard had had to admit defeat. When he reported back to the nick, he'd been surprised to learn that DCI Jackson wanted to see him straight away. Ma Robertson had evidently become less important as the day had gone on and he was to see Jackson immediately. The DCI had not asked him to sit down when he arrived in his office, which was always ominous, and sat looking at him for some time with an unreadable expression on his face before he spoke. It was certainly long enough for Barnard's sense of foreboding to grow exponentially and he could feel himself beginning to sweat.

'Sergeant,' Jackson had said at last. 'I've just had a call from the Assistant Commissioner for Crime at the Yard. He'd seen the first report of the death we attended this morning at Robertson's gym and decided that as you have been so closely connected with the man, who has to be regarded as a major suspect, you are not to work on this case. You'll be diverted to other duties and I'll take charge of this investigation myself.'

Barnard's sense of anxiety turned in a moment to anger, which he swallowed down with difficulty.

'So the ACC thinks I can't be trusted?'

'You're too close to that family,' Jackson said flatly. 'I never know where I am with you and your East End friends.'

'I was close to Rod Miller, guv,' Barnard came back quickly. 'He trained me as a kid. He was a diamond bloke and I know that's what Ray Robertson thought too. There's no way Ray could have shot him.'

'That's your opinion,' Jackson said. 'But it is nothing more than an opinion. Which is precisely why the ACC doesn't want you on this case. You obviously think I have jumped to a conclusion, but you have obviously jumped to the opposite conclusion. When did you last see Robertson to talk to?' Barnard shrugged wearily.

'It must be a month ago, at the Delilah Club. I was making inquiries about some betting scam which I thought he might have information on. It was nothing out of the ordinary and he said he couldn't help me pin down the organizers.'

'Couldn't or wouldn't?' Jackson asked, but didn't wait for an answer. 'And Miller? When did you last see him?'

'Not for months,' Barnard said. 'I don't think I've been to the gym since the end of last year.'

'You're too close,' Jackson said again. 'Go and draft a statement about your recent contacts with Robertson and Miller and let me see it before you go off duty. Did you talk to his mother, by the way?' Barnard allowed himself the faintest smile.

'She was off on a crusade to stop the council pulling down her street, guv,' he said. 'I don't think she likes that sort of progress. She'd rather be back in the 1930s when it wasn't Ray who ruled the roost down there but her husband, Jim. But maybe after this it won't even be Ray. It sounds to me as if the Yard believes the reign of the Robertsons in the East End is nearly over.'

'And isn't that something we should be devoutly hoping for?' Jackson asked, his Scots accent thickening with emotion and his colour rising. 'Isn't that what we're here to achieve?'

Kate O'Donnell got back to the Ken Fellows Agency by four, feeling slightly deflated. Tom, her acquaintance from the Red Cow, had done as he had promised and guided her round the island in his battered-looking Ford, stopping at places of particular interest or, more often, tragedy. They had looked at the sea wall that failed so catastrophically in 1953, inspected the restored houses and chalets, some of which still looked desperately insubstantial, and ended up outside the new block of flats which was to be opened in a couple of weeks' time. The builders were still working there, the scaffolding only just coming down. A group of women stood outside watching a dumper truck busy removing debris from what was obviously intended to be a forecourt.

'What are they looking for?' she asked. Tom shrugged.

'They built this block where some damaged properties had stood. Some people complained that people had died there and no one had thought to search the place for personal stuff that might have got left behind. They wanted a proper search done. A lot of them never came back here to live, but while the building work's been going on, especially while the foundations were being dug, they've been coming in from Southend or one of the Wakerings, or wherever they ended up. But I don't think much has been found. Whatever was there got washed away or buried back then and isn't likely to turn up now. Do you want to talk to them?'

But by this time Kate had lost her enthusiasm for the project. The light had been poor all afternoon, the weak sun never really breaking through the mist and low cloud, and it was now fading fast. She took a few more shots but was afraid that her prints would be barely usable and she would have to make this trip again in better weather. She knew that Ken would not be pleased if she had wasted the best part of a day.

'I need to get back,' she said. 'It's getting too dark already.'

'I'll run you up to Benfleet station,' he offered. 'It's a long walk.'

Back at the agency she shut herself in a dark room and processed the film, looking critically at each print as it emerged to dry off. She made two sets of prints of shots that were not too affected by the weather, thinking that as well as showing them to Ken Fellows she would show them to Barnard as he had had such a close encounter with Canvey Island and its traumatized residents after the wind and sea had done their worst. It was different now, she thought, tidied up and sanitized, but still bleak and to an outsider, especially one brought up in another port and only too aware of the worst the sea could do, very sad.

She was surprised when she got back to Highgate to find that the lights were on and Harry Barnard was already at home. She found him slumped in his favourite revolving chair in the living room, tie loosened, cigarette in one hand and a generous glass of Scotch in the other, swinging aimlessly from side to side. She did not need him to speak to guess from his expression that there was something seriously wrong.

'Whatever's happened?' she asked.

'The roof fell in,' he said with a weary shrug, and he told her briefly how he had discovered Rod Miller's body and the DCI's implacable conviction that Ray Robertson must be the prime suspect.

'It doesn't sound like Ray,' Kate said. 'I can't say he's my favourite person, but since I met you he's done me some favours and begun to move in slightly less dodgy circles.' She tried a tentative grin but Barnard didn't respond.

'No, it doesn't sound the least bit like Ray. I've never known him carry a gun, let alone use one. Not like his crazy brother.'

'So surely they want you to redouble your efforts to find him?' she asked.

'No, that's exactly what they don't want. They want him found, but not by me. The Yard have apparently told Jackson to take me off the case. Although I wouldn't be certain that he didn't make the decision all on his own.' Kate looked at him, appalled.

'You're joking?' she said. 'Don't they need all the knowledge you've got about the Robertsons?'

'Apparently not,' Barnard said angrily. 'I've made a statement about my inquiries so far and that's it. Finished. I'm confined to other cases and I guess if I step out of line they'll suspend me or sack me. They've wanted me out ever since Jackson took over Vice. This is just the excuse they're looking for.'

'So what are you going to do?'

Barnard shrugged and sipped his Scotch.

'I don't know,' he said. 'I could still keep on looking for Ray, I suppose, but if I find him I'll have to turn him in. Anything else and I'd find myself in the dock with him, if that's what it comes to in the end.'

'In a way they're right, aren't they?' Kate said gently. 'You're too close to him to go hunting for him for murder.'

'So what do I do?' Barnard snapped. 'Nothing at all? Let them hang him out to dry? There's no way Ray would kill Rod Miller. The trouble is that the brass at the Yard don't understand how the East End works.'

'Can't you just keep an eye on Jackson's inquiries? Or an ear open, maybe? If you're in CID every day that would let you keep in touch, wouldn't it? They couldn't keep the whole inquiry under wraps, could they?'

'My first reaction was to jack it all in,' he said. 'But I reckon that's what they want, so I won't give them the satisfaction. It's not as if I'm the only dodgy officer in Vice. They're all at it one way or the other, but it's small stuff, kickbacks, favours, finding a way to rub along with small-time crooks and get information without bringing Soho to a halt. It's not about turning a blind eye to gangsters with guns. At least not unless you're a much bigger fish than me. You remember DCI Venables?' Kate shuddered. She remembered Ted Venables only too well.

'That's all very well but you're still the only one who's known the Robertson brothers since you were kids,' Kate said. 'Your bosses are never going to like that. Even with Georgie out of the way they're going to think you're too close to Ray, especially if they want to question him about this murder.'

'Well, I can't undo what happened during the war. We were thrown together then but in the end I decided I didn't want to follow them down their road. I kept well clear for years and in the end helped put that bastard Georgie where he belongs. That obviously doesn't count for anything with the Yard.'

Kate sighed. 'Sleep on it,' she said. 'Come on, I'll cook us a meal and then I'll show you the pictures I took on Canvey Island.'

'Oh yes, what did you think of it?' Barnard sat up straighter in his chair, more than ready to be distracted.

'Pretty bleak,' Kate said. 'But I did find a few people willing to talk to me, so I got some material for my captions. The trouble was the weather – misty and dark, so I'm not sure the pictures are really usable. I think I may have to go back on a better day and take some more. I'll have to see what Ken thinks on Monday morning.'

'Let's have a look at them before you start cooking,' Barnard said. Kate pulled the prints from her portfolio, glad to distract him, and he riffled through them quickly.

'I see what you mean about the weather,' he said. 'Who are these three?' He stopped at a clearer print of the three men she had met in the Red Cow. She smiled.

'My new-found admirers. I met them in the pub. They couldn't get their heads round my accent but in the end they were very helpful, showed me round and took me back to the station to catch the train. But I could see that they didn't think it was a suitable job for a woman. Dead old-fashioned they were.' But Barnard seemed to have stopped listening to her. He held another print in his hand, transfixed.

'Who are they?' he asked, holding out one of the last pictures she had taken showing the group of women on the edge of the building site, some of them scrabbling through what looked like a rubbish tip set apart from the new building.

'Just locals,' she said. 'They think the builders may have dumped some of the remains of their houses that used to be on the site. They reckon they've lost things that could have been saved. I can imagine that must be pretty awful if you've seen your home washed away. Though they didn't look as if they had much hope of finding anything useful. It was just a gesture, I think.' Barnard nodded and jabbed a finger on the print.

'I don't think this woman is – or was ever – local. I think this woman used to be Ray Robertson's wife. I saw her the other day in Regent Street, all dolled up to the nines then, which she's not here. Looks as if she's got her second-best mac on with the headscarf. But I'd swear that's Loretta, and she told me she was looking for Ray. But why she thinks he might be on Canvey Island I can't imagine. It's the last place I could imagine either of them being. She doesn't look as if she's searching for anything very hard. She's just watching. Did you get the names of any of these women?'

Kate shook her head.

'I hardly spoke to them, and I didn't need lots of names,' she said.

'It's Saturday tomorrow,' Barnard said quietly. 'Do you fancy another little trip to Canvey? On my behalf this time. We could go together, and if it's a better day you can take some more pictures to keep Ken Fellows happy.'

'Are you sure that's a sensible thing for you to do? Isn't it a big risk if it has anything to do with Ray, or even his ex-wife?'

'It may be,' Barnard said, his face bleak. 'But I really don't think I can sit this one out and let them pin something on Ray that I'm pretty certain he'd never do. If Loretta has been down there for some reason, we may get a lead of some sort. Canvey is about the last place anyone would look for Ray – or for Loretta, for that matter. What do you think?'

FOUR

Harry Barnard was up early the next morning and brought Kate a cup of coffee in bed.

'Did you get any sleep?' she asked, looking at his slightly haggard face and knowing that he had not been in bed beside her for the whole of the night.

'Not a lot,' he said. 'I thought if we are going out and about we could drop by Ray's house in Epping, the one Loretta said he'd bought for her, though she doesn't seem to be getting much benefit from it now. If anyone from the local nick is around, we'll just drive by. If not, we'll try to work out if he's been there recently. It would give me a lead.'

'Are you sure?' Kate asked, sipping the strong brew he had given her. Italian coffee was a taste she was acquiring slowly, though she preferred it sweet. Coffee where she came from came out of a Camp bottle or was never seen at all. 'Your car's a bit conspicuous. People will remember it.' Barnard took the point.

'I'll see if I can borrow something more anonymous if you like,' he said. 'Give me half an hour. I know a bloke with a garage in Archway who owes me a favour or three. And we'll potter along at a very sedate pace so as not to attract the attention of Traffic. We'll go to Epping first and then Canvey, then I'll buy you some winkles in Southend. Bring your camera with you. It looks as if the sun might come out today.' The idea of doing something possibly constructive – although Kate doubted that his boss would look at it that way – had obviously energized Barnard. He drank his coffee quickly, put on his coat and hat, and disappeared before Kate had even got out of bed.

By mid-morning he was back with a slightly dilapidated green A40, which they set off in with much muttering from Barnard when it failed to start first time and more colourful language as he crunched the gears and it failed to accelerate as sharply as desired.

'Take your time,' Kate said mildly as he did an emergency stop behind a bus that had pulled up unexpectedly. 'There's no hurry, is there?' Barnard shrugged and slowed down to something nearer the speed limit on the next clear stretch of road beyond Crouch End.

'I suppose not,' he said. But his anxiety obviously gnawed at him. They both knew that it was not just Ray Robertson's future on the line but Barnard's own as well, and this time he might not be able to keep Ray or himself out of trouble.

Kate watched the landscape change as they worked their way out of London and everything became greener. The houses got bigger, the golf courses more frequent, and the woodland began to close in on them. Eventually Barnard slowed down and turned into a narrow unpaved lane which was not signposted and looked like a track through the woods.

'Somewhere down here,' he said, as the car bumped over the rutted road. 'On the right, set back a bit behind a high fence. I came here once years ago when he was still married to Loretta. He had a party to celebrate some deal he'd done.' The houses along the lane were substantial and well scattered, and there was little sign of life apart from the large cars parked on the long driveways and a single gardener clipping a front hedge. Eventually Barnard slowed to a crawl.

'That's it,' he said, stopping outside wrought-iron gates beyond which a large red-brick house with white window frames was visible. There was no sign of life. He continued slowly then turned the car round to face the way they had come before parking a couple of houses further up the road.

'We'll walk back,' he said. 'There's no sign of anyone from the local nick, so maybe they've not got out here yet.'

'But they might still turn up?'

'I'm sure someone will, though they're probably a bit slow out here in the sticks. After all, it is Saturday morning. We'll do a very quick recce to see if there's any sign of Ray. But be prepared for a quick exit. I don't want to have to explain to PC Plod what I'm doing here.'

They walked slowly back to the Robertsons' gate, still seeing no sign of life, and then up the short gravel drive where no cars were parked. The gardens were neatly kept and the grass short but the ground-floor windows were securely shuttered. Taking a deep breath, Barnard knocked at the front door and listened carefully. But there was no response beyond a hollow echo.

'We'll have a quick look at the back,' he said and led her on a circuit past the tall ground-floor windows to a paved yard with three garage doors on one side, the gated entrance to an extensive garden at the end, and what was obviously a kitchen door at the back of the house. He tried the handle but it was firmly locked, as were the garages. The rear of the house had a slightly neglected air that was not apparent from the front, as if no one had been there for a while or spent any time tidying the place up. Leaves had blown against the walls and back door and not been swept away, and a couple of dustbins had blown over.

'Come on,' Barnard said abruptly. 'There's nothing doing here.' He did not seem much more relaxed, and Kate wondered what he would have said to Ray Robertson if he had found him holed up here in his mansion, but when they got back into the car and he succeeded in starting the engine at the third attempt she could see the obvious relief on his face. He drove slowly back down the bumpy lane, and as they waited to turn back towards London a police car approached from the opposite direction and turned into the narrow entrance. Barnard whistled quietly.

'That was a bit close,' he said with a grin. 'Bloody good job we didn't come in my car. The registration number on this won't get them very far, even if they noticed it. It doesn't really exist.' Kate glanced at him as they swung south again and wondered how he had learned to be quite so devious.

It took them another hour to weave round East London and out into Essex, but finally Barnard took the bridge from Benfleet on to Canvey Island and slowed right down to take in the scene.

'I've not been back since the week or so I spent here as a squaddie,' he said. 'It looks a bit more civilized now.'

'The new building we talked about is down that way,' Kate said, pointing to a side road leading away from the sea wall. Barnard pulled up by the almost completed block and sat staring at it for a moment, but the site was completely deserted.

'That's where I took that shot of the women,' Kate said. 'There were half a dozen of them milling about talking to a man who looked like a foreman or something.'

'Perhaps your friends will be in the pub again,' he said. 'What's it called, the Red Cow? They might know the names of some of the women in your picture.'

'It's worth a try, I suppose,' Kate said doubtfully, thinking that it was not like Barnard to chase wild geese. Ray Robertson's disappearance was really getting to him and she didn't think it could possibly end well.

'I could do with a drink,' she said. 'Though I warn you the food there is dreadful.'

But when they went into the Red Cow they found the lounge bar deserted and only a couple of young men playing a desultory game of darts in the tap room. The same heavily built man was leaning on the counter as on Kate's last visit, this time intent on the *Sporting Post*. He showed no sign of recognition as she approached with Barnard. Eventually he looked up as if they were an inconvenience and raised an eyebrow. Barnard ordered a pint for himself and a shandy for Kate, but instead of going to a table he leaned on the bar as if willing the barman to take notice of them.

'Quiet this morning?' he said. Unable to avoid a direct question, the barman shrugged.

'Always is this early on Saturday. The women like to go into Southend shopping and take their men with them, don't they? Them that don't are too decrepit to get out of the house mainly.' His eyes flicked back to the racing news.

'I was here yesterday talking to three old boys,' Kate said bluntly. 'Do you know if they're likely to be in today?'

'Nah, they don't come in till later Saturdays. One of them's got a boat and they sometimes go fishing if the weather's good and the tide's right. That's where they'll be this morning now the sun's put in an appearance.'

'Were you here in the flood in '53?' Barnard asked, so sharply that the barman looked startled.

'I was, but we were OK here. We sat it out upstairs till it was safe to come down.'

'Show him your picture, Kate,' Barnard said. 'Do you know any of these women? They were all here in the flood apparently, and I want to talk to one of them. It might be to her advantage financially – a bit of late compensation, as it happens.'

The barman cast his eye over the picture without enthusiasm but shook his head.

'One or two of them I've seen around.' He indicated a couple of the women, but not the one who Barnard thought might be Loretta Robertson.

'Not her?' he persisted.

'Nah. I've never seen her before in my life.' Barnard's shoulders slumped and he drank his pint down quickly.

'So she's not local?'

'Well, she might be,' the barman said. 'There's new people moving in now the place is getting tarted up. But I don't think she was here in the flood. She's a bit of all right, isn't she? Or would be if she smartened herself up. I'd have noticed her.' He leered at Kate and Barnard put his arm round her, obviously annoyed.

'Come on, honey,' he said, guiding her away from the bar. 'Let's go. Have you ever been to Southend?' Kate shook her head.

'I'll take you on the roller coaster,' he said. 'There's a funfair there. We used to come out here when we were kids, once it'd opened again after the war.'

'We used to go to New Brighton, on the other side of the Mersey.'

'Sounds like the same sort of thing,' he said. 'Let's go.'

Kate woke up late the next morning. She and Harry Barnard had not got back to the flat until after midnight, after an evening in Southend sampling the delights of the only half-functioning funfair and a fish-and-chip supper wrapped in newspaper and eaten on the pier. Surprised Harry had not woken her, she got up and found him in the kitchen frying bacon but his attention held by a Sunday paper spread out on the worktop.

'That's going to burn,' Kate said, taking the fork out of his hand and turning the rashers over. 'What's so interesting in the paper?'

'They've got a story about Rod Miller's murder,' he said. 'Apparently he trained some quite well-known youngsters in his day. The boxing correspondent reckons he's a serious loss to the sport. I wouldn't have thought that myself, but there it is in the *Sunday Express* so I suppose it must be true.' Kate looked sceptical. Her recent contact with a Fleet Street crime reporter had not impressed her very much.

'Do you want an egg with this?' Kate asked and turned back to Barnard when he did not reply.

'Bloody hell!' he said, more to himself than to Kate.

'What's the matter?' she asked.

'They've got a bit about Ray Robertson in here as well. I know he owns the gym, but the way it's written . . .' He shrugged. 'It says the police want to speak to him. And everyone knows what that means.'

'They don't know where he is, but they think he did it?'

'And they want everyone to know they think he did it,' Barnard said angrily. 'The Yard must be behind this. I don't reckon DCI Jackson's that devious. The last time I spoke to him there wasn't a shred of evidence against Ray and no witnesses who claimed to have seen him at the gym at the right sort of time. But after this every gangster and petty crook in London will be looking out for him. Some of them will be his mates, but an awful lot of them won't. He's made a lot of enemies in his time with his social climbing and he can be an arrogant bastard.' Kate turned back to the bacon, which really was burning now. She tipped it into the sink and ran water on the smoking pan.

'So much for breakfast,' she said. 'What about toast? It might be less of a fire hazard.'

Barnard shrugged and ate what she put in front of him, but as soon as he had finished he put his coat on.

'I'll get all the papers,' he said. 'I want to know if this is just in the *Express*, just a boxing story basically, or whether they've all latched on to it.' He was not out long and came back with a bundle of Sunday papers which he set about searching for any mention of the murder. Kate watched as he cut out bits from some of the papers and made a neat pile of them on the dining table. When he'd finished he looked slightly nonplussed.

'Most of them have a bit about the body being found, but it's only the man at the *Express* who mentions Ray as anything other than the well-known promoter who owns the gym. The *Sunday Times* says he has friends in high places, which is true enough, but no one else says the police want to talk to him. I wonder who the *Express* man's contact is.'

'You could ask him,' Kate suggested.

'And have it get straight back to whoever he talked to? No thanks. I'm officially off this case, remember?'

'So you are,' she said quietly. 'And if you ask me, you've already taken enough chances. Why don't we have a quiet drink at that pub you took me to at the top of the hill and a lazy Sunday afternoon? I think you've done all you can for now. If Ray wants to stay out of sight, I'm sure he's got plenty of places he can hide. He'll reappear in his own good time I dare say, but probably not until they've arrested someone else for Rod Miller's murder. That would be the sensible thing to do, wouldn't it?'

The phone call came after they had come back from standing close to the braziers at the front of the Flask where families with children, who were not allowed inside, congregated to keep warm. The low bars in the old building were packed with adults, and after failing to find a space inside among the Sunday lunchtime crowds they carried hot toddies outside and were put off by the cold from staying very long. They walked briskly back down Highgate Hill to Barnard's flat, flushed from a combination of the icy wind and the whisky, and could hear the phone ringing as Barnard put his key in the lock.

The conversation seemed monosyllabic at first, as if Barnard was unsure of who he was speaking to, but eventually he seemed to relax and appeared to be making plans for a meeting at a pub near Fenchurch Street with whoever was at the other end of the line.

'Seven o'clock will be fine,' Barnard said at length. 'They'll only just have opened then and it'll still be quiet on a Sunday night in the City. You obviously know what I look like. I'll see you then.'

'Who was that?' Kate asked.

'A bloke who wants to talk to me about Rod Miller,' Barnard said. 'Says there was more to Rod than the trainer dedicated to helping lads from the back streets make it with their fists. That could well be right, seeing that Ray took him on. It's not as if either of the Robertsons was ever squeaky clean. Even as kids their pockets were stuffed full of goodies they'd nicked from the corner shop. I remember Georgie working the bomb sites for scrap metal and anything else he thought he could flog. Some poor beggar's false teeth once, but he didn't care.' Kate pulled a face.

'Do you really need to see this man?' she asked. 'How do you know he's genuine and not someone trying to catch you out? It's not as if you're short of enemies at the nick by the sound of it, quite apart from trying to run a freelance murder investigation.'

'Well, he seems to have prised my phone number out of someone at the nick, so it might be a good idea if you came with me,' he said. 'I might need a witness if it comes to the crunch. No one will know me at the Wellington. I don't think I've ever been inside the door and he certainly won't have. Apparently he's coming in from Essex.'

'Essex?' Kate said quietly. 'Not Canvey Island, surely?'

'No, I don't think so,' Barnard said. 'But would you believe it? He mentioned Southend.' Kate met Barnard's eyes but said nothing. She could see the same anxiety there that she knew was mirrored in her own and could think of nothing encouraging to say.

The Wellington was an unprepossessing pub close to Fenchurch Street station, a brick building on a corner, facing the railway arches under the line that took the trains east, the windows half-obscured by engraved glass that looked as if it hadn't been cleaned for years. Barnard parked his car some distance from the entrance and sat in the driver's seat for a long moment before getting out, but the street outside was deserted at this time on a Sunday.

'Come on then, let's see what this bloke wants. If he's taken the trouble to come all this way, it must be something important.'

'Shouldn't you tell him to talk to DCI Jackson?' Kate said, gripped by a sudden feeling of panic.

'In theory yes, but he didn't seem very keen on that idea,' Barnard said. 'Mind you I didn't tell him I'd been pulled off the case. Don't worry, sweetheart, I'll tell Jackson tomorrow if it's anything relevant. I'm not looking to put my head into a noose deliberately.' Kate shrugged, thinking that DCI Jackson might be only too happy to see him hang. But she had never seen Barnard so morose and didn't quite know how to handle him in this mood.

'Let's get it over with,' she said without enthusiasm.

There was only one customer in the lounge, a chilly, dusty-looking room with smeared tables and nobody behind the bar at all. He was a heavy-looking, broad-shouldered individual who scanned the newcomers with a slightly hunted expression as if he did not really want to be there. He was sitting in a corner, back to the wall, with an empty whisky glass in front of him and had the collar of his topcoat pulled up round his ears and a scarf tucked in tightly. The eyes he turned in their direction were focused and cold.

'Barnard?' he asked.

'Harry,' Barnard said.

'Les Greenwood, also a DS once upon a time,' the stranger said, waving his empty glass in the direction of the bar. 'And I'll have another double Scotch.' He glanced at Kate.

'Who's this? Your dolly bird?'

'I brought her for the ride,' Barnard said. 'We're going up West later. She's very discreet.'

He saw Kate into a seat then turned towards the bar, where a boy who didn't look old enough to be serving alcohol had appeared to deal with his order. Greenwood stared at her silently, loosening his scarf slightly to reveal the several chins it had concealed, and Kate realized that his eyes were bloodshot and the veins in his face reddened. His breath had the smell of a man who was seldom sober. She knew the signs only too well after a childhood spent on Liverpool's Scotland Road and she realized that she still hated men like this, even after being away from those slums for years now.

'What's a nice girl like you doing going out with a dodgy copper like him?' Greenwood asked in the end, in the gravelly tones of a committed smoker, but he did not seem to expect a reply and she did not offer one. He shrugged and glanced up at Barnard and took the whisky from his hand with enough enthusiasm to suggest he did not just want it, he needed it.

'I was in the Met once,' he told Barnard. 'Went out to Essex just before the Yard had one of its purges. Not that they had anything on me, mind. The Essex force was only too pleased to have someone with my record of arrests.'

'So what about Rod Miller?' Barnard asked impatiently, sipping his pint. 'Did you arrest him?'

'I did, as it goes, Sergeant,' Greenwood said. 'But he wriggled out of it. We couldn't persuade him to talk, though we tried hard enough.'

'I can imagine,' Barnard said.

'As if the Met's squeaky clean,' Greenwood snapped. 'Anyway, we couldn't crack him or his alibi, so in the end he walked. But I knew he was guilty as hell. You can always tell.'

'So what was he guilty of?' Barnard asked sharply.

'This is ten, eleven years ago, you understand. I've been retired for seven. Must have been '52. There was a nasty robbery in Southend – a gang raided a post office on pension day, an armed gang waving two sawn-off shotguns. They terrorized the customers, got the keys off the postmaster, emptied the safe, and scarpered with the postmaster as hostage. They dumped him later on in the marshes with a cracked skull. He bloody nearly died and they say he's never been the same since. Anyway, we got the two main men – bloke called Sam Dexter and a bit of a nutter called Barrett. Bomber Barrett they called him, because of his rep from the war. He was some sort of explosives expert who liked big bangs. Those two went down for fifteen years apiece, though I hear they've just got out for good behaviour. But two others got clean away. We reckoned Rod Miller was the driver and a lad called Bert Flanagan, Dexter's brother-in-law, was there on the day as well. Miller wasn't charged and Flanagan was acquitted. He claimed he was visiting his sister Delia on Foulness Island that day, and as the military keep an eye on who comes and goes there and hadn't seen him leave we couldn't prove he could have been in Southend with the others. Not to the jury's satisfaction, anyway. Later on, people told me you can get on and off Foulness without troubling the checkpoints if you know how. But it was too late by then.'

'Miller didn't buy his way out of it, did he?' Barnard asked. 'If he grassed his mates up, that might explain why someone'd come for him now. He wasn't just shot, you know. He'd been badly beaten up before he died. It could be revenge that had to wait until they came out of prison.'

'No he didn't grass anyone up,' Greenwood said sharply. 'If you knew Barrett, you'd know no one would grass him up in a hurry.'

'So why are you telling me all this now? How's this robbery connected to Miller's murder?' Barnard asked.

'Dexter and Barrett have just been released, haven't they? And nobody ever recovered the loot from that raid and some similar ones we suspected they were involved in. Believe me, we've kept an eye on Flanagan in particular, but there's been no sign of him living it up. Though I hear from my mates in CID that he's not been seen around much recently. But we always reckoned that there's at least a quarter of a million stashed away somewhere, waiting for Dexter and Barrett to come home and claim it. Unless it's been half-inched already by someone who didn't go down. The Great Train Robbery it was not, but it's a tidy sum all the same. Quite enough for someone who might have stashed it away somewhere to get roughed up.'

'And you think one or other of them might have come looking for Rod Miller to see if he knows where the money is?'

'Exactly,' Greenwood said. 'You need to look up the records down in Southend.'

'As far as I know, Rod Miller hasn't put a foot wrong since he went to the gym in Whitechapel to work for Ray Robertson,' Barnard objected. 'And he's certainly never shown any sign of being loaded with cash.'

Greenwood got to his feet unsteadily and ordered another whisky at the bar without offering Barnard or Kate a refill.

'Robertson? There's another name to conjure with,' Greenwood said when he came back and slumped into his chair. 'Maybe he's picked up the loot somewhere along the line. If I remember rightly, Robertson had some connection with one of the Flanagan sisters. He married one of them and Dexter married the other.'

'Ray Robertson and his wife were divorced years ago,' Barnard said. 'Though I did see her in Oxford Street recently.'

'You're not suggesting they're not dodgy as a three-pound note?'

'The brother's gone down and Ray's gone AWOL as it happens, and my DCI has him down as prime suspect for killing Miller. But I don't see it myself,' Barnard said thoughtfully. 'Ray Robertson and Rod Miller have been partners for years at the gym. And Miller, as far as I know, is officially clean as a whistle.'

'Well, he wasn't back then,' Greenwood said flatly. 'You need to talk to CID in Southend. There must be records of the little chats I had with Miller about that robbery, even if they haven't filtered back to the Met. I just hope they've been cleaned up a bit for public consumption.'

'Can the DCI contact you?' Barnard asked, but the older man shook his head wearily and drained his glass.

'No way,' he said. 'I'm retired and want to stay that way. I'm not in Southend any more, as it goes. I moved to Canvey to get away from all that. It was only by chance I noticed Miller's name in the papers. I thought I'd better remind someone about what happened back then. If Dexter and Barrett are on the loose again, I want to stay as far away from them as I can.'

'Can I contact you? You don't have to do anything official but it might help,' Barnard persisted.

'Don't even think about it,' Greenwood said. 'This meeting never even happened.'

FIVE

DCI Keith Jackson called Barnard into his office mid-morning. Barnard put his jacket on, straightened his Liberty-print tie, a flowery job that provoked much derision around the station, and gave DC Peter Stansfield an unenthusiastic smile.

'Thanks, Pete, you're a mate,' he said. The younger detective had just been regaling him with the final results of the post-mortem on Rod Miller, and Barnard was puzzled. Apparently it confirmed that the trainer had not just been shot at close range but systematically beaten first, which in Barnard's book could only mean that whoever had attacked him had wanted information. The shot to the head might have been retribution for some slight, imagined or otherwise. Broken ribs and cigarette burns said something very different. But as he wasn't supposed to be on the case he would have to keep his thoughts to himself, at least for now. In the end, he suspected, they would have to turn to him for advice if not practical help. Of all the detectives in the West End, he was the one who had been born in the East End and lived and breathed there for most of his life, and the two areas of London were as different as chalk and cheese.

The DCI waved him into a chair, which Barnard reckoned was a good sign after his previous uncomfortable meeting.

'Have you stumbled on anything that might help locate Ray Robertson?' the DCI asked. 'I know you've got the contacts.'

''Fraid not, guv,' Barnard said. 'The local CID came back to me to say there's no sign of him at his house in Epping, though they'll keep an eye on the place in case he turns up. And I called in at the Delilah as I was passing on my way in this morning, but he's still not put in an appearance there.'

'Right, well you can leave it to the murder team now,' Jackson said. 'I want you to concentrate on your home ground from now on. We're getting more and more complaints about queers in certain pubs and there was another vicious attack on one of the street girls over the weekend. I want you to follow that up. Though I sometimes wonder why we bother when they all so obviously ask for trouble.' Barnard drew a sharp breath at that but thought it wise not to disagree right now with his career seemingly on a knife edge.

'Did you want me to have another go at Mrs Robertson?' he asked.

'I'll send someone from the murder squad,' he said. 'Or maybe someone local in Whitechapel. We're working closely with them on this one obviously.'

'She hates the police with a passion, guv,' Barnard said quietly. 'She just might open up to me as she's known me since I was a kid.' Jackson hesitated for a moment, obviously calculating the costs and the benefits of this suggestion in the light of Scotland Yard's clear antipathy to Barnard. Eventually he nodded.

'Go down there this morning, and take DC Stansfield with you,' he said, looking pleased to have found a means to cover his own back if not Barnard's. 'We want any ideas about where he might hide out. Does he ever go abroad? Has he even got a passport? I've put a call out to the ports and airports just in case he tries that on. Both of you report to me as soon as you get back, I want to know exactly what you get out of his mother. Then you can resume your normal duties in Soho.' Barnard gritted his teeth and took another deep breath. If Jackson was covering his back so blatantly, things must be serious and he probably needed to cover his own.

'There's one other thing you need to know, guv,' Barnard said. 'I went down to Canvey Island with my girlfriend this weekend. She's a photographer and she's taking some pictures down there for some sort of magazine article on the big flood in '53. We got talking to a bloke in the pub who turned out to be an ex-copper who used to work in Southend. He'd read about Rod Miller and told us he'd interviewed him years ago after a series of armed robberies in Southend. Before the flood, this was. He reckoned Miller was the driver for a particularly vicious post office raid. They left the postmaster half-dead. Two men called Dexter and Barrett went down for that and some other attacks, but Miller had an alibi they couldn't break and wasn't charged. I reckon it might be worth having a chat with Southend CID.'

'Leave that to me,' Jackson said irritably. 'I'll put someone on to it. If Miller was involved in anything dodgy down there, it's highly likely Robertson was as well. You let me know what Robertson's mother has got to say for herself. And then get back on the streets. I don't want another working girl murdered if there's some nutcase out there carving women up. It gives us all a bad name.'

'Guv,' Barnard said and got to his feet, thinking that the DCI vastly overestimated how much the great British public cared about dead prostitutes. 'I'll go down to Ma Robertson's straight away.'

'And take Stansfield with you,' Jackson said again. 'Don't forget.'

'Sir,' Barnard replied through gritted teeth, thinking that Stansfield would be about as much use talking to Ma Robertson as a vegetarian at Smithfield market. Ray's mother would chew him up and spit him out if the fancy took her and he was afraid he himself might inadvertently be included in the feast.

When Barnard parked outside the familiar terraced house from which Mrs Robertson's long-dead husband had run his East End empire for years, this time there was a light visible in the front room.

'Looks like she's at home,' Barnard said to his companion in the passenger seat. 'This is a bit of East End history, Pete. I was only a kid when Ray and Georgie's father was running the place – extortion, illegal betting, a bit of this and a bit of that. But not girls. They didn't go in for vice and Ray Robertson doesn't either, as far as I know. I don't know if that was where Ma Robertson drew the line. Her husband was technically the big man, but that didn't mean she didn't think she was in charge. The tragedy was that when the old man died Ma Robertson thought she could keep control, but the two boys wouldn't have that. They were only teenagers but they both went their own ways, as pig-headed as their mother, as it goes. I don't think she's ever really forgiven either of them, especially Ray. He took himself off and built a new empire in Soho where she never got a look in. I can remember their father's funeral, plumed black horses, a whole column of mourners behind the hearse, all in black, crowds lining the streets, hats off, respect. If ever there was a time I might have gone down that road, that was it.'

'But you lived happily ever after,' Stansfield said, with a sly sideways glance at Barnard.

'I wouldn't go as far as that,' Barnard said. 'But I guess it's better than having the shadow of the Scrubs looming over your head all the time.'

'And there's me thinking you had that as well,' Stansfield said, attempting a grin.

He flinched as Barnard gripped his arm just a fraction too hard.

'Don't push your luck, constable,' Barnard said. 'I knew the Robertson boys when we were all kids. They went their way and I went mine. That's it. Now come on, we'll see what Ma Robertson knows about Ray's movements. If DCI Jackson reckons I'm the right officer to do this interview, there's no reason why you should have another opinion. Let's get on with it.'

Ma Robertson opened her door within seconds of their first knock and looked at both her visitors cold-eyed and stony-faced.

'It's you,' she said to Barnard, glancing over his shoulder at DC Stansfield. 'And who's this? Your apprentice?'

'Something like that,' Barnard said with a smile that signally failed to melt Mrs Robertson's icy suspicion. 'Can we come in?'

She led the way into the main living room, where a coal fire smouldered in the grate and a clothes horse of damp washing filled the air with steam.

'You'd better sit down,' she said ungraciously, waving them into chairs each side of the fire and moving her laundry infinitesimally so that she could face them from a hard chair on the other side of the room. Ma Robertson had always been renowned for refusing to move from the small terraced house where she had started her married life, however lucrative her husband's criminal enterprises had become, and it was obvious that neither of her sons had persuaded her to change her mind since their father's death. And as she aged, Barnard thought, she was becoming more set in her ways and the house was beginning to decay around her.

'Have you seen Ray recently?' Barnard asked. Ray Robertson's mother pursed her lips.

'Not since my birthday,' she said. 'He brought me a bloody great bunch of flowers, the silly sod. As if that would make any difference. I chucked them in the bin when he'd gone.'

'Why was that Mrs Robertson?' Peter Stansfield asked, all wide-eyed innocence.

'Brothers are supposed to help each other,' she said. 'That bastard's not lifted a finger to help Georgie for years. Why are you looking for him, anyway? He's fallen off his pedestal at last, has he? The king of Soho, God's gift to boxing, friend of Lord Muck and Lady No-better-than-she-should-be. His father must be turning in his grave.'

'So this was when? Your birthday?' Barnard asked.

'Week last Sunday,' she said.

'And is that what he usually does? Sees you on your birthday?' She shrugged.

'Usually,' she said reluctantly. 'Yes, usually.'

'But he's not been round here since then?'

'Nah,' Ray's mother said. 'And he won't be round no more. I gave him an earful, didn't I?' Barnard nodded, guessing that this could only be the truth. Legend had it that East End families stuck together through thick and thin, but this one had been spectacularly disintegrating for years.

'But if he wanted to drop out of sight, have you any idea where he would go?' Barnard persisted. 'Does he use the house in Epping he bought when he got married?'

'That was another silly thing Ray did, marrying that bloody gypsy from Essex. I told him no good would come of it. However she dolled herself up in silk and mink, she never had no knickers on underneath.'

'You mean Loretta?'

'Course I mean Loretta. Who do you think? She's the only one he ever married and she had to have it done in a bloody great church in Southend. Claimed she was a Catholic. Even so, it didn't last. I was expecting half a dozen nippers, but none appeared. A waste of space that woman was. Couldn't even give me a grandson, could she? Couldn't or wouldn't, I don't know. Anyway, Ray threw her out in the end.' Ma Robertson had evidently brought the honing of grievances to a fine art. He wondered if the council that had had the temerity to threaten her home would meet their match here.

'I saw Loretta recently up West,' Barnard said. 'Still all dressed up to the nines. Has she been to see you at all? She said she was looking for Ray.'

'What does she want with Ray after all this time? He won't want to set eyes on her.'

'I've no idea,' Barnard said. 'She didn't say.'

'Has Ray ever been abroad, Mrs Robertson?' Stansfield asked, obviously feeling left out of the interview.

'He was in the army, National Service. Went to Germany, didn't he? Don't think he liked it much.'

'But not on holiday or anything like that?' Mrs Robertson shook her head.

'Not as I know. What would he want to go abroad for? All those foreigners and greasy food. Southend was always good enough for us. Or sometimes Margate, if we fancied a change.'

'Has he got a passport, do you know?' Barnard persisted.

'How the hell would I know that?' Ma Robertson was losing patience and her voice took on a whining note which reminded Barnard that, however belligerent she liked to appear, she was an elderly woman who must be nearer seventy than sixty. He sighed.

'So you've no idea where Ray might be holed up? No bolt hole he uses when it gets too much for him?'

'When did anything ever get too much for Ray?' she asked. 'Or for Georgie for that matter. They ran me ragged when they were small, the little sods. And it looks like they're going to run me into my grave, if the council doesn't do it first. I've told them, they'll have to carry me out of this house in a box.'

'So Ray's not giving you much help with that, Mrs Robertson?' Stansfield asked, suddenly all sympathy. But the old woman was not for buttering up.

'I told you,' she snapped, 'I've not seen him for two weeks. And if you're that keen to find him, it can't be for his own good, can it? Why would I tell you, even if I knew? Which I don't. You always were a conniving little weasel, Harry Barnard. You never knew which side you were on, so you can sod off now and leave me in peace.'

Kate O'Donnell got back to Barnard's flat after a frustrating day spent in various picture libraries in central London looking for photographs of the flooding of Canvey Island dramatic enough to satisfy Ken Fellows. He didn't say much as he went through her own pictures of the reconstructed island but she could see he was disappointed.

'It's a dreary-looking place, isn't it, even when it's not awash?' he said eventually.

'It was a very gloomy day, but it's not very picturesque anyway,' she admitted. Ken glanced out of the window.

'The weather looks like it's settled now,' he said. 'I think you should go back there tomorrow and have another go at it in sunlight. And while you're there, you could look at the picture library at the local rag. What is it? The *East Anglia News* or something like that? They'll have an office in Southend I should think. Check it out anyway, and see if they'll let you in. They probably took far more pictures than they used at the time and will be glad to flog some of them to us. These local rags run on a shoestring but they're usually quite good at archiving stuff. I don't suppose they have the time or the energy to sort stuff out and throw it away. I know the feeling.'

'Right,' she said. 'I'll check them out and get an early train down there in the morning.'

When she had made the necessary arrangements it was time to fight her way on to the busy Northern Line to Archway in a subdued mood that was not improved by the sight of Barnard's distinctive red Ford Capri parked outside the flat unusually early. She guessed that maybe he had had a bad day coming to terms with the fact that he had been excluded from the murder inquiry into Rod Miller's death.

She found him already in the kitchen, with a savoury smell coming from a large pan.

'That smells good,' she said. She was still slightly surprised every time she saw him toiling in the kitchen. Where she came from, that was strictly woman's work and not very exciting work at that. Meat and two veg was all her father had ever demanded, on the table whenever he chose to roll in. Until eventually he had ceased to bother rolling in at all.

'Just a sauce for some pasta,' Barnard said. 'There's nothing like Italian food to cheer you up.'

'Do you need cheering up?' she asked, although she could hear the strain in his voice and see it in his eyes.

'Jackson is really serious about keeping me off the case. I managed to persuade him to let me interview Ma Robertson today, but that's as far as it'll go. I told him she wouldn't be likely to talk to anyone else, which is true enough. But he made me take a minder with me to keep me on the straight and narrow.' Kate nodded, her own face glum.

'I'm going to Essex again tomorrow. Ken Fellows wasn't very impressed with the pictures I took on Canvey. Too dark he said. And after that he wants me to trawl through the archives at the local paper in Southend. They'll probably have pictures we could use of the flood and of that new development.' Barnard left his pan and picked up a bottle of Chianti in a raffia basket and waved it in Kate's direction.

'Want some?' he asked as he got two glasses out of the cupboard.

'Why not?' she said. He sat down on a tall stool at the breakfast bar and looked at her consideringly.

'You could do something for me if you're going to the local rag,' he said. 'You could look up their coverage of the robbery Greenwood told us about, and any others that were connected. Jackson reckons that if Rod Miller was one of the suspects, Ray Robertson could well have been involved as well. And if that's true, Ray might have had a motive for killing him, even after all this time. I think it's nonsense myself, but there might be something in the reports of the robberies and the trial that would give me a clue. Could you bring me the cuttings?'

'You're not going to give up on this, then?' She tried to keep her voice light but could not pretend she wasn't worried. He shrugged.

'I won't step on the murder team's toes,' he said. 'But if I can track Ray down, I will. The longer he stays below the radar the more suspicious it's going to look. I don't want to see his face on the front of the *Globe*. Ray was good to me when we were kids, kept that paranoid brother of his off my back. I owe him.'

'It was a long time ago,' Kate said.

'I know,' Barnard said. 'I promise I'll be careful. Will you help me, Kate? I don't think I can do it on my own.'

SIX

Kate O'Donnell had finished taking her second set of photographs on Canvey Island by lunchtime, this time in fitful watery sunshine which she hoped would satisfy Ken's demand for greater clarity. She strolled past the Red Cow, decided against indulging in one of their stale cheese sandwiches, and made her way back to Benfleet, crossing the bridge from the island with few regrets. As she stood on the station platform for ten minutes waiting for the Southend train, she smelled the salt on the breeze and thought nostalgically of the Mersey ferry that used to take Liverpool families across the water to New Brighton. She had made an appointment to meet the picture librarian at the *East Anglia News* and didn't quite know what to expect.

The library turned out to be a rambling warren in a semi-basement where issues of the paper were stacked in precarious-looking heaps held together by wooden clamps on broad shelves marked with inky labels according to the year of publication, the newsprint yellowing with age and the stacks looking more precarious with each year further back they went. Cuttings on specific subjects were packed into cardboard folders and she seriously wondered how anyone could find anything in the apparent jumble. She gazed around in search of assistance, but when a tall thin man with straggly grey hair, thick-lensed glasses and an expression of puzzlement glanced in her direction it was clear he was not expecting her. He ran a hand through his hair, which looked almost as dusty as his groaning shelves.

'Are you Frank Garside?' Kate asked.

'No, dear, I'm not,' the man said. 'I'm Bob Little, the librarian. Can I help you? Are you here about the filing job? If so you should be upstairs, not down here.'

Kate flashed him her most brilliant smile.

'No,' she said sweetly. 'My name's Kate O'Donnell. I made an appointment to see Frank about some picture research I'm

doing. I'm a photographer with a picture agency in Soho. We're
working on something about the East Coast floods.'

Little looked somewhat nonplussed by her explanation.

'I've never met a lady photographer before,' he said. Kate bit
back a retort about life obviously being very sheltered in Southend
and forced another smile.

'Is Mr Garside here?' she asked.

'Not yet,' Little said. 'He rang to say he'd had a puncture and
would be late in. Do you want to wait for him?' Kate glanced
at the stacked files.

'I have to or my boss won't be best pleased,' she said. 'Perhaps
I could look at some of your editions from 1953? It would give
me an idea of what pictures you had back then.' Little looked
slightly relieved at the suggestion.

'That sounds like a good idea,' he said, obviously keen to rid
himself of any responsibility for her. He shuffled towards the
back of the stacks and with slow deliberation began to assemble
the unwieldy files for the year of the flood.

'Of course it happened early in the year,' he said, 'so you
won't need to go too far through. Though there was a lot of
activity for months afterwards, rehousing people who'd lost their
homes, rebuilding the sea defences, all that. You have a browse,
dear. I'm sure Frank won't be long.'

Kate set to work, glancing only quickly at the flood reporting
and looking instead for any coverage of the armed robbery at
the post office that the police believed Rod Miller had been
involved in. It was not difficult to find. Both the robbery itself,
in January, and the trial of three men in the autumn of the same
year had been splashed across the front page of the paper. Sam
Dexter, described as a farmer from Foulness, Sid Barrett – better
known as Bomber and obviously something of a criminal celebrity
in Essex – and a man called Bert Flanagan, described as a
showman, had been arrested and charged soon after the robbery
and tried after the flood.

Bob Little took no further notice of her, pottering around in
the further recesses of his dim and dusty kingdom and making
himself coffee in a corner containing a kettle and a collection of
grubby-looking mugs. Kate wondered if she would be offered a
cup but to her relief no offer was forthcoming. It was another

half hour before another person entered the library – as short and plump as Little was tall and thin, but the same sort of age and with the same look of slightly harried anxiety. He bustled over to her as she closed the file she was looking at and put her notebook away in her bag.

'You must be Miss O'Donnell,' the new arrival said, holding out his hand. 'Frank Garside. So sorry I'm late, so sorry. I had to mend a puncture. Some little hooligan is going around letting tyres down and running away with the valves as a bit of fun. It's the third time this month. Bike locks don't deter them, you know.'

Kate took in this tale of woe, slightly taken aback at the revelation that he was talking about a bicycle rather than a car. Local newspapers were obviously run on a shoestring in Essex.

'Come into the picture store,' Garside said cheerily. 'I've got better lights in there. But you've been looking at the files, that's good. So you know what we were using back then. Of course there were very few pictures of the night itself. Too dark and no one had time to take photographs. It wasn't until daylight that we got any real idea of what had happened. And some places were cut off for days. They had to go out to Foulness by boat, not expecting any survivors . . .'

He led the way into his sanctum and handed her the files of the night of the surge and its devastating aftermath – black-and-white images of death and destruction, rescue and escape, almost every picture a frozen drama that she felt she would never forget. Kate spent more than an hour going through the prints and with difficulty selected a couple of dozen that she thought would interest Ken Fellows. She carried them over to Frank Garside tentatively, almost afraid of the power of the images she had selected.

'Could you let us have copies of these?' she asked. 'Do you still have the negatives?'

'It'll be plates in most cases, we were still using those massive cameras back then. They might have moved on in Fleet Street and such by that time, but down here in the sticks we were way behind. You'd have had difficulty carrying one of those great things around. But the answer is yes, we should still be able to give your agency prints. Why don't you take the ones that interest you back to London and get your boss to have a look, then let us know what he would like to use?'

'Are you sure?' Kate asked, surprised at this generous offer.

'You'll return them safely, won't you?' Garside said.

'I promise to let you have them back in a couple of days. In case you need to contact me . . .' She handed him one of the cards that the agency provided for their photographers. 'But I should be able to ring you tomorrow. Thanks very much for your help.'

And she left, aware that in the notebook tucked away in her bag the *News* had provided Harry Barnard with rather more help than it realized.

Kate came out of the newspaper office and for a moment stood in a chilly breeze from the east to take stock. It was still too early in the year for the town to have attracted many visitors on a cold Monday morning and she glanced longingly at a sign pointing to the railway station and the option of a warm – or at least warmer – ride back to London. But she reckoned that at least some of the information she had garnered at the *News* on Barnard's behalf might be worth following up straight away. She made her way down to the pier and was surprised to see one of the little trains that took passengers to the end – more than a mile out into the estuary – trundling out of the station, though there didn't seem to be more than a handful of intrepid visitors bundled up in winter coats on board.

Close by stood the other main attraction on the seafront, the funfair, but that looked almost completely deserted and silent, with many of the stalls shuttered, the rides not moving, and fish-and-chip papers and other rubbish being tossed around in the wind. Even so, she walked towards the rides and stalls, wondering if Bert Flanagan, the 'showman' who was acquitted at the trial of the post office robbers, had left any sort of trail from ten years ago. What sort of a showman was Flanagan, she wondered, and had he worked right here on the seafront where, so the ex-copper Les Greenwood had said, the gang was also suspected of carrying out a robbery, although that had not been on the charge sheet at the crown court? But perhaps ten years on Flanagan had decamped to New Brighton or Blackpool, or some other resort where the show families would look after their own.

She walked slowly down the path into the fairground, which was dominated by the roller coaster that swooped high above the other rides. In a couple of months, she thought, the place would be filled with screaming overexcited children and teenagers enjoying the thrills and spills and the cheap food and fizzy drinks. Now, at the end of the winter, the place looked faded and neglected and there was nobody to be seen. But she stopped suddenly as she looked at the dodgem cars parked silently on their gloomy unlit rink, autumn leaves still rustling where they had been blown into dark corners. Over the top was a banner flapping forlornly in the wind advertising FLANAGAN'S DODGEMS FOR BUMPER FUN. Her heart jumped uncomfortably in her chest as she took on board the fact that just possibly the man who seemed as if he had got away with it all those years ago was still here, plying his trade in the same place as he and his family probably always had.

Uneasily she stood close to the steps up to the dodgems, not sure what to do next, and she only gradually became aware that she was being watched. A woman in what looked like a boiler suit, over a dark sweater, was standing half-concealed by the pay booth at the far side of the rink smoking. It was the thin stream of smoke from her cigarette that had revealed her hiding place.

'Hello,' Kate said, almost shouting above the wind, which flung her words back in her face. 'When does the fairground open again?' The woman shrugged and walked slowly across the shiny floor towards her. She was not tall and wore sturdy boots beneath her stained boiler suit. She wore no make-up and her dark hair was tied back from her face in an unflattering pony tail. There was nothing to conceal the fact that she looked careworn and tired out.

'At the weekend,' she said. 'We don't bother during the week at this time of the year. More often than not it's bloody raining, isn't it?' She didn't come close, but instead stopped by one of the cars and stepped on to the bumper with one hand on the upright with the ease of someone used to collecting the fares. She looked hard at Kate's bulging briefcase and seemed to realize straight away that this was not a casual inquiry. There was no way that Kate looked as if she was desperate for a bumper fun ride.

'Actually I need to speak to a man called Bert Flanagan and I saw that this was Flanagan's dodgems. Does he still run it?' The woman's face visibly hardened. She stubbed out her cigarette on the mottled paintwork of the car she was leaning on and flung the butt in Kate's direction, where it fell on to the muddy ground.

'Tell me when you find the bastard,' she said. 'I'm his wife and I've not seen him for months. And I've got three kids to keep.'

'Ah,' Kate said. 'You have no idea where he is?'

'Who are you, anyway?' Mrs Flanagan asked sharply. 'You don't look like a copper. So what? A lawyer? What do you want Bert for?'

Kate hesitated.

'I work for an agency in London,' she said. 'I'm doing some research about fortunes that seem to have gone missing, and one of them was the proceeds of the robbery of which your husband was acquitted. I wondered if he had any idea what happened to the money when the two guilty men went to jail. He did know them, didn't he?'

'Yes, he knew them. Of course he did, and more's the pity. But none of the money came our way. It wouldn't, would it? Bert wasn't involved. We wouldn't still be scraping a living here if we'd made anything out of it.' She came to the edge of the rink and sat down wearily on the top step.

'Connie,' she said, lighting another cigarette and drawing deeply.

'Kate.'

'Was Bert really not involved?' she asked cautiously. Connie Flanagan looked away and did not answer.

'You can't be tried twice for the same offence,' Kate said, a bit of legal information she had picked up from Barnard.

'It's not the law he's worried about,' Connie said. 'It's Dexter and Barrett. Those two nutters are out now and Bert wants to stay as far away from them as he can. He didn't tell me when he was going or where he was going, but it was easy enough to work out why.'

'So he's not as innocent as the jury thought?' Kate said quietly. Connie Flanagan shrugged, her face bleak.

'Sam Dexter's his brother-in-law,' she said. 'Married to his sister Delia. He never told me what he got up to with Sam, but he's easily led, is Bert. He's a bit of a fool and I can imagine he'd follow where Sam led. He spent months in jail on remand but they never found anyone who could identify him as having been there at the post office. So he got off, didn't he? He was happy enough with that, but the other two didn't look too happy when the verdict came in. Barrett went raving mad, shouting at the jury. They had to take him back to the cells . . .'

She stopped and drew deeply on her cigarette again. 'I'll have to give up this place if Bert doesn't come back for the start of the season at Easter,' she said. 'There's no way I can run it on my own.'

Kate was conscious of the fear that lay behind Connie Flanagan's eyes.

'There was another robbery, wasn't there? Here at the fair-ground. Was Bert involved in that?'

Connie shook her head violently.

'We were all hit by that robbery,' she said angrily. 'The takings – everyone's takings – were on the way to the bank, so we all lost out. Bert wouldn't have got involved with that, would he? We all ended up losers. It was our rent money.'

Kate said nothing for a moment, thinking that the family connection might have been convenient for the robbers. They could easily have persuaded or perhaps forced Flanagan to tell them what they needed to know. She sighed.

'If it wasn't Bert who told them about the takings, who was it?' she asked.

'Bert always thought it was his sister Delia. The Flanagans were all brought up here, and she'd have known that the money was taken to the bank once a week. I don't think the silly beggars had changed their routine for years, so in theory anyone with a pair of eyes in their head could have worked it out. But Bert thought it was Delia. He wouldn't shop her, would he, but he's kept well clear of her ever since. Like everyone else, he's scared of Sam Dexter and that madman he was sent down with – Bomber Barrett.'

'Why Bomber?' Kate asked.

'I think he was in bombers during the war. I don't know really. That's just what people call him.'

'Do you think Dexter and Barrett will come looking for Bert? Seriously?' she asked.

'I only know that Bert's gone and I don't know where. He must have had a reason for going, mustn't he? He must have been scared of someone or something. I've tried to contact his sister out on Foulness but she never seems to be there. Not that she'd tell me anything, I don't suppose. She's stuck by Sam Dexter all these years. Maybe she's sitting on a pile of cash. Who knows? All I know is that we certainly aren't.'

'So what do you think you can do?' Kate asked.

'Pack up the kids and move out,' Connie said. 'But I haven't a clue where to go. I'm living in one of the vans here at the moment, but it's too small. My eldest boy is eleven and needs some space. We did have a house for a few years on Canvey Island, just me and Bert, but it got washed out by the flood and we never went back. I was pregnant by then and I thought it was too risky to stay. Kiddies died in that flood.'

She glanced over Kate's shoulder and suddenly seemed to stiffen, her eyes wide. She took Kate's arm in a tight grip and pulled her on to the rink and into the shadows on the far side.

'Two blokes getting out of that green car over there,' she whispered. 'One of them's Sam Dexter and I guess the other's his mate – Barrett. Come with me. Quick!'

She half pulled Kate over to the far side of the dodgem rink and behind the pay booth. And then, constantly glancing over her shoulder, into the fenced-off area almost under the pier where the showmen's caravans were parked.

'Luke and Sally are at school,' she said. 'And Liam, the little one, is old enough for nursery now, so they're all safe. We'll go to my van and I'll get some of the men to see them off. No one's supposed to come in here. We should be safe.' She dragged Kate behind her as she led the way through the parked caravans, where there was almost no sign of life, until she stopped close to a covered area where a group of men, muffled up against the cold, were sitting or standing around a wooden table playing cards.

'Stay here,' Connie said, and she left Kate on the edge of the small crowd while she approached a burly man in a sheepskin jerkin, no shirt but an array of blue-and-white tattoos on every exposed bit of flesh and a pork-pie hat pushed back on his head, with whom she had a brief conversation. At a sign from the man in the hat, he and half a dozen of the others got up and strode off together in the direction the two women had come from.

'They'll see them off,' Connie said. 'That's my uncle, Jasper Dowd. We have to look after ourselves down here. There's no love lost between us and the townies. Half the time we get the blame for stuff we had nothing to do with. And the police don't want to know.'

'Is that why they arrested Bert?' Kate asked quietly.

Connie looked away.

'Bert got in too deep with those bastards,' she said eventually. 'My family won't let anyone near me and my kids, but I'm not sure they'd lift a finger for Bert. He's a Flanagan, not a Dowd, and there's no love lost. It didn't go down well when I married him.'

Kate got home before Barnard that evening. To her relief, she'd got a better reception from Ken Fellows when she showed him the pictures she'd taken on Canvey Island in pale sunshine, plus the ones she'd culled from the files of the local paper.

'That's good,' he had said flicking through the prints. 'I can see a sensible before-and-after scenario now. All we'll need to complete it are some photos of the grand opening of the new buildings. I think the *Evening Standard* might go for it, or one of the colour magazines. Give your mate at the *News* a call in the morning and ask him to give us permission to use these six. I think they will meet the bill.'

Pleased that her efforts had met with approval this time, Kate pushed the cuttings she had acquired for Harry into her case and left early, hoping to avoid the worst of the crush on the Northern Line. When she arrived at the flats, she was not too surprised to find his car was not outside. After taking off her coat and making herself a cup of tea, she unloaded her collection of cuttings on to the dining table and sat down to sort through them. In the light of what Connie Flanagan had told her, she was pleased she had taken the time to collect together reports of the robbery at the fairground as well as the post office robbery, although these had petered out quite quickly as the crime remained unsolved and police interest seemed to have declined quite fast. There were only rough estimates of how much the robbers had got away with, but it was a relatively small amount compared to what had disappeared in Dexter and Barrett's getaway car, which Rod Miller may or might not have driven after the post office raid. And perhaps Connie Flanagan was not exaggerating when she suggested that the local community might not make much effort on behalf of the showground families. But nothing Kate had discovered in chilly Southend seemed to throw much light on the murder at the gym that was bothering Barnard more than ten years later.

She took her cup into the kitchen and was wondering whether to start cooking supper when the phone rang. She hesitated for a moment, knowing that it was very unlikely to be for her, but finally picked up. For a couple of seconds there was silence at the other end, then a voice that was low and tentative, as if the caller didn't want to be overheard. It sounded familiar.

'Is that the lovely Katie?'

'Who's that?' she asked, almost but not quite sure who the caller was.

'It's your Uncle Ray. Is Flash Harry there?'

'Ray!' she breathed. 'Harry's been looking for you everywhere.'

'Has he now?' Robertson said. 'Or is it that poker-up-the-arse Scotch DCI of his? I know what he'll be thinking.'

'Harry's not back yet,' she said, not answering his question. This was a web she did not want to stray into, let alone try to untangle. 'Can I get him to ring you later when he comes in?'

'Oh, I don't think so, sweetheart,' Robertson said. 'That wouldn't do. Tell him I'll call him later this evening, unless you've got plans . . .'

'I'll tell him,' Kate said, her mouth dry and as she waited for a response she realized the line had gone dead. Feeling slightly shaken, she went back into the living room and slumped into Barnard's revolving chair, spinning slowly round as she tried to make sense of what had just happened. From what he had said, there was no doubt that Robertson didn't want to talk to the police officially or give any clue as to where he might be. So what did he want Barnard for? She hardly dared think. Whatever it was, she guessed it was unlikely to be anything legal.

She was still in the revolving chair when she heard Barnard's car draw up outside and then his key in the lock. He was whistling faintly as he came into the living room, but when he saw her his cheerful expression quickly turned anxious.

'What's wrong sweetie? You look as if you've lost a tenner and picked up a brass farthing. What's happened?'

So she told him.

SEVEN

Harry stalked around the flat all evening like a caged lion, waiting for Ray Robertson to call back as promised. While Kate cooked a quick meal, he glanced with little apparent interest at the cuttings she had collected for him in Southend. When she put it in front of him, he just picked at his pasta and poured himself a generous Scotch. He had said very little since Kate finished her story, apart from asking her if Ray had said anything at all about Rod Miller's death.

'I told you, he didn't say much about anything. It wasn't me he wanted to talk to, was it? But yes, I think he knew. He said something rude about your boss being the one who'd be looking for him anyway.'

'But he didn't give you any idea where he might be?' he asked for what must have been the sixth time. And for the sixth time Kate said no, Robertson had not given any clue.

'He was only on the line for a minute or so at most,' she said.

'Did you ask him where he was?' Barnard persisted.

'No, of course not,' Kate said, getting more edgy by the minute. 'There was obviously no way he was going to tell me that. I told you, it wasn't me he wanted to speak to, it was you. He sounded worried but he didn't give anything away.'

'With Miller dead, he must be worried. He must think he might be next. Maybe we could arrange a meet—'

'But if you do that, how can you avoid telling the DCI what's going on? You can't cover for him. You'll lose your job, if not worse.'

Barnard drained his glass and got up to pour himself another. Kate watched him anxiously. She had never known Barnard so uncertain and felt her own stomach clench with tension.

'So what do you suggest?' he asked angrily. 'Leave the phone off the hook?'

'Probably,' Kate said. 'It's one thing going to Essex and trying to track down Miller's connections there. I've been doing most of the legwork anyway. But it's something else to interfere in the DCI's murder investigation when you've been warned off. You can't do that. I'm not even sure you should speak to Ray at all. Leave him alone. You're in too deep with him already. You're officially off the case and you shouldn't get involved with one of the suspects. You know that. You shouldn't need me to tell you.' Kate's face was flushed and Barnard pulled her on to the sofa and put an arm round her shoulders.

'I know, I know,' he said. 'But the Robertson brothers have haunted me since I was a kid.'

'Well, maybe this is the moment to break the link completely,' Kate insisted. 'Ray may be involved in the murder or he may not, but you can't interfere because if he turns out to be guilty he'll take you down with him. And if he's not, you'll still be in trouble for disobeying orders.'

'Right,' Barnard said, but she could tell he was not really convinced. He got up and paced around the flat anxiously until eventually the phone rang again.

'Go into the bedroom and listen in on the extension,' Barnard said quickly, his hand hovering over the receiver. Knowing she had failed to convince Harry to ignore the call, Kate hurried into the bedroom and picked up. Robertson's voice was faint but he sounded as if he was trying hard to be cheerful.

'Watcha, Flash,' he said. 'I spoke to your little bird earlier. Did she tell you?'

'Where the hell are you, Ray?' Barnard said, his voice sharp, not wasting any time on the niceties. 'Where the hell are you? DCI Jackson's got the whole of the Met out looking for you. Your mug will be on all the police noticeboards soon. You need to talk to him about Rod Miller. You can't stay out of sight on this one for ever.'

'Prime suspect, am I?' Ray said. 'Well, sod that for a game of soldiers. I thought it was time to take a little holiday for one reason or another, and if that's what your boss thinks he can whistle for me. I didn't kill poor old Rod. As it happened, I popped into the gym the other day and got the shock of my life when I found him dead. Poor bastard. And if the people who knocked him off are the people I think, it's possible they'll be looking for me too.'

'So who the hell are these people?' Barnard asked. 'If you've got an idea who did it, you need to fill us in. Why do you think he was killed? And who by?' There was a groan at the other end of the phone.

'I don't know, do I?' he complained. 'But long before I took Rod on at the gym he had a record. He lived down Southend way, did a bit of training on his own account, which is how I met him. But he was in with some of the local bad boys, a bloke called Sam Dexter among them. If the local cops thought Rod was the driver for the post office robbery they were probably right, though he managed to wriggle out of it. Anyway, by then I'd taken him out for a few bevvies and persuaded him to come to Whitechapel and run the gym for me. I knew he was good and by then I didn't want to do all the training myself. I had other plans. But that was the end of it as far as I was concerned. And as far as Rod was concerned, I thought.'

'But,' Barnard asked, 'clearly it wasn't, as it turned out?'

'Just recently Rod seemed to be getting edgy. I had a long talk with him in the boozer one night and he said he knew that Dexter and Barrett were getting out of the nick soon. I said, so what, that's all old history. But he said no, it wasn't. They'd be looking for their haul, and he reckoned they wouldn't find it. He reckoned someone in the know had nicked it and they wouldn't see a penny.'

'Did he say who he thought had nicked it?' Barnard asked.

'Well, the obvious person apart from Rod himself was a bloke called Bert Flanagan, the member of the gang who was acquitted. If he knew where they'd hidden the cash, he might have helped himself. He's Dexter's brother-in-law. Might have found out more from his sister Delia than Dexter realized.'

'Right,' Barnard said cautiously. 'But surely, if he'd got his hands on the cash he wouldn't have hung around waiting for them to come out of jail? He'd be long gone.'

'You'd think so, yeah,' Robertson said.

'I take it you want me to pass this on to the DCI? It'd carry much more weight if you came in and told him yourself.'

'No way,' Robertson said. 'I'm not taking that chance. I know the Yard want me banged up with Georgie and I'm not taking that risk. If you can use what I've just told you, that's fine.'

'I'll have to think about it,' Barnard said. 'But you're too well known to hide for ever. The longer you stay out of sight the more likely the Yard is to think you are up to your eyes in this. One way or another.'

'Don't you worry about me, Flash. I can look after myself. But there's no way I'm going to help your boss with his inquiries and finish banged up in a cell on remand just because he doesn't like my face. Do they know exactly when Rod died? He looked to me as if he'd been dead a while. He didn't smell very sweet.'

'I'm not sure,' Barnard said. 'I told you, I'm not working on the case myself. Too close to you, Jackson reckons.'

'Well, I dropped into the gym that Sunday afternoon. I was on my way back from Scotland, as it goes. I'd been catching a few salmon in the Highlands and talking to contacts about a boxing gala up there. All above board and legit, so if it's an alibi they want mine's rock solid. I was three hundred miles away that weekend and I reckon I can prove it easily enough. But I'm not rushing to implicate my business acquaintances in all this nonsense. You find out when Rod was killed and I might consider giving your boss an alibi. But I'd want to be very sure he wasn't aiming to arrest me regardless. You can't tell me that's not easy enough if the mood takes the bastards.'

Kate heard Barnard sigh heavily.

'By the way, I ran into your ex the other day, swanning across Regent Street all dolled up,' Barnard said eventually. 'She'd been to the Delilah looking for you, she said. Do you want to talk to her if she gets in touch again?'

'No I bloody don't! I won't lose any sleep if I never see that woman again.'

'OK, OK. I only asked. I gave her my number, so she may call me back.'

'Don't even tell her you've spoken to me, Flash. I need her around like a hole in the head. Do you understand?'

'Well, as you haven't told me where you are there's no risk of her finding out anything from me, is there?' Barnard snapped back. 'How do I contact you if I need to?'

'You don't need to,' Robertson said. 'Leave it to me, I'll do the contacting.' And the line went dead.

Kate hung up and went back into the living room to find Barnard sprawled in his revolving chair looking shell-shocked.

'You heard all that?' he said.

'Do you think what he said was true?' Kate asked.

'I haven't a bloody clue,' Barnard said. 'It sounds plausible, especially as we know that this Bert Flanagan has scarpered. But who knows? Ray's had years of sounding plausible enough to wheedle himself into high places. He's as slippery as an eel, and I doubt Jackson's going to believe a word he says.'

'What about his alibi?' Kate asked. Barnard gave a hollow laugh.

'You can buy alibis, sweetheart,' he said. 'Scotland sounds a bit far-fetched to me. Do you think they really do boxing galas in kilts? Or that Ray Robertson could catch a salmon? In the meantime I've got to decide how much to pass on to Jackson. If I can convince him that Ray approached me I might get away with it, I suppose.'

'I took the call,' Kate said, but Barnard only scowled.

'I don't want you involved in this,' he said. 'It's bad enough as it is. Anyway, if Jackson so much as suspects I've persuaded you to make inquiries for me, I'll get the blame anyway. You, my love, have done nothing more than take a few photographs on Canvey Island for your agency. The rest never happened. OK?'

'OK,' Kate said. 'I suppose.' But she felt uneasy. Nothing to do with Ray Robertson was ever as simple as it seemed.

Barnard was not able to see the DCI until lunchtime the next day as Jackson had been called to a meeting at the Yard, which he suspected might be about the progress – or lack of it – being made on Rod Miller's murder. When he was finally called into Jackson's office, he found the DCI in an obviously unreceptive mood. Barnard's stomach clenched.

'You wanted to see me?' Jackson snapped.

'Yes, guv, something unexpected happened last night. It's relevant to the murder case.' Jackson's expression darkened even further. He said nothing, clearly waiting for him to jump off the teetering chair and hang himself.

'I had a phone call from Ray Robertson last night, guv. Completely out of the blue.' Jackson steepled his hands in front of his face, as if praying, and waited some more. Barnard took a deep breath.

'He knows you want to talk to him, but he doesn't seem at all keen to talk to you. He thinks you'll tar him with the same brush as his brother.' Jackson's face hardened.

'Did you find out where he's holed up?' he asked.

'No I didn't, guv. There was no way he was going to tell me that.'

'Did you not think we could have traced the call?'

'I'd no way of doing that without hanging up on him and I doubt very much he'd have called back. He's got away with things for years by being very, very careful—'

'So what did he say? What did he want you to do? Help him in some way?'

'No, guv,' Barnard said firmly. 'He didn't want me to do anything except tell you certain things that Rod Miller had told him. He said Miller was obviously worried about something, and it seems he had reason to be. His past was catching up with him.'

'Tell me,' Jackson said and listened carefully to Barnard's summary of Miller's involvement in the Southend robbery before Robertson gave him a job at the gym, the convicted men's recent release from jail, and the disappearance of the proceeds from the post office robbery and possibly others. The scepticism in Jackson's eyes did not noticeably diminish as he listened, but nor did it obviously increase.

'Write this all down,' he said when Barnard had finished. 'I want a full report for the murder team. If necessary, we'll liaise with the Essex police. But it sounds to me like a bit of a fairy story which Robertson thinks might get him off the hook. Did he give you no clue where he was? No hint? You should have some idea where he might hide out, you've known him long enough.'

Barnard shrugged wearily.

'I've absolutely no idea, guv,' he said. 'I know you think he's my best friend, but he hasn't been that since I was ten years old. We went our separate ways long ago.'

'Have your report on my desk by three,' Jackson said. 'The Press Office at the Yard are keen to give Robertson's details to all the papers. So far no one seems to have followed up on that squib the *Daily Express* ran. I'm not at all sure how they'll react to what you're telling me. I may get them to put their plans on hold for another day or so – or maybe not.'

Ken Fellows called Kate O'Donnell into his office that same lunchtime. He still had the prints she had brought back from Southend on his desk.

'I've just had a call from the picture librarian at the East Anglian rag,' he said. 'He wanted me to know that he's uncovered another batch of shots we might be interested in. I think maybe you'd better go down there again and have a look. You can take this bunch back with you, as he seemed a bit anxious about them. And tell him which ones we definitely want to buy. Here, give him a call and nip down there again this afternoon. You've not got anything else urgent on, have you?'

Slightly surprised, Kate shook her head and took the folder containing the prints that were to be returned. She called Frank Garside from the phone in the photographers' room, which at that time of day was almost deserted. Garside picked up quickly but sounded slightly distracted.

'Yes, you can pop in,' he said. 'Leave it until about four. I'm a bit busy at the moment. There's some big story on the go at the fairground and I'm being asked for all sorts of pictures to illustrate it.' Kate pricked up her ears.

'I had a look at the fairground yesterday,' she said. 'It was very quiet then. What's the problem?'

'The police aren't saying very much, but it looks as if a little boy has gone missing. I don't know all the details. We're a bit cut off down here in the library. But the final edition will be out soon, so I'll know exactly what's amiss.' She heard the sound of urgent voices in the background.

'See you about four o'clock then,' she said. 'Thanks again.'

She left the office just after two, slightly worried that Barnard had not called to suggest lunch, which he often did. But she pushed that anxiety to the back of her mind as she made her way to the train from Fenchurch Street that took her on the now familiar ride to Southend. It was a short walk to the offices of the *News* and she was soon back in the library, where Frank Garside was waiting for her. She filled him in quickly on which of the prints Ken Fellows was interested in buying and then flicked through the new folder of flood pictures that he had unearthed.

'These are the ones we didn't use at the time,' Garside said. 'Some of them are very dark, as you can see, and the news desk no doubt thought some of the pictures were too graphic. Like this one of the woman carrying the baby. That baby turned out to have drowned.'

'Sad,' Kate said, looking at the woman's face frozen with cold and grief, the child limp in her arms.

'I shouldn't think Ken will want to use that either,' she said. 'This is supposed to be a celebration of the recovery of Canvey Island, a new beginning and all that. It's not intended to upset people. I don't think it's going to be too explicit.' She handed back the photograph. 'What's all this about a child missing from the fairground?' she asked. Garside picked up the latest edition of the day's paper and handed it to her.

'Set off for school but never arrived,' he said. 'The police are saying privately that he's probably been picked up by his own father. There have been some marital problems, apparently. Father walked out some time ago. They're not exactly treating it as a kidnapping. More a family affair.'

Kate quickly read the story tucked away on an inside page about eleven-year-old Luke Flanagan with a feeling of foreboding which was quickly enough confirmed when she realized that the blurred photograph of the boy's mother was undoubtedly Connie, looking distraught, with two younger children clutching at her hands.

'Well, I don't suppose he'll come to any harm if he's with his father,' she said quietly although she already had a conviction, based on no more than a gut feeling, that that was not necessarily the case. 'But when I went down to the fairground yesterday I happened to meet Mrs Flanagan and she gave the impression that there was more going on than just a bit of marital trouble. I only chatted to her because she said she'd lived on Canvey Island when the flood came.' Garside looked at her curiously as she picked up the folder containing the new photographs.

'There's always trouble with the showmen's families,' he said. 'It's nothing new. People who live in houses don't like them much.'

'They're very firm they are not gypsies,' Kate said.

'As good as,' Garside said coldly. 'Or as bad. There's a big chap – Jasper I think he's called – who rules the roost down there. The police are always hauling him in for threatening the young local lads, but he never seems to get more than a caution. It's my belief they don't mind him laying down the law at the fairground. It saves them having to do it themselves.' Kate nodded and buttoned up her coat. She wouldn't like to cross Connie's Uncle Jasper, she thought, but if he was on her side he might be a good man to rely on.

'We'll get back to you if Ken wants to use any of these,' she said. 'Thanks again for all your help.'

Once outside she hurried towards the fairground, which was as empty and windswept as the previous time she had been there. There was no sign of life around the dodgems this time, so she headed towards the area where the show families' caravans were parked beneath the shelter of the pier. The same tall man in the sheepskin jerkin and jaunty hat spotted her: Jasper Dowd, who Connie Flanagan had claimed was her uncle. This time he hurried over, putting out a heavily tattooed arm to prevent her continuing.

'What do you want now, petal?' his voice was soft but his eyes were hard.

'It's Connie's boy Luke who's missing, isn't it?' she asked.

'So what if it is?' the man said. 'She doesn't need the likes of you interfering, does she? We've told the police and that's good enough. Though they won't stir themselves more than they have to. They say if he doesn't come home tonight they'll start a proper search in the morning. We'll have to see, won't we? If they don't do anything, we'll have to start looking ourselves. We don't need them.'

'It seems very slow. Do you really think his father's taken him?' Kate persisted.

'Most likely, it's the sort of thing Bert would do if he was in the mood.'

Behind the man's back she suddenly spotted Connie herself, standing beside a caravan with the two younger children, Sally and baby Liam, clinging to her skirts. She guessed that Connie had seen her, but she made no move in her direction. She could hardly push past the man who had obviously appointed himself Connie's heavyweight guardian, but she could think of nothing that would persuade him to let her through.

'Tell Connie I'm sorry for her trouble,' she said quietly. 'If she wants to talk to me, this is my phone number.' She wrote Barnard's number on the back of her photographer's card and handed it to the man, who glanced at it sceptically and put in his pocket. The chances of Connie getting hold of it seemed remote, but Kate could do nothing except swallow her anger. She turned on her heel and made her way back through the amusements towards the road. No one seemed to be taking the disappearance of Luke Flanagan very seriously and she was sure that was a horribly big mistake.

EIGHT

After they had exchanged news of two very unsatisfactory working days, cooked a meal and drunk half a bottle of red wine in time to watch the television news, the evening stretched ahead and Kate could see just how uneasy Barnard was. He kept glancing at the phone as if expecting a call.

'He won't ring again,' she said. 'If what Jackson said about tracing the call was serious, they're probably listening in by now. It's not that difficult to tap the line, is it?'

'It's not that difficult at all,' Barnard said. 'They're supposed to get permission, but I don't think the Yard or Special Branch bother too much about that.'

'Do you think they'd go that far?' she asked.

'Oh yes, the Yard would go that far to pin something on Ray Robertson. All that effort he made to make friends in high places through the boxing galas and the other charity stuff he's done over the years doesn't impress the Met one bit. Jackson's not the only one who's been panting to get Ray as well as Georgie for years. I'm just a side issue. A means to an end, maybe, but nothing more than that.'

'An innocent bystander?' Kate asked, almost offering a smile.

'I wouldn't go quite as far as that,' Barnard said with a grin which fleetingly reminded Kate just why she was sitting here in his flat. He had, she thought, been fun once though not right now. He seemed as close as she had ever seen him to giving up.

'I'm useful at the moment, but ultimately expendable,' he said.

She took his hand tentatively. He responded by putting an arm round her shoulders and kissing her.

'I'm sorry I've got you involved in all this nonsense,' he said. She moved closer and returned the kiss more passionately than perhaps he'd anticipated. Reluctantly they pulled apart when the phone rang. Barnard half stood, hesitating.

'Shall I answer it?' he asked quietly.

'You'll have to make up your own mind about that,' she said

cautiously. 'It depends if you think someone might be listening in.' He nodded, spun on his heel and went to the phone. As he listened to the caller she was surprised to see the tension ebb away.

'Yes, she's here,' he said handing the receiver to Kate. 'It's for you.'

The voice at the other end of the line was muffled and Kate did not recognize it at first. But when Connie Flanagan identified herself she realized that it was because the woman at the other end of the line was in tears. She instantly knew why.

'Have they found Luke?' she asked.

'No, they haven't. Everyone thinks his father's taken him – my uncle, the police, everyone. They're not taking it seriously. But I know Bert wouldn't do that. I thought I was safe here with my family, but obviously I'm not. And I'm frightened they'll try to take Sally and Liam as well. I found your number on the card you gave Jasper.'

'But who would take the children?'

'Someone who wanted to find Bert badly enough. I need to get away from here but I don't know where to go.'

'Isn't it better to stay with people you know? Your uncle and his friends look as if they would be able to protect you.'

'They didn't protect Luke, did they? Someone got hold of him.'

'So is there anywhere else you could go? Somewhere you'd be safe?'

There was a silence at the other end of the line and for a moment Kate thought Connie had rung off.

'There's my Auntie Vi in Clacton,' she said eventually. 'She married a man up there and runs some of the amusements on Clacton pier. She lives in a proper house, not a van. She might take us in, just until they find Luke.'

'Can you ring her?' Kate asked, but there was another silence.

'She's not on the phone and I don't know how to get there by train. Not with the kids . . .'

'Can you ring me back in ten minutes?' Kate said glancing at Barnard who looked mystified, but she had had an idea and looked determined.

'What the hell's going on?' Barnard asked after she hung up.

'It was Connie Flanagan, from the fairground in Southend. I

left her this number in case she needed to get in touch. She wants to get herself and two children from Southend to Clacton as fast as she can. She's scared out of her wits that whoever's got the little boy will try to take the other children as well. If it's the husband who's taken Luke, I suppose he might well come back for the other two. She's terrified.'

'Can't the Southend police help her get there?' Barnard asked, reasonably enough.

'I don't think she trusts them,' Kate said. 'And she certainly doesn't want anyone in Southend to know where she's gone, not even the police. It doesn't sound as if they're trying very hard to find Luke.'

'So what do you want to do? Drive out there and rescue her? Take her to Clacton?'

'Would you?' Kate said quickly. 'If only I could drive . . . I don't think I'll sleep a wink unless I know she's safe.'

Barnard sighed and looked at his watch. It was nine thirty.

'It wasn't quite the way I planned to spend the evening,' he said ruefully.

'I know,' Kate said. 'But can we do it? She's going to ring back soon. If we say no and anything happens to her and the kids, I'd never forgive myself.'

'Your problem is that you think you can solve the problems of the world single-handed.' He glanced at his watch again. 'Tell her to meet us at the end of the pier at eleven. We should be able to make it by then, the roads will be quiet.'

She kissed him again.

'Thank you,' she said. 'I wish we didn't have to.'

They seemed to Kate to have been driving for half the night when a car with a blue flashing light passed them and cut in front, forcing Barnard to stop. A uniformed police officer waved to him to open the window and stuck his head inside curiously, taking in Kate in the front seat and Connie Flanagan and two sleeping children in the back.

'Pushing it a bit hard, weren't you sir?' the traffic officer asked. Barnard nodded wearily.

'Sorry,' he said. 'It's late and I was keen to get these kids to bed.'

'Have you been drinking, sir?' the officer persisted.

'Not for hours,' Barnard said. 'I'm not drunk if that's what you're thinking.'

'Perhaps you'd like to get out of the car for me then, for a little chat?' Barnard shrugged and got out.

'Look,' he said quietly. 'I'm in the job myself, with the Met. You could give me a break. This was a family emergency. My girlfriend's cousin had her bag stolen and couldn't get home to Clacton, so I offered to take them. You don't realize quite how fast you're going when the road's as empty as this.'

'You'd realize if you had to scrape people off the road after a smash,' the officer said, his eyes cold, making a note of the Capri's registration number. 'Name and address?' he asked. For a wild moment Barnard thought of lying although his name could be easily traced through his car's number plate. He shrugged and gave his details, cursing the persistence of the Essex police.

'Can't we leave it at that?' he asked. 'Perhaps if I bought you and your mates a drink?'

'I don't think so, sir,' the officer said. 'But maybe we'll forget you made that suggestion. This isn't the Met, this is Essex. We tend to be straight up and down in Essex, and we don't much like foreigners tearing up and down the A12 at seventy-odd miles an hour. Would you like to walk in a straight line towards my car? Let's see how much I think you've been drinking, shall we?'

Barnard did as he was told, conscious of being carefully watched by the officer behind him and his mate behind the wheel of the patrol car. To his relief, all he got in the end was a pat on the shoulder rather than the heavy hand of an arresting officer.

'Mind how you go the rest of the way, sir,' the officer said. 'And keep your speed down. Remember you've got kids in the car.'

Barnard got back into the driving seat, leaned back and shut his eyes for a second.

'What was that all about?' Kate asked.

'Speeding, drinking. I think they were just looking for something to break the monotony of a quiet night. But if they'd decided to arrest me, it could have been nasty. It would have gone straight back to the Met and questions would have been asked.' He watched the police car set off towards the turn-off for Clacton at a sober pace, which he knew he would have to follow.

'Let's go,' he said, glancing at the sleeping passengers in the back seat. 'I'm more than ready for bed myself.'

Terry and Kevin sat on the shingle eating jam sandwiches. The boys were wearing wellington boots but their grey school shorts were already spattered in mud, and the coats that concealed the rest of their school uniform were also liberally smeared. Terry, the smaller boy, finished his sandwich and groaned, rubbing his stomach dramatically.

'I'm still starving,' he said. 'We should have brought something else.'

'If I'd taken anything else, my mam would have noticed. She'd guess we were bunking off and not having school dinner,' Kevin said.

'I didn't realize it was so far,' Terry said, rubbing his calf above the boots and turning his leg black with mud.

'If you want good worms you have to come right out here, my dad says. This is where he comes. He'll give me sixpence if we take a bucketful back. Anyway, it's worth it for a day out of school. I'm fed up with being called a pikey or a gyppo and getting thumped all the time by Ricky Raymond. I hate him and I hate the place. The sooner I can leave school and help my da on the big dipper the better. You don't need to read and write to do that.'

'Adding up is useful, though,' Terry said with a thoughtful expression. 'For doing the change.'

'Most of them don't even count their change,' Kevin said scornfully. He threw away the paper bag his sandwiches had been wrapped in and picked up a long metal fork. 'Come on,' he said. 'You bring the bucket. Let's see what we can find.'

They plodded out on to the sands again, with the wet mud sucking at their wellingtons.

'What's that?' Terry asked, pointing slightly to one side. They both stared at something sticking out of the mud.

'It's just an old log,' Kevin said.

'Looks like a boot,' Terry said uncertainly.

'Nah,' Kevin said. 'Just a log. Come on. Let's get digging.'

The two boys worked hard and silently for half an hour before Terry gave a wail. Kevin looked across the wet sands, which lay not far below the grassy edge of what passed here for dry land and laughed. The younger boy was standing on one leg with his other wellington boot wedged firmly in the mud. He wobbled precariously for a moment, then put his bare foot down with a squelch.

'Oh God,' he said. 'My da will murder me if I go home like this.'

'Here, I'll help you pull it out,' Kevin offered, plodding through the increasingly liquid surface towards Terry, using his fork to help keep his balance. But with each step he could feel less of a firm base beneath his feet and by the time he reached the younger boy he was becoming seriously worried.

'Hold on to me,' he said, and felt his own feet sinking deeper. Terry grabbed his arm and Kevin could see the watery mud rising up his own boots. He reached for Terry's wellington and gave it a tug. At first it refused to move, but when he stuck the fork into the mud close to it he was able to lever it back to the surface. He rubbed his sleeve across his forehead, leaving another dark smear.

'Come on,' he said urgently. 'I don't know about the tide out here. We'd better get back to dry land. It feels as if the water's getting deeper.' He turned and began wading through the mud but soon realized that Terry had moved no more than a couple of steps and had stopped again.

'What's wrong?'

'I'm stuck,' the younger boy said. 'I can't get my feet out.' Kevin turned and plodded back towards Terry. He could feel the pull of the mud getting stronger and grabbed Terry under the arms. As he tried to pull him upwards, he realized that the more he tugged the more the sucking black stuff was pulling him down as well. He let go and extricated his own feet. Panic was beginning to seize him and he felt sick.

'I can't lift you out, mate,' he said. 'I'll have to get someone to help.' He glanced at the shoreline and, some distance back, could see a white van that had stopped close to the water's edge.

'Look,' he said. 'There's someone up there. I'll go and get them.'

'Don't leave me,' Terry screamed, tipping over into panic. 'Don't leave me, please don't leave me.'

'I have to,' Kevin said. 'It'll only take five minutes if I run like the clappers. Promise.' Gritting his teeth, he turned away from Terry and began the long, tortuous struggle back to the grassy bank, the fork in one hand and the bucket with a puny catch in the other. As he scrambled up on to dry land, dropped the fork and bucket with a clatter and began to run, he could hear Terry's wails. There were two men sitting in the front of the van drinking mugs of tea. Kevin banged on the window and shouted incoherently for help.

'Calm down, calm down,' one of them said. 'What's the panic?' But when Kevin told them, they quickly opened the back door, shoved the boy inside, and drove along the shore to the point where the boys had embarked on their adventure. Kevin could see that Terry had now sunk up to his waist and could hear him screaming hysterically.

'Ladders,' one of the men said sharply to the other, waving at the roof of the van, where ladders were stored. 'Quick, mate.' Silently they lifted the ladders down and began to wade towards the trapped boy until the mud came almost over the top of their boots. Then they placed the ladders flat on the surface, one man holding the end steady while the younger, lighter man began to crawl purposefully towards Terry. The boy clung to his rescuer as soon as he succeeded in reaching him, and for a moment it looked as if he would pull him into the mud instead of being pulled out. But the man quickly got a grip and began to ease backwards very slowly, bringing Terry with him.

As soon as they got to the shingle edge, Kevin sank to the ground and began to cry. The men helped the boys up the shallow bank and the four of them sat on the grass panting, gazing over the flat expanse of the sands where a muddy black tide was now gurgling towards them.

'Dangerous, that,' the van driver said, watching as Kevin emptied the water out of his wellington and pulled it on again and Terry tried to scrape the mud out of his.

'So where do you little beggars come from?' he asked. Kevin told him reluctantly.

'So how the hell did you get out here?' the man asked, surprised.

'We walked,' Kevin said. 'My da comes out here to dig for worms.' The other man was gazing out at the mud flats with a curious look on his face.

'Is that a log?' he asked his mate. The other man shook his head.

'I noticed that,' he said. 'I think it's a log. Maybe.' He shook his head slightly and glanced at the boys.

'I thought it was a boot,' Kevin said. 'Maybe someone got stuck and couldn't get out. Ugh.' The two men exchanged a quick glance.

'Come on, we'll take you home,' the driver said.

But Terry, covered in thick mud and now shivering, just glanced into the bucket.

'D'you think we got enough worms to get sixpence?' he asked.

'I should think you're more likely to get a bloody good hiding,' the driver said.

DS Harry Barnard took his time going into work the next morning. He'd driven sedately back to Highgate after delivering Connie Flanagan and her children, together with a couple of battered suitcases, to a sleepily bemused Auntie Vi in Clacton, and it was almost three o'clock when he and Kate had fallen into bed exhausted, any lingering thought of doing anything but sleep driven from their minds. By the time Barnard surfaced, Kate had already gone to work and he decided to take a leisurely stroll around Soho to see if he could pick up anything there that the DCI might be remotely interested in. He called into a couple of booksellers, legitimate as far as their window displays were concerned, but much less so if you chose to have a look in their locked back rooms. There had been a rumour that a new source of supply had been located by some of them in the Netherlands and he wondered if his best contact – a man called George, whose tweedy bulk and permanently smoky briar pipe suggested nothing but intense respectability – would be prepared to help. George would either be buying some of the allegedly extreme pornography himself, in which case Barnard might get a sniff of discomfort amongst the tobacco fumes. Or he would not, in which case he might be prepared to grass up some of his rivals and hint to the Met which storerooms would be worth raiding. But he was not

giving much away this morning and Barnard left the fug of the
overstuffed shop convinced that George was probably already
buying from the new source and would tell him nothing unless
and until the deal went sour.

On his way back towards Oxford Street he called in at the
queer pub, another of DCI Jackson's monotonously frequent
targets, but found only cleaners and a solitary barman inside.
Like the street girls, who generally slept until noon, seekers after
illegal sex went to bed late and rose even later. He needed, he
thought, to have another prowl around later in the day. He knew
he was being watched from high windows in the narrow streets,
but at this time of the morning no one of any interest was talking.

Even so, Barnard felt reassured by the familiarity of the Soho
streets and the myriad doorways offering services from the exotic
to the everyday. If you wanted illicit pleasures or jazz, foreign
cuisine or late night boozing, this was the place to come and it
was where he felt most at home.

Cutting through close to the Delilah Club, doors firmly closed,
his pace quickened as he saw someone he did recognize. Ray
Robertson's ex-wife Loretta was sweeping up the road towards
him, the same hat with a tiny veil perched on top of her red hair
and a fox fur round her neck with lifelike eyes that seemed to
Barnard almost as searching as Loretta's own.

'Ha!' she said with some belligerence as he approached. 'Have
you found him yet?' Barnard reluctantly stopped as she was
effectively barring his way.

'No, I haven't,' he said. 'He's gone to ground for some reason
that I don't understand. The only way he's going to sort this out
is to talk to us.'

'Well, you know what a slippery bastard he is,' Loretta said,
smoothing the tawny fur more tightly around her neck to keep
out the wintry wind. 'Are you going to let me know when you
find him? Or are you holding out on me? Do you really not know
where he is?'

'Not if it annoys my boss. No, I'm not going to let you know,'
Barnard said, thinking he'd had enough of Loretta's pestering.
'And no, I don't have a clue where he is. You know about Rod
Miller, I take it? It would be more than my bloody job's worth
to cover for him now.' Loretta's lips pursed tightly.

'I read about it. Is that why they want to find Ray? Does your boss really think he whacked Rod? That's ridiculous. They've been thick as thieves for years.' It was, Barnard thought, an unfortunate choice of words.

'My boss was told by the Yard to offer Ray some sort of protection with the big trial coming up. But now the picture's changed. They obviously want to talk to him about Rod and the longer he stays out of sight the more suspicious they're likely to get. If you do track him down, Loretta, let us know. Did you by any chance go down to the gym the other day? Someone told us they saw someone who could have been you trying to get in? If that was you, you need to tell us.'

'I've never been near the place,' she said angrily. 'I thought you were his best mate in the force. Can't you do something to help?'

'There's no way I can help him now or I might end up in the dock with him,' Barnard snapped.

'Ha!' Loretta said again. 'Maybe no more than you deserve.'

'Thanks a lot, darling,' Barnard said, suddenly furious. He side-stepped round Loretta and hurried towards Oxford Street. She was, he thought, almost more of a liability than her ex-husband. He didn't look back, but he felt her fury like an unexploded bomb just behind him all the way to the nick.

Barnard walked into the CID room, hung up his trench coat and hat carefully, and went over to his desk. DC Stansfield was the only person who glanced in his direction.

'The DCI's looking for you,' he said. 'Though with that tie you're likely to give him a heart attack.' Barnard was used to banter about his fashion sense, but this morning he did not feel like offering even a faint smile of apology over the flowery Liberty's job he had chosen to put on. He pulled his jacket back on and walked down the corridor to the DCI's office, suddenly feeling the dispiriting effect of his late night. He knocked on the door and went in when summoned, to find an even more unfriendly welcome than usual.

'You wanted to see me, guv?'

'You're late,' Jackson snapped. 'I got Stansfield to ring you at home but there was no reply.'

'I came down through Soho,' Barnard said more equably than

he felt. 'I hoped I might get a lead on this Dutch pornography that's supposed to be coming in. But there's not a whisper yet.'

'Keep on with that inquiry,' Jackson said. 'Have you heard any more from Robertson?'

'No, guv. Not a dicky bird. I don't think he liked what I said to him very much when he called me.'

'Which was?'

'To come in and talk to us.'

'I want to know if you have any contact, any contact at all,' Jackson said. 'Is that clear?'

'Crystal, guv,' Barnard said. 'I did bump into his ex-wife again this morning, still hanging round the Delilah Club. She's not managed to track him down either, apparently.'

If it had been possible for DCI Jackson to look any angrier, he would probably have exploded. 'If you bump into her again, bring her in,' he said. 'I think maybe it's time we had a chat with that lady, don't you?'

NINE

I t took Essex police and fire service most of the afternoon to extricate a man's body from where it had been buried on Maplin Sands.

After waiting for the tide to fall, they had to establish a firm platform around the waterlogged boot that the boys had tentatively and their rescuers with more certainty identified as attached to a leg. The first police constable on the scene had seen nothing but churning muddy sea water and had not rushed back to the nick. But when he did eventually call in at the end of his shift, his inspector had been sufficiently concerned to investigate a bit further and, wearing waders, had satisfied himself that the boot contained a foot, although no more of the body was visible from the surface. It had become firmly wedged beneath the mud, though whether by accident or design it was impossible to tell.

By then the tide was at its lowest and the mud at its firmest, but it still took more than an hour to dig the body out. When it had been dispatched to the morgue, so caked in mud and sand that not much could be seen by the naked eye, Inspector Fred Weston made his way back to the nick in Southend and poked his head round the door of CID.

'Possible suspicious death down on the sands,' he said to DCI Jack Baker, a heavy man who looked very comfortable behind his many chins and rolls of fat. 'Almost buried, though he could have dug himself in deep if he fell in and panicked. I've sent it to the morgue and asked for a post-mortem as soon as. Could be nothing.'

'Close to the Broomway, was it?' Baker asked lugubriously as he smoothed almost invisible strands of hair over his bald head. 'There are still idiots who think they can use that path. Should have more sense if they're local. I don't think it's been properly maintained for years. It certainly wasn't during the war. The military have always hated it.'

'Not far from the end, anyway,' Weston said. 'Could be

someone trying to walk to Foulness. But I don't think anyone's been reported AWOL apart from the young boy from the fairground. And his dad, though everyone seems to think he's working away. Anyway, I'll check.'

The post-mortem was not scheduled until the next morning and, now aware that no one had been reported missing over the last few days, Baker felt his curiosity piqued and decided to attend. Uncomfortable in an overall that was too tight round his paunch, he stood at the end of the table where the unknown man, now washed clean of the clinging mud, lay naked under the bright lights. The closer he looked at the body, the more sure he became that he had made the right decision. Call it instinct, he told himself, or luck, but he had become certain in his own mind overnight that this death was not natural. The confirmation was now spread out in front of him as Reg Stephenson, the pathologist, gave him a nod.

'Not an accident then,' Jack Baker said flatly, gazing at the tall gangling corpse whose pale skin was cut and bruised and had been damaged by what looked like burns almost all over. Only the reddish hairy legs had been spared.

'Not an accident,' Stephenson said lugubriously. 'Look here.'

Baker went round to the far end of the table, where the pathologist was pushing the corpse's thinning red hair away from his scalp. 'He was beaten, tortured even, and then shot. At close range. Entry wound here. And exit wound here.' When Baker went to the other side of the table, he could see that part of the victim's jaw was missing.

'No chance of finding the bullet?' Baker asked, although he already knew the answer.

'Must be under all that mud, I should think. It's certainly not here. Straight in and out, as you can see. Unless he was shot somewhere else and it's conveniently lodged in a door or a wall somewhere.'

'No ID, I don't suppose?'

'His clothes are over there.' The pathologist waved at a couple of buckets of mud-encrusted clothing. 'We'll get them cleaned up, but nothing fell out of the pockets when we took them off. Looked as if they'd been emptied. Well-worn corduroys, vest and shirt, and a donkey jacket. Nothing out of the ordinary for a working man.'

'And any idea when he died?'

Stephenson shrugged. 'That's an interesting question. I've no idea how well bodies are preserved when they're buried in salty sand and mud and kept wet by the tide twice a day. Not something I've come across before. There's not much decomposition or bloating, as you can see, but that could mean he was buried there very recently or that the body has been preserved unusually effectively. I'll have to do some research and come back to you on that.' Baker sighed and put a hand in his pocket to pull out his cigarettes, but then thought better of it.

'So all we know is that we've got an unidentified bloke, shot through the head and badly injured, with no identifying features except red hair? Not much to launch a murder inquiry on, is it?'

'I'll let you have my report as soon as I can,' Stephenson said irritably. 'It's pretty obvious what killed him, but you never know what I might find when I open him up.'

'Thanks. I think the best thing I can do is talk to the local rag. Someone must know who this bloke is and that he's gone missing. Dead bodies don't turn up buried on the sands without someone knowing where they came from. Can I send in an artist to give us some sort of likeness? That would help.'

'Feel free when I've finished and tidied him up,' Stephenson said. 'His face isn't too badly damaged if you hide the bullet wound.' And with that Baker had to be satisfied. He glanced at his watch. 'We won't get anything into the paper until tomorrow morning now, anyway. They were bloody slow getting him out.'

'Time and tide,' Stephenson said heavily, picking up a scalpel. 'Especially out there on the sands.'

When Harry Barnard and Kate got back to the flat after a rare visit to the cinema, to catch up with the new Bond film, the phone was ringing.

'Damn and blast!' Barnard muttered, flinging his coat carelessly on a chair and letting his hand hover over the receiver. 'If it's Ray Robertson again, I'm in trouble. Jackson told me he wanted to tap the phone, and I've no doubt he will already have arranged it.' Kate pulled him away and picked up the receiver herself.

'Hello?' she said. 'Who's that?' But to the surprise of both of

them no one responded, and after a couple of seconds the line
went dead.

'Wrong number? Or someone who doesn't want to talk to
me?'

'Or someone canny enough to know the sound of a wiretap
kicking in,' Barnard said. 'I get the distinct feeling that I'm being
set up, but whether it's by the Yard and Jackson or Ray, or
someone else entirely, I haven't a clue.'

Kate pulled him on to the sofa and took his hand.

'Don't get paranoid,' she said. 'I don't think this is anything
to do with you personally. It's about Ray Robertson and his crazy
brother. They're just hoping you'll lead them to him. But as you
don't have a clue where he is that's not going to happen, is it?
So relax.'

Barnard shrugged and got up to pour them both a drink but
before the Scotch had even hit the glass the doorbell sounded,
making them both jump. Barnard topped up his drink and took
a gulp.

'Who the hell is that?' he said. Kate's stomach tightened as
she wondered whether Ray Robertson had decided to turn up in
person, but as she listened to Barnard opening the door she realized that the husky voice was unmistakeably female. 'You again!'
she heard him say.

He came back into the room closely followed by a tall buxom
woman in a fur coat and high heels, heavily made up and with
her red hair in a fashionably short style. She looked slightly
startled when she saw Kate.

'I didn't realize you had company, darling,' she said to Barnard.

'This is my girlfriend, Kate,' Barnard said with a very thin
smile. 'Kate, this is Loretta, Ray Robertson's ex-wife.' Kate
nodded, uncertain how to react.

'How did you get this address?' Barnard asked Loretta, obviously
furious at her unexpected arrival. 'Have you tracked Ray down?
Did he tell you where I live?'

'No, I haven't tracked him down,' Loretta said. 'I wondered
if you had.'

'If I had, he'd be at the nick by now,' he said. 'The top brass
aren't going to give up on this, so if you do find Ray you can
tell him that from me. He can run but he can't hide for ever. Why

do you want to see him so urgently, anyway? It's years since you
split up. You haven't given me a clue what this is all about.'

'Well, you can whistle for that sort of information, Harry. But
I can tell you that Ray'll be furious if he finds out what I know
and he's not been told in time. Let's just say there's a pot of
gold for him at the end of the rainbow and I know where it's
hidden. Anyway, I won't keep you from your bed. I'm sure
you're having lots of fun there. You always did.' And she spun
on her heel and left as quickly as she had entered. Within seconds
they heard a car accelerate away, and by the time Barnard had
pulled back the curtains and looked out of the window all that
could be seen was a cloud of exhaust fumes hanging over the
small car park at the front of the flats.

'That woman is a pain in the neck,' Barnard said angrily. 'I
wonder where she got my address from? It must be someone at
the nick. I'm not in the phone book for obvious reasons.'

'She's something else,' Kate said thoughtfully. 'But I did
wonder why she's wearing that red wig. She's a bit long in the
tooth to be trying to look like Cilla Black.'

DCI Jack Baker extricated himself wearily from the patrol car
that had given him a lift to the fairground. He scanned its windswept and almost deserted depths and pulled his coat collar up
more tightly around his neck. The sharp wind and flecks of rain
didn't offer much hope of trade for the stalls and rides, some of
which were making preparations to open their shutters and ticket
offices. Like most of the locals, he regarded the showmen and
their families with more suspicion than respect. And the feeling,
he knew, was mutual.

'Come on, lad,' he said to the young plain-clothes officer who
accompanied him, carrying a handful of papers in a folder that
inadequately protected the contents from the rain. They skirted
around the amusements and headed for the caravans parked in
the lee of the sea wall and the pier. His lumbering approach was
being watched, he knew, and he was not surprised when the tall
figure of Jasper Dowd appeared at the door of one of the larger
and more ornate vans and headed in his direction.

'Jasper,' Baker said, holding out a conciliatory hand to the
man who towered over him. 'We need some help.'

'Oh yes?' Dowd said. 'That makes a change from the way you usually come here mob-handed. You'd better come in. I'll get my lass to make some tea.' He made his way back to the caravan he had come from and led them up the steps into a spotlessly clean space where it was obvious that everything had its place and was firmly in it. A pale young woman who had been washing cups at the sink turned round towards her father.

'Tea,' he said and within seconds the kettle was on and beginning to whistle. Dowd waved the two policemen on to a bench seat in front of a table and reached for a bottle of whisky from a shelf above the cooker.

'You'll join me, gents?' he asked when the three cups were poured and the girl who had made them had put her coat on and left. Baker opened his mouth to object but it was too late. Dowd had topped the cups up with the spirit regardless.

'So how can I help you?' he asked, leaning back in his seat and appearing completely relaxed. Baker took the file from his DC and opened it.

'A man was found dead on Maplin Sands yesterday,' he said. 'He was buried so deep in the mud he'd not have been found in normal circumstances, but it was a neap tide and it uncovered his boot. We don't know who he is, but we've got an accurate sketch of his face.' He pushed a copy of the sketch towards Dowd and drummed his fingers on it.

'Anyone you know?' he asked. Dowd picked up the sheet of paper and took a swig of his well-laced tea.

'Oh yes,' he said. 'That's Bert Flanagan, who runs the dodgems. Not much doubt about that, Inspector. We wondered where he'd got to. We thought he was working away.'

Irritated by Dowd's casual manner, Baker scowled.

'The father of the lad who's missing?' Baker snapped.

'Yes, we thought he must have picked Luke up from school and taken him off somewhere. The parents have not been getting on too well lately. Bert's wife is my niece, Connie.'

'So how long exactly has Bert been away?' he asked.

Dowd shrugged and looked vague. 'A few weeks, I reckon,' he said. 'It's not unusual at this time of the year. You can't make a living just opening at the weekends. Some of the men go off to work somewhere else.'

'And they don't keep in touch?'

'No reason to,' Dowd said. 'When the season starts, they generally come back.'

'So tell me about the family.'

Dowd hesitated for no more than a split second, but it was enough for Baker to make connections he knew he should have made as soon as he had learned the dead man's name. He'd not been nearly quick enough there, he realized – and he wondered, not for the first time, if half a bottle of Scotch a night was slowing him down.

'So a young boy's gone missing,' he said. 'You didn't rush to tell us and, anyway, everyone said maybe he's gone to his dad. So now his dad's been hauled out of the sinking sands, what do you reckon? Should we be looking for Luke out there as well in that bloody bog?'

Dowd stiffened and pushed his hat even further to the back of his head while the ensuing silence lengthened. 'I don't know,' he said at last. 'I have no idea.'

'If someone wanted to get rid of Bert, is there any reason you know of why they might kill the lad as well?'

'I don't know who might want to get rid of Bert,' Dowd said angrily, 'so how would I know if Luke was in danger? Why would anyone want to hurt an eleven-year-old boy?' Baker did not respond to that and changed tack.

'Is his mother here?' he snapped.

'Connie? No, she did a flit the other night with the other two kids.' Baker froze.

'What do you mean, did a flit? Don't you know where she's gone?'

'She didn't say,' Dowd said angrily. 'I'm her bloody uncle, aren't I? I was supposed to keep an eye on her while all this was going on. They were staying in my van and I was sleeping in another. When I got up yesterday morning they weren't there. She's always been a law unto herself, has Connie.'

'So it was not last night? It was the night before when she did a flit?'

'Yeah, the night before,' Dowd muttered reluctantly.

'Did she not leave a message, or give any indication where she'd gone?' Baker's patience was at breaking point by now.

'She couldn't have gone far without some help, with two kids in tow.'

'She took most of the kids' stuff with her,' Dowd said reluctantly. 'She must have got a taxi, or maybe someone she knew gave her a lift.'

'We'll check the railway station and the bus station,' Baker said. 'Have there been any strangers hanging around here recently?' Dowd gave that infinitesimal hesitation again.

'There was a young woman talking to Connie last week, said she was doing research or something and wanted to take some pictures of the fairground. Sounded a silly sort of story to me. When Luke went missing, I wondered if she was involved in that.'

'Did she leave a name?' Baker asked, although he guessed that if she did it might not be genuine. But to his surprise, Dowd nodded.

'She left it with me, as it happens. On a bit of card, but I gave it to Connie. There were phone numbers in London.' He glanced away, crushing his hat down on his head as if it might help him. 'I don't read very well,' he mumbled.

'Anything else you can remember about this woman?' Baker insisted.

'She told Connie she'd been to the local rag, looking for something. Maybe they'll know who she was.'

'Right,' Baker said. 'If you hear anything from Connie Flanagan, I want to know about it. Without fail, understand? In the meantime, we'll step up the search for Luke and see if we can track down this mysterious visitor Connie had before she left. And we'll try to find out who dumped Luke's father on Maplin Sands, though there can't be much evidence out there with the sea washing over the sands twice a day. I just hope to God the boy's not out there as well.'

Harry Barnard answered the summons from DCI Jackson with a certain weariness. A conference with his boss every day, he reckoned, was over the top. But as soon as he opened the door to Jackson's office he realized that this was something new in the scale of things. There were two men in the office – Jackson himself, who was standing by the window, looking out, with his back to the room, and a man Barnard did not recognize wearing the uniform of a commissioner at Scotland Yard sitting comfortably in Jackson's chair.

'Ah,' the stranger said, and there were layers of meaning in the tone, by no means any of them encouraging. 'You're DS Barnard. I've heard a lot about you.'

Jackson turned back into the room.

'This is ACC Cathcart, who initiated the search for Ray Robertson recently, for reasons which we discussed. That search has now become a top priority.'

'Sir,' Barnard said, his mouth dry.

'I know you have been kept at arms length from the murder case in Whitechapel, for very good reasons,' Cathcart said, his eyes like flint. 'But in the light of some information that has just come to hand from Essex, I need some information from you which may be relevant to the inquiry into Rod Miller's death. Have you been to Essex recently, Sergeant?' Barnard took a deep breath before concluding that there was no easy way out of this. Kate, he thought, would probably never forgive him.

'A couple of times,' he said. 'I went to Canvey Island with my girlfriend on Saturday, to keep her company while she was taking some pictures, and then we had a night out in Southend. Took me back a bit.'

'Is that all?' Cathcart pressed. Barnard sighed.

'No,' he said. 'I gave my girlfriend a lift out there again the night before last,' he said. 'She can't drive and she wanted to help a friend – well, not a friend exactly, someone she'd met through work in Southend. This woman wanted to get herself and two kids from Southend to Clacton in a hurry. It sounded like an emergency, so I agreed to help.'

'And you got stopped on the A12 for speeding, in your red Capri,' Cathcart said.

Barnard nodded. 'Stupid thing to do,' he said.

'So where exactly did you drop this woman and her children?' Cathcart snapped.

'At her aunt's house,' Barnard said reluctantly. 'I don't know the address exactly but it was close to the pier. She just told me where to turn. We watched her go to the door with the kids and a couple of bags she had with her. When someone let her in, we left.'

'And does she have a name?'

'Connie Flanagan,' Barnard said. 'Her boy's disappeared and she was trying to drop out of sight. She was very scared. The Essex police know all about it.'

'That's not all the Essex police are concerned about today, Sergeant,' Cathcart said. 'There have been some major developments since Mrs Flanagan unexpectedly took herself off with your help. I'm sure they'll now want to talk to her urgently.'

'So how did your girlfriend come to be in contact with her?' Jackson broke in, his face flushed and angry.

'She was taking some photographs on Canvey Island and then did some research at the local paper in Southend. It was initially all to do with the 1953 floods. There's some redevelopment on Canvey that her agency is interested in.'

'Did you go to Essex on any other occasions, Sergeant? With your girlfriend, maybe?'

'No, sir,' Barnard said. 'I talked to her about Canvey before she went. I was in the army in '53 and ended up trying to get people out, then filling sandbags for days afterwards . . . It's not a place you volunteer to go back to if you saw it then. I talked to her about the flood, obviously, but she went there and to Southend on her own, apart from those two occasions.'

'The Essex police will want to talk to Miss O'Donnell,' Cathcart said. 'We'll let them make their own arrangements. They don't like interference from the Yard. You can warn her that there will be questions, probably later today.'

'Have they found Connie's son?' Barnard asked, fearing the worst and suddenly feeling very cold.

'Not her son, Sergeant, it's her husband who has been found dead. So, as you can imagine, they want to talk to his wife urgently.' Barnard stared at the commissioner, a whole raft of wild possibilities running through his mind.

'And on the other matter, Sergeant?' Jackson broke in. 'Have you heard anything more on the whereabouts of Ray Robertson?'

'No, guv,' Barnard said. 'I saw his ex-wife again last night. She's haunting me. But I told her the same as the last time. I've no idea where Ray Robertson is. For all I know he could be dead too.'

*   *   *

Two police officers from Southend arrived at the Ken Fellows Agency at midday. Harry Barnard had already warned Kate that they would be contacting her, but it didn't make her feel any more comfortable when they arrived. The news that Connie Flanagan's husband had been pulled out of the marshes dead had shaken her, and the two men did not look enchanted when they realized that the limited space Ken and his photographers worked in would give then no privacy at all.

'The local nick?' the younger man, the one who had introduced himself as Sergeant Mason, asked. Mason shook his head.

'Don't think the boss would like that,' he said. 'I think, miss, it would be better if you came back to Southend with us. This may take some time.' Kate shook her head angrily.

'It's a long way to go, for not very much,' she said. 'Can I ring my boyfriend to tell him what's happening?'

'That would be Sergeant Barnard would it, miss?' Mason asked. Kate nodded, startled that they already knew so much about her.

'In that case, best to leave him out of it,' Mason said. 'We'll need a statement from him eventually, so we'd rather you talked to us first. We don't want you comparing notes, do we?' He gave her a smile which was not really a smile at all. It reminded Kate of an anticipatory shark. 'Sorry,' he added, as an apparent afterthought. 'Do you have a coat?'

Kate turned towards Ken, who was standing in his office doorway looking bemused, but she could see little encouragement there. Angrily she pulled on her coat, picked up her bag and followed the two policemen down the stairs and out on to the street, where they had parked an unmarked car half on the kerb. Mason held open the back door for her and got in beside her.

'Chin up,' he said, with an attempt at a smile. 'It's no worse than going to the dentist.'

TEN

Kate O'Donnell sat in an uncomfortably hard chair in a small, slightly smelly interview room with only an opaque window high in the wall opposite her. She had been there, becoming increasingly impatient, for an hour, delivered by a smirking Mason and his taciturn colleague, then apparently ignored. She had nothing to read and had not been offered anything to eat or drink, or even a visit to the lavatory. As the hand on her watch flicked up to the hour she decided that enough was enough, got out of her seat, and opened the door on to an empty corridor. She listened carefully before heading in the direction of faint voices to her left.

The corridor led her to a door and when she opened it she found herself facing a busy office where plain-clothed officers mostly had their heads down over files or glued to telephone receivers. For a second no one appeared to notice her standing at the open door, but eventually it was DS Mason who realized she was there and who hurried over to her.

'What the hell are you doing here?' he asked, evidently not best pleased to see her. 'Have you finished with the DCI?'

'I haven't even started with the DCI!' she said. 'I've been sitting there like a lemon doing nothing for an hour. I need a drink and a visit to the lavvy, la, before I burst.' Mason glanced at his watch and winced.

'I'll show you where to go,' he said. 'And see if I can find the guv'nor. He's a busy man.'

Kate scowled at him and followed him back down the empty corridor, where he indicated a door.

'Go back to the interview room after, petal,' he said, looking faintly embarrassed, though not as much as Kate thought he should be. 'I'll get you a cuppa.' He was as good as his word and came back with tea and a packet of biscuits.

'The DCI says he'll be ten minutes,' he said, though it was twenty before DCI Jack Baker opened the interview-room door

and came in, surrounded by a cloud of cigarette smoke, closely
followed by Mason.

'Right, young lady,' Baker snapped. 'I want a statement from
you about your contacts with Connie Flanagan and an explanation for why you've been interfering in police operations in this
part of the world. So let's have it. What were you doing in
Southend in the first place?' Kate placed her empty mug in front
of her carefully and met Baker's belligerent stare full on.

'I was working,' she said flatly before outlining her assignment
on Canvey Island and how she had come to move on to Southend
to seek some help from the *East Anglia News*.

'Right, I've had a word with that old fool Frank Garside,'
Baker said. 'I hope you're paying him a decent whack for his
help. I can't see how they came to send a dolly bird like you to
do a man's job. Anyway, that's by the by, your boss's problem
I suppose. How did you meet Mrs Flanagan, then?'

'I'd never been to Southend before,' Kate said, ignoring Baker's
insults with difficulty. 'I walked down to the seafront and had a
look at the pier. It's famous, after all, isn't it? And then I thought
it would be interesting to take some pictures of the funfair, but
it was mostly closed. But Connie Flanagan was there and we got
talking. The next time I came to see Frank Garside, to look at
some more pictures, I found her son had disappeared.'

'There was no real panic over that at the time,' Baker said
defensively, not meeting her eyes. 'His mother thought he'd
probably gone off with his father. The parents weren't on the
best of terms, it seems.'

'So Connie said,' Kate agreed. Baker ran his hand over his
bald head, slightly nervously, then lit another cigarette. He had
got it wrong about Luke, she thought, and she hoped the boy
had not suffered for that misjudgement.

'So tell me how and why you and DS Barnard became the
good Samaritans and took Mrs Flanagan all the way to Clacton.'

'She was terrified,' Kate said flatly. 'According to her it all
went back to some robbery years ago, with the two men just out
of prison. Her uncle was supposed to be looking after her and
the kids, but she still didn't feel safe. With her husband and the
boy missing and, as far as she could see, the police not taking
any interest, she wanted to get out. I'd given her my phone number

and she rang me and asked if I could help her get to Clacton. She sounded desperate, so we took her. I can't drive, so Harry Barnard offered to take us all in his car.'

'Well, she's back now, silly cow,' Baker said with no vestige of sympathy. 'And for all I know, you have significantly slowed down a murder inquiry by interfering. Give DS Mason a full statement of everything that happened after you met Connie Flanagan, including what your boyfriend got up to. I hear he's not flavour of the month at Scotland Yard. So don't leave anything out, young lady. I'll be passing a copy of your statement to the Met in case they want to take any action of their own.'

'What we did wasn't illegal,' Kate said fiercely. 'She was in trouble and had two small children with her. Why couldn't we help? Nobody knew her husband was dead at that stage. Although I wouldn't be surprised if she thought he was, and Luke as well. If you'd taken the boy's disappearance seriously from the start, none of this would have happened.'

Baker stood up ponderously and for a moment Kate thought he might hit her, but he did no more than thump the table hard, his face the colour of a ripe tomato.

'You and your dodgy boyfriend – and don't think they haven't filled me in on him from A to Z – are riding for a fall.'

'What's going to happen to Connie now?' Kate persisted, even as DS Mason flinched in his chair.

'At this moment she's downstairs in a cell getting ready to answer some questions,' Baker said. 'And her uncle will be next. They think they're a law unto themselves, these fairground families. It's about time they learned they're not.' He turned on his heel and slammed the interview-room door behind him.

'And where are the children?' Kate asked Mason, who looked slightly embarrassed.

'They're being looked after. For the time being at least, they're staying with their auntie in Clacton.'

Mason allowed himself a glimmer of a smile. 'Where's that bloody awful accent from? Glasgow, is it?' he asked.

'Liverpool, la,' Kate said. 'Where I come from you don't mess with anyone who comes from Scotland Road. Or anyone who knows John Lennon, for that matter. Which I do. So now what more can I tell you about a law-abiding drive – well, nearly law-abiding – from Southend to Clacton that you don't know already? We did someone I'd met down here a favour, that's all, and I don't see why I had to be dragged back like a criminal for no reason at all. Do you?'

Kate took the train back to London and strap-hung on the Northern Line back to Highgate and Barnard's flat. He was not there and she made herself a cup of tea before coming to a decision she had been mulling over on the rackety train journey back from Southend. Decision reached, she phoned her flatmate in Shepherd's Bush and spelled out her plans.

'Are you sure?' Tess Farrell asked. 'You and Harry have been through a lot together.'

'True,' Kate said. 'But being dragged down to Southend and interrogated like that was a step too far. He didn't even make a phone call to see what was happening to me. He must have known I was there. They wouldn't have come to London to pick me up without telling the local police, would they? I've not heard a word from him.'

'You used to say he couldn't call you from work,' Tess said. 'Talk to him when he gets home.'

'No,' Kate said firmly. 'I want to give him a shock. And I want a break from the blasted police and all their works.' Kate was slightly surprised herself at the depth of her sudden anger. Tess was right, she and Barnard had a history of trouble which in large part stemmed from her own insatiable curiosity about the new world he had introduced her to. But they had always been on the side of the angels and had had backup from his colleagues when it was needed. Yet this time she'd been scooped up by the Essex police with little excuse, bullied and spat out again, with not a glimmer of an apology and without so much as a phone call from Harry to reassure her. Enough was enough. He could see what it was like to come home to an empty flat and not know where his lover was.

'I'll see you in an hour or so,' she said.

She went into bedroom, flung most of her clothes into a suitcase, left a brief note on the kitchen table for Barnard and within ten minutes was making her way back down the hill to Archway underground station lugging her heavy suitcase, not quite sure whether she felt relieved or devastated by what she had done. By the time she arrived at the flat she still technically shared with Tess, her friend had cooked a meal and put clean sheets on her bed.

'I assume you're staying the night,' she said. 'Although Harry's been on the phone already. He's obviously seen your note and he says he'll come over later when you've calmed down a bit.'

'I'm perfectly calm,' Kate said, knowing she sounded far from it, and dumped her suitcase on the bed. 'It's not about calmness, it's about how I want to live and this was definitely not the way I wanted to spend the afternoon – being harassed by policemen, essentially because we did a woman a favour. I think I've had enough of cops for a bit.'

'Even Harry?' Tess asked as she presented Kate with sausage and mash. 'Are you quite sure?'

'Even Harry,' Kate said. But when push came to shove and Barnard was sitting in his car outside the flat hooting his horn, Kate pushed the curtains back and stared intently into the ill-lit street outside unsure what to do. He flashed his lights and then got out of the car and stood on the pavement with his arms wide looking up at her. Kate shrugged helplessly and went downstairs to meet him. Even in the poor light, she could see that for the first time since she had met him he looked crumpled and defeated.

'What did I do, honey?' he asked. 'I knew nothing about what had happened until the DCI told me just before I was leaving. I didn't know what had happened and I didn't know where you were. Then Southend said you'd gone back to London and wouldn't tell me any more. I'm so sorry, Kate. They're all bastards.' Kate could feel the tears running down her cheeks, although she did not seem to be in control of them or anything else.

'You can't get so involved,' he said putting a tentative arm around her shoulder.

'I wasn't involved,' she said. 'I just felt sorry for Connie and the kids. What she wanted to do seemed sensible to me. They needed to get away for a bit.' Barnard nodded, though she could see even in the dim light that he was no longer convinced what they had done was wise.

'There's more bad news from Southend,' he said. 'Some DS called Mason called me. Did you meet him?' Kate nodded.

'He was marginally better than the DCI,' she said grudgingly. 'So what's happened now?'

'They've found Luke's coat out on the mudflats near where his father was found dead. And they are looking at his mother and his uncle very hard. They reckon they must be involved in some way. If they arrest them, they'll take the other children into care for their own safety.'

'Oh, no!' Kate said. Barnard sighed.

'Stay here tonight if that's what you want to do. Take some time out. I'll call you in the morning, if that's OK.' Kate gave him a half-hearted hug and turned away while Barnard got back into his car and watched her go up the steps and into the house.

'Hell and damnation!' he said to himself as he revved the engine and pulled away from the kerb, anxiety tearing his insides to shreds. 'Don't do this, Katie. Please.'

Kate did not wait for Barnard to call her the next morning. She rang him at eight o'clock, knowing he would not yet have set off for work. The phone rang for a long time before he picked up, and she guessed from his slurred voice that she had wakened him and that he had drowned his sorrows the night before.

'Are you all right?' she asked tentatively.

'What do you think? Are you coming home?'

She hesitated for a moment before answering, not sure how much to tell him about what she planned to do.

'I'll have finished this Canvey Island assignment by the end of tomorrow,' she said. 'Then I'm going to ask Ken for a few days off. I'll tell him I need to go home to Liverpool for a christening or something.'

'And what are you really going to do?' Barnard asked. Kate could hear the growing anxiety in his voice as he recognized a lie when he heard it.

'I want to go back to Southend to check out that Connie Flanagan is all right and she's got her children back.'

'That's crazy, Kate,' Barnard said. 'There's nothing you can do down there, and if DCI Baker trips over you he'll be even more furious. You really can't interfere in a murder investigation. You'll end up in a cell. It sounds as if you've already annoyed him big time.'

'Well, I didn't let him intimidate me, if that's what you mean. But I feel responsible for Connie. She can't possibly have killed her husband and dumped him in a bog, and if it wasn't for your stupid driving they'd never have found her in Clacton. I don't think she's safe in Southend, I don't want her to lose her children, and I don't like that uncle of hers. I wouldn't trust him an inch if push came to shove.'

'You're not being very rational, Kate,' Barnard said and she could hear the weariness in his tone.

'Did you hit the bottle last night?' she asked.

'What do you think?' The silence between them lengthened.

'I'm sorry,' she said. 'But I really want to do this. And I don't think you should be involved. I'll stay here with Tess for a few days and then you're in the clear. Let's talk next Monday.' The silence at the other end of the line deepened and Kate thought for a moment he had hung up.

'I love you Kate,' he said eventually. 'I don't think I can live without you.' She took a deep breath at a declaration she never thought she would hear and sat down, her heart thumping.

'I'll think about that,' she said eventually. 'Let's talk at the weekend.' And feeling slightly dizzy, she hung up.

ELEVEN

Kate finished her assignment on autopilot and asked for three days off to go to Liverpool to see her family. That, she was sure, would give her enough time to find out what was happening to Connie and her children. She knew that Harry was right, what she was planning to do was not rational. The woman was a complete stranger and the police might be right to suspect she was involved in her husband's murder. Or if not her directly, then her overbearing and slightly menacing uncle. But she did not believe Connie was a killer, and Luke was still missing. After seeing the Essex police at first hand, she did not believe that they were likely to be doing anything very energetic to find the boy even now. She guessed that if at first they had thought his father had taken him away, they would now think that the child had probably died with him in the mud of the estuary and his body would never be located. What disappeared into the sands, she thought, more often than not stayed disappeared and Connie must be distraught if she thought Luke had been swallowed up by the mud.

The next day dawned dark and dismal and Kate rolled over in her unaccustomed and too narrow bed, taking a moment to realize from the traffic noise outside that the bed was her own not Barnard's. As she came round, her decisions of the day before crowded in on her and she became increasingly reluctant to move. She lay for a moment wondering if the course she had decided to take was remotely sensible, but convincing herself in the end that it was something she had to do. She got out of bed and made herself a cup of instant coffee in the tiny kitchen and concluded that it was a pale imitation of the intense Italian brew she had got used to with Barnard. She smiled slightly. Maybe she would miss Harry's coffee more than she missed the man himself. Of Tess there was no sign and she assumed that her friend was sleeping in after a hard week at school.

An hour later she was back on a Southend train, heading

through a misty morning to Essex. In the summer the train would no doubt be crowded with day-trippers, but on a bleak weekday the train carried few passengers as far as Southend and on a dank morning like this there was little to look at, with the temperature barely above freezing and banks of mist blotting out anything but brief glimpses of the docks, close to the stations where the train stopped briefly, and the ever present river winding its course to the sea. The occasional mournful wail of fog horns and sharp blasts of ships negotiating their way to and from the Port of London reminded her of home. Back home, a favourite – and free – outing had been a trip to the Pier Head to watch the ships on the Mersey, even if there had not been enough in the kitty to take the ferry across to the other side.

Benfleet station was at least recognizable through the murk, but Canvey Island itself, across the bridge, was barely visible through what had now turned into thickening fog. She gathered her belongings together and prepared to get off at Southend, still unsure of the best course to follow. As she came out of the station she took a deep breath, but instead of the salty tang of the sea all she could detect in the thick damp air was a slight whiff of fish and chips.

She slowly made her way through the ambling shoppers towards the pier, which looked deserted, visibility reducing it to little more than a short narrow track heading into a grey blanket where sea, sky and sands dissolved into each other. Below the trailing clouds of fog, it was difficult to see across the fairground and almost impossible to pick out the showmen's caravans parked close to the pier. She took a deep breath to bolster her courage and set off to where Connie Flanagan's uncle was supposed to be looking after her welfare. But she did not get as far as the caravans before a group of men loomed out of the semi-darkness and she recognized Jasper Dowd in the lead.

'Who the hell—' he began. 'Oh, it's you, is it? What are you doing here again?'

'I was in Southend and wondered how Connie was getting on. Is she all right?'

'If you call being harassed by the police all right. They wanted her back at the police station again this morning. She spent half the day there on Thursday, so I don't know what the hell more they can ask her.'

'Have they found Luke?' Kate asked.

'No, they haven't. I reckon they think he's buried out in the sands like his father. They should be looking for his father's dodgy friends, not making his mother's life a misery.'

Dowd glanced at his companions and shrugged.

'Anyway, we've got work to do. We were hoping to open up this afternoon, but in this weather I wonder if it's worth the effort.'

Kate gazed at the tall showman and as he crowded in on her realized he was not giving her any option but to return the way she had come. She spun on her heel and was aware of the men following her off the fairground and watching as she headed back into the town centre. That, she thought, had been a fruitless call and although she did not entirely believe what Dowd had told her she could think of no way of penetrating the barrier that they seemed to have erected between her and Connie Flanagan.

Kate stopped for a coffee in a small café close to the station, hot and steamy and almost empty on a foggy morning, and considered her next move. It was obvious that Jasper Dowd was determined that she should not talk to Connie again if he could help it and she wondered why. She also wondered whether he was lying about Connie being at the police station. That was one place where she certainly would not be able to get hold of her, so it could be a very convenient lie. She drained the indeterminate brown liquid in her cup and decided to try to find out.

But when she got to the police station she hesitated on the opposite side of the road, reluctant to go inside the bleak building again in case she should bump into DCI Jack Baker or even the slightly less aggressive DS Mason for a second time. That, she thought, might be more than she could stand and she began to think that this excursion on her own was a lost cause. She should have listened to Harry. But as she hesitated, she noticed a woman in a formal suit and carrying a briefcase coming out of the main entrance. She could, Kate guessed, be a detective, although she knew that would be unusual. Barnard had more than once told her that very few women succeeded in joining CID. Alternatively she might be a lawyer, or even a social worker, who had some contact with Connie.

She crossed the road and waited for her to come down the steps then tried to catch her eye. The woman, who looked only slightly older than Kate herself, glanced at her curiously. She was as blonde as Kate was dark and smartly turned out in a blue suit over a red shirt.

'Are you a cop?' Kate asked tentatively, putting herself directly in the path of the woman so that she had no choice but to stop.

'God no!' the woman laughed. 'I'm a solicitor. But they won't eat you, you know, the cops,' she offered with a sympathetic smile.

'I'm not so sure about that,' Kate said with feeling. The woman looked at her for a moment.

'Do you need help?' she asked. 'I'm Janet Driscoll. I spend quite a lot of my time here at the nick for my sins. Or other people's.'

'It's not for me,' Kate said quickly. 'I had a session in there a couple of days ago. And I'm not at all sure DCI Baker wouldn't swallow me whole if he got the chance. But I'm looking for someone else this time.'

'You didn't get on?' the solicitor asked. 'He doesn't react well to what he considers uppity girls and you look as if you're that just as much as I am.'

But although she smiled, her smile did not reach her eyes. 'So who are you looking for?' she asked and looked even more concerned when Kate told her.

'Ah,' she said. 'Now you've put me in a difficult position. I've just been talking to Connie Flanagan as it happens. I was the lawyer on call this weekend and she's being questioned under caution about her husband's death. But of course I'm not allowed to tell you anything more than that about a case I'm involved in.' Kate's face must have revealed her disappointment because Janet took her arm. 'But that's not to say that you can't tell me about your connection to Connie and anything you know about what's been going on in her life recently. Any – or all – of that I can listen to as it may help my client, and I'd certainly not be breaking any rules by admitting that she needs some help right now. Come on, let's have a coffee and a chat.'

Janet led the way to a coffee bar in a side street, where Kate was relieved to see they made Italian-style coffee. Harry Barnard had certainly done a good job on her taste buds if nothing else, she thought as the lawyer ordered two espressos.

'So,' Janet said thoughtfully as they sipped their coffee and she pulled a notebook and pen out of her briefcase. 'You don't look as if you work at the funfair. How do you come to know Connie Flanagan? And even more important to her at the moment, have you any idea where her son Luke is?' She listened carefully as Kate went through her contacts with Connie right up to the moment she and Barnard dropped her and the two younger children at her aunt's in Clacton.

'I shouldn't think DCI Jack Baker appreciated that intervention,' she said. 'Especially as your boyfriend's a cop with the Met.'

'He didn't appreciate it,' Kate said feelingly. 'Far from it. He dragged me all the way back to Southend to bully me into telling him essentially what I've just told you. And my boyfriend's not very popular with his boss in London, either.'

'There's no love lost between different police forces,' Janet said. 'And the country cousins out here especially hate the Met. So why are you back in Southend today?'

'I haven't seen or heard from Connie since we left her in Clacton and I wondered if she and the children were OK. I had to come in person. There's no way I can ring the nick here and ask about them, is there?'

'You'd get short shrift, I think,' Janet agreed.

'Just like I did from her uncle when I went to the fairground to see if she was there. He practically ran me off the place.'

'Well, that's worth knowing. I was going to tackle Jasper Dowd myself. I wondered why he hadn't been to the nick to see why they're keeping Connie so long.'

'I don't believe Connie could have killed her husband. It's nonsense,' Kate said fiercely. 'How could she have pushed him into the quicksands? She's only a slip of a thing.'

'I can't comment on that. But there are different sorts of involvement in crime,' Janet said, her expression neutral. 'I can't discuss what's going on in there. But I promise you I'll do the best I can for her. And what you've told me about the background will help. If the worst came to the worst, I might need you as a witness at a trial. But that's a long way off and hopefully it won't happen at all if I do my job properly. Now I have to go and talk to her family on the fairground, however unhelpful they are. If I were you, I'd go back to London. If you give me your phone number, I'll call you tomorrow to let you know what's happened.

They're not allowed to question her indefinitely. They have to either charge her with something or let her go, and I'll do my best to make sure she's out of there by then.'

Janet Driscoll hurried off and left Kate sitting savouring the dregs of her coffee, unsure what to do next. In the end she decided that, having come this far, there was at least one more avenue of inquiry she could follow. She went back to the station and took the train to Benfleet, determined to comb Canvey Island and try to find the former detective Les Greenwood. With all that had happened since she and Barnard met him in London he would surely be more ready to help find young Luke Flanagan, if not his father's killer.

Tentatively Kate opened the door of the Red Cow and scanned the lunchtime crowd. In one corner of the lounge bar she spotted two of the regulars she had met before – Tom, who had given her a tour of the island, and Ken, who had lost his son in the flood. She wriggled her way through the busy lounge to their table and smiled at both of them.

'You again?' Tom said, looking slightly surprised. 'You'll be settling down here if you keep this up.'

'I'm only passing through this time,' Kate said. 'I'm looking for someone in particular. Do you happen to know someone called Les Greenwood? He said he lived on Canvey but I can't find him in the phone book.' Neither of the men responded immediately, but they both glanced at each other and then round the bar.

'It's unusual for Les Greenwood not to be here by now,' Tom said reluctantly.

'Used to be a copper,' Ken added. 'Spends a lot of time in here now he's retired.'

'Sounds like the man I'm looking for,' Kate said quietly. 'He can certainly knock it back.'

'Why do you want to talk to him? He didn't move to the island until long after the flood. He was a detective in Southend, I think, though I've never heard him talk about that very much. In fact I've never heard him talk about anything very much. Keeps himself to himself does Les, even when he's plastered.' That sounded like the Les Greenwood she and Barnard had met in an obscure City of London pub and she wondered, as they had then, quite why an ex-cop should have been quite so reluctant to be open with Barnard.

'Do either of you know where he lives?' she asked, but neither of the men answered immediately until Tom nodded towards the open door, through which a familiar figure was entering the pub.

'There he is, coming in,' Tom whispered. 'But for God's sake don't rile him. He's a bad-tempered beggar at the best of times, and if you catch him when he's seriously thirsty he'll snap your head off.'

'Why don't you have a drink with us for a while and wait until Greenwood's had a few and mellowed out a bit? That's what I'd do. Safer that way.' Ken winked at her. 'What can I get you, sweetheart?'

Glancing cautiously at Greenwood, who was scowling heavily as he settled into a seat near the bar, Kate decided that following local advice was probably the safest course and accepted the offer of a shandy. But she parried all attempts the two men made to uncover why she was so keen to talk to Greenwood – that sort of gossip would do Connie Flanagan no good at all, she thought.

She sipped her drink slowly, wondering how long it would take Greenwood to mellow out. He was ordering whisky with such regularity that she suspected he would pass out before he mellowed. But as she sipped her shandy and listened to the two men chatting about their most recent fishing trip, she suddenly realized that Greenwood had fixed her with a bleary-eyed stare and within seconds had clearly recognized her. He got unsteadily to his feet and started towards Kate before evidently having second thoughts as Tom and Ken got to their feet too, obviously planning to intercept his threatening approach. When he realized Kate was not alone he spun round, teetering precipitously close to another table of young men, who shouted abuse in his direction, before he eventually reached the door and disappeared from view.

'You want to ban that old fool,' one of the lad's shouted at the barman, who laughed and shrugged his shoulders.

'We'd make no profit and then how far would you have to go for a drink? Bloody Benfleet, that's where,' he said. Amid the general jeers and laughter, Kate got up and headed to the door herself. Having got this far, she wasn't going to let Les Greenwood disappear into the mist without making a serious effort to talk to him.

She had only just moved in time, she realized when she got outside. Greenwood was making erratic but speedy progress down one of the roads leading right from the pub forecourt, but visibility was still poor and she had to hurry to keep him in sight. She had no doubt that he was heading home, but she had no idea how far away that was or whether she would be able to catch him before he disappeared inside and maybe refused to answer his door. She speeded up and at one of the junctions where Canvey's generally straight roads intersected, she caught up with him and he finally stopped, panting as he leaned for support against a garden wall. He was sweating heavily and, Kate thought, looked seriously unwell.

'What are you doing here?' he asked. 'How the hell did you find me? I told you and your boyfriend I wanted nothing to do with all that old history. I knew no good would come of it, and who did I see yesterday? Those bastards who went down for the robbery.'

'Dexter and Barrett?' Kate asked. 'Here on Canvey?'

'Here on Canvey,' Greenwood said. 'I told you Dexter and his wife lived here before the flood for a while, down by where they're building the new flats. He'd gone to prison before the place was inundated, so he wasn't here. But his house was wrecked. His wife got out in time, apparently. Dexter was here for a time after the robberies, and the Flanagans too. Mrs Flanagan didn't want the kids living on the fairground any more. At least that's what I was told. They're related, you know, the Dexters and the Flanagans. I don't know how Bert Flanagan got away with that robbery. He was thick as thieves with Dexter, everyone knew that. Now I hear they've found him dead.'

'On the sands, and his son's still missing,' Kate said. 'That's why I'm here. They're holding the boy's mother at the police station, which is ridiculous. There's no way she could have been involved in her husband's murder or the disappearance of her son. She was distraught about that.'

'Well, I know nothing about it. But if you'd been a copper as long as I was, you'd know that families lie through their teeth if it suits them. Especially those gypsies from the fairground. They say they're not gypsies but I can't tell the bloody difference. And the women are as devious as the men.'

'Connie was looking after two small children and was desperate about the missing boy,' Kate said obstinately. 'She's hardly likely to have gone out on the sands and pushed her husband into the mud. Can you help me find out what's going on with her at the police station?'

'Not bloody likely,' Greenwood said. 'Your boyfriend would stand a better chance of that than I would. But I will say, I reckon if Dexter and Barrett are mooching about Canvey they can only be looking for the proceeds of God knows how many robberies. And if they're here, I'm not taking any chances. It's quite likely they remember me and might feel like settling old scores. I interviewed both of them at one time or another, as well as Rod Miller, and we didn't pull any punches back then.'

'Nor now as far as I can see,' Kate added, thinking of her interview with DCI Baker.

'I'm off this afternoon for a long holiday, just in case Barrett is still bearing a grudge. He's a nutter, that one. I told you.'

'Where will you go?' Kate asked.

'Never you mind,' Greenwood said. He hauled himself upright and began to follow the road to another gate, which Kate guessed was that of his own house.

'Where did Dexter's wife end up?' she asked as he struggled to open the latch.

'I don't know, do I?' Greenwood growled. 'I expect she went back to Foulness. That's where she came from, I think. They bought a farm out there before the robberies. Bloody wilderness that is. The population got completely cut off in the flood. The rescue people thought they'd all drowned.'

'So could Dexter have gone back there himself?'

'I don't think they're on speaking terms any more, those two,' Greenwood said. 'I heard she divorced him while he was in jail, though she managed to keep the farm apparently. But that might be just another rumour. And it wouldn't stop him or Barrett beating her to a pulp if they thought she knew where the money was. My guess is that's why Flanagan's dead. She's his sister, after all.'

Kate suddenly felt very cold and she didn't think it was simply because the fog had begun to thicken and the warnings had begun to sound again out on the estuary. Greenwood looked at her.

'I'm off,' he said. 'And I tell you, girl, you should get back to London and keep right out of this. That's my advice. Stay well clear.' He went into the house and slammed the door behind him, and she realized that she would not get anything more out of him.

She turned and began the long walk back to Benfleet station. The fog was still hanging in swirls above the road and she had to keep an eye out for the few cars that loomed through the murk, most of them without lights in spite of the gloom. Back on the train to Fenchurch Street, feeling deflated at the results of her inquiries, she knew she would have to swallow her pride and talk to Harry Barnard. There was no alternative.

TWELVE

Ray Robertson was twitchy. Swathed in a heavy camel coat plus a muffler and with a broad-brimmed fedora pulled down to shield his eyes, he stood close to his Jag on the forecourt of a garage on the A11 heading north out of London. He had made his arrangements very carefully and was furious that his contact was late. He lit another cigarette and pulled the smoke into his lungs gratefully, but he flung it away when he saw the man he had persuaded to drive out here for him pull off the main road in what looked like a clapped out Ford. He wrenched open the driver's door and almost pulled him on to the tarmac.

'You're bloody late,' he said, handing him the keys to the Jag. 'I hope this old banger moves a bit smarter than looks likely.'

'You can bank on that, guv,' the driver said. 'It's been well fixed.'

'I'll call you when I want to swap back,' Robertson said. 'Probably tonight, possibly tomorrow.'

'Any time, Ray, any time.'

'And for God's sake get the Jag out of sight as soon as you can. It's not just the filth who might recognize it, though I don't think they'll be looking for me around here.'

And with that he slid into the Ford's driving seat, switched on the engine, and revved it for a moment, evidently to his satisfaction, before accelerating on to the main road without a backward glance. He drove north for a short distance before swinging east and then south, cruising just below sixty to avoid attracting unwanted attention, then finally turned east again, with the Thames just in sight, towards Southend-on-Sea. He stopped briefly on the seafront, close to the pier, and parked. After downing a Scotch at one of the cluster of pubs close to the amusement arcades, which were the only places that looked busy, he indulged in fish and chips, which he took back to eat in the car, stuffing the greasy papers into the footwell on the passenger side with a sigh of satisfaction when he had finished. Then he pulled out into the traffic stream and continued his journey.

He followed his route more slowly now. He knew the terrain but it was years since he had followed these increasingly narrow roads over increasingly flat country, and as he got closer to his destination he was particularly anxious not to draw any unwanted attention to himself. Beyond the two villages of Wakering, set back from the estuary, the landscape flattened out even more and he could see across the featureless fields towards the equally featureless Thames. There was little or no traffic out here and he had little fear of being seen. Safely over the first of the two bridges that crossed to the island, first over the River Roach, slow-flowing and muddy at low tide, and then the two creeks that helped cut Foulness off from the mainland of Essex. The movable Scherzer bridge, which looked like something out of science fiction, was fortunately in place. He slowed for the military checkpoint where the army controlled access, particularly when artillery firing was taking place, but the sleepy-looking squaddies on duty waved him through although Ray was certain that they would have made a note of his number plate. Good job it was a fiction, he thought. He prided himself on leaving nothing to chance.

Once safely on Foulness Island proper, he relaxed and headed down the narrow road to Churchend, the only village on the island with its own church, the stubby steeple of St Mary the Virgin serving as a landmark for miles around, as well as a substantial pub – the weather-boarded George & Dragon – and a post office to serve the scattered farming community that shared the desolate space with the military. Beyond that, he would have to be more circumspect as he approached the isolated farm where Delia and Sam Dexter had set up home before Dexter's incarceration. One fork in the road veered left in the direction of the north coast and the River Crouch, but Robertson kept right on along an increasingly rutted track. After a mile or so, he pulled off the road into a barnyard and eased the car out of sight behind a dilapidated wooden barn, where it would be concealed from any passing traffic. He sat for a moment breathing heavily and surveying the rutted mud that lay between him and the Dexter farm.

'I should have brought my bloody wellies,' he muttered as he began to plod towards the huddle of house and barns, trying to keep out of the more liquid puddles of mud. 'My God, I hate the country.'

There was no sign of life at all around the farm. He could see there was no livestock kept here, only apparently endless ploughed arable fields with few hedges or trees to break the monotony, not even a dog to give useful early warning of a stranger's approach or a cat to keep down the rats and mice. There were no lights on inside the house that he could detect and the solid wooden front door was closed and, he guessed, locked.

'It's like the bloody *Marie Celeste*,' he muttered and began to wonder if he was not too late and Delia Dexter's body was lying in a shallow grave somewhere in this endless God-forsaken flat muddy landscape, the latest victim of Bomber Harris's rage. If it was, he thought, it could lie buried for weeks if not months before anyone even noticed she had gone.

While he was still considering what to do next after what appeared to be a long wasted journey, he picked up the sound of a car engine on the road he had just travelled down. He thought he had concealed his own car carefully enough, but he himself would be clearly visible once the approaching car came round the last bend and in through the farm gate. With surprising speed for a man of his bulk, he dodged inside one of the empty barns and crouched behind some bales of hay or straw. He heard the approaching car pull up outside, the slam of two doors, and then heavy footfalls as, he guessed, the visitors made their way across the yard to the farmhouse door.

The hammering on the door did not last long before Robertson heard a scream of frustration and then the start of a second assault, which was clearly being carried out with more than just fists. The sound of wood splintering and a heavy weight falling to the ground told its own story, as the door was demolished. Then a long silence fell. Robertson moved to the barn doors, which he had left slightly ajar, and peered carefully out. There was no sign of the two men who had arrived in the black Rover parked in the yard. Cautiously, keeping the barns and outbuildings between him and the farmhouse, he hurried back to his own car and drove quietly away. If Delia Dexter was in the farmhouse, which he doubted, he did not give much for her chances.

Kate O'Donnell got back to the flat in Shepherd's Bush to find it empty and no sign of much in the fridge from which to make a meal. She sighed. She knew it was her own fault, as she had not left Tess any details of where she was going or when she expected to be back. If she was going to move back here permanently, she thought, she would have to get used to flat-sharing on a different basis from the life she had become accustomed to with Barnard. Tess liked order in her life, the result she guessed of a home life in Liverpool even more disorganized than her own. Flinging herself down on her bed to rest, Kate did not find the prospect enticing. In any case, she needed to talk to Harry about her trip to Southend.

She glanced at her watch. It was six thirty and if Barnard had decided to go to the pub after work for want of anything better to do on a dismal evening without her, he would probably not be home for a while. Unless, she thought with a slight sense of guilt, he decided to make a night of it. She was not so naïve as to imagine he would avoid female company if he was still in Soho, if only to pass the time. Almost reluctantly she dialled his flat and to her relief he answered so quickly that she was certain that he had been waiting for her to call.

'You're back,' he said and then hesitated, obviously realizing that the statement was unnecessary.

'Can we meet for a drink?' Kate asked. 'I need to talk to you.'

'You're not coming back here then?'

Kate took a deep breath before she replied. 'Not yet,' she said. There was a long silence at the other end of the line and she could imagine Barnard struggling with the implications. But she couldn't help him. She had not worked out the implications for herself yet.

'OK,' Barnard said at last. 'I'll pick you up in half an hour and we'll go to one of the pubs in Notting Hill. That suit you?' Kate settled for that and hung up.

An hour later they had found a table in a corner at the Windsor Castle and Barnard had delivered a pint of bitter and a half pint of shandy to the table before sitting down opposite Kate.

'What did I do, honey?' he asked. 'What did I do to deserve this?'

'You didn't do anything but I decided I'd got in too deep, far deeper than I wanted to be,' she said. 'Why the hell did I get carted off to Essex like that? Like a criminal? That man DCI Baker thinks he's God Almighty. Maybe you all do. I think I want a break from playing cops and robbers. That's not my job.'

'Is that what it is, you and me?' Barnard asked. 'Playing cops and robbers?'

'That's what it feels like sometimes,' she said.

'The Southend business was your call,' he said mildly. 'You persuaded me to go and rescue Connie Flanagan, remember?'

'I did, but we didn't know then that her husband was dead, did we? Which links it all to those robberies in Southend and quite likely to the murder in Whitechapel and your missing friend Ray Robertson. It's wheels within wheels, isn't it, Harry? It's all escalating and I don't know what's going on or who to believe. I've had enough. To be honest, I want nothing to do with any of it any more.'

'I'm sorry,' he said. They stared at each other in mutual incomprehension for a moment.

'I think we should have a break,' Kate said at last. 'I don't know where I am any more. I told Ken Fellows I was going up to Liverpool to see my family. Maybe that's what I should do.'

'You know I'm not officially working on this murder case in Whitechapel,' Barnard said. 'I can leave it alone. Maybe we could go away together—'

'You won't leave it alone, though, will you? You don't want to. You're too tied up with Ray Robertson. As far as I can see, you always have been. The man's a crook, a gangster, and maybe a murderer. And yet you still make allowances for him. You feel you owe him something. No wonder your DCI doesn't trust you.'

'It all goes back a long way,' Barnard said, looking uncomfortable and lighting a cigarette.

'So it should be over.'

'Maybe you're right,' Barnard said, though there was not much conviction in his voice. 'Why did you want to meet up anyway?' he asked. 'If you're not planning to come back?'

Kate finished her drink.

'I wanted to fill you in on what I did today, so you know where we stand,' she said. 'I bumped into Les Greenwood on Canvey Island. He was the one who really spooked me. He's getting out, he said. He says it's too dangerous to stay while Dexter and Barrett are tearing around looking for their money. He thinks they may have it in for him as he was one of the officers involved in the investigation into the robberies back before the flood. I asked him if he knew what was going on with Dexter's wife and he said he didn't want to know, you were best placed to ask DCI Baker about that. But you can't do that, can you? It would get straight back to your boss. And I certainly can't go anywhere near the Southend police again, even if I wanted to, which I don't. Connie Flanagan has got a lawyer. I managed to speak to her. Connie should be all right with her, I think.'

'You take too much on your shoulders,' Barnard said.

'That's what Greenwood told me,' Kate admitted. 'I was thinking about what he said while I was on the train coming back to London and I realized that if he was getting out maybe I shouldn't be going down there asking more questions. I suddenly felt very scared.'

Barnard drew a sharp breath.

'I think Greenwood's right,' he said heavily. 'Come back to my place for tonight and I'll put you on a Liverpool train first thing in the morning. Can you phone your family, tell them you're coming?'

'They're not on the phone,' Kate said.

'When did you tell Ken Fellows you'd be back?'

'Tuesday,' she said.

'So have a couple of days in the north and call me on Monday before you set off back and I'll tell you whether I think it's safe,' he said. There was no doubt that Barnard was taking her worries seriously now.

'What are you going to do on your own?' she asked.

'I'll see what I can find out in Southend when I've dropped you at the station,' he said. 'Just a quick check.'

'Are you sure that's sensible?' she asked, suddenly as anxious for him as for herself, and wondered what that told her about her own feelings.

'What I do in my own time is my business,' he said.

THIRTEEN

Kate woke up early the next morning, slipped out of bed without disturbing Harry, and made herself coffee in the kitchen. She was drinking it slowly at the kitchen table when Barnard came in and put his arms around her.

'Couldn't you sleep?' he asked. She shook her head.

'Too much to think about,' she said. 'But if you are going back to Southend, I want to come with you. I never really intended going to Liverpool. That was just an excuse.' Barnard tensed before letting her loose.

'I don't think that's a very good idea,' he said. 'I thought I'd go out to Foulness to try to track down Delia Dexter, but if her husband's around it might get nasty.'

'I thought it was difficult to get on to the island,' Kate said.

'It is, but it should be OK today. It's very foggy again, so I don't think they'll be firing artillery shells. Anyway, if they don't let me in they won't let me in. But I think it's worth a try. And if it looks as if there's anyone else at the Dexters' farm apart from Delia, I won't go near. I don't want to tangle with Dexter or Barrett if I can help it.'

'If I come with you, we could try to find out what's happened to Connie and her kids. Greenwood said you might be able to find out at the nick.'

'I don't think so,' Barnard said. 'They'd boot me out and report back to the DCI before I got through the door. What about her lawyer? He should know what's happened to her.'

'She,' Kate said sharply. 'The lawyer's a woman, Janet Driscoll.'

Barnard grinned. 'Is there no end to female ambition?' he asked. 'You'll be wanting to be prime minister next.'

'And why not?' Kate said tartly, although it was not an idea that had ever entered her head any more than the idea of a female photographer had ever crossed her boss's mind until she walked through the door and talked herself into a job. But time would tell, she thought. Barnard sighed and she knew he would give in.

'Well, how's this for a plan?' he asked. 'We go to Foulness first and see if we can find Sam Dexter's wife. Someone must know where he and Barrett are, and she sounds the most likely person if she's still around. She may be the only person who knows if they were looking for Rod Miller when they came out of jail. If they were, maybe that would get Ray Robertson off the hook. We don't need to get too close if there's any sign that her husband's there. Though if Greenwood is right and they're divorced now, I should think it'd be the last place he would go.'

'Greenwood thought that if her husband and Barrett believed she knew anything about the money disappearing from wherever they stashed it, they might do her some harm. He seemed quite sure they lived on Canvey for a while before the flood, so I suppose they might have left it with Delia if they trusted her enough and then everything got overtaken by the flood on the island.'

'All the more reason to pay a very cautious visit to Delia,' Barnard said. 'It's very remote out there and access is difficult. For all we know, she could be lying dead if they've been out there to find her.' Kate shuddered. The thought of a woman's body left to moulder was horrifying enough, but it could be that her brother's killers had dumped her out on the sands and she would never be found.

'Isn't your car a bit conspicuous for driving out into the wilds?' Kate said doubtfully.

'Doesn't matter,' Barnard said. 'The military check traffic in and out because of the danger zones. No one gets in or out unnoticed.'

'Afterwards we'll go to Southend and ask the lawyer where Connie is. Right? It's outrageous if they've still got her locked up in a cell without her children.'

'We'll talk to the lawyer,' Barnard promised, 'if we can find her. And let's hope DCI Baker is safely at home or having a round of golf, well out of our way. The lawyer will certainly know what's happened to Connie. We don't need to visit the nick at all.'

Kate and Harry whiled away the tedious drive east by disputing the respective merits of the Beatles and the Rolling Stones, with Kate preserving a little space in her heart for the Kinks whose single *You Really Got Me* had just made a spectacular entry into the charts.

'I think they could be as big as the Beatles,' Kate said recklessly. 'Don't laugh, they're really, really good.'

'Maybe,' Barnard said, not for the first time wondering at Kate's ability to bounce back from whatever life threw at her. He had to admit that since they met life – and maybe he himself – had not treated her very kindly. Her insatiable curiosity and her determination to point her camera where powerful, and often dangerous, people did not want it pointed had not made for an easy ride for either of them. This time, he thought, he would keep her out of trouble.

Foulness Island lay flat and apparently deserted when they approached the bridges and the military checkpoint that guarded the island. No warning flags flew and the soldiers on duty took no more than a cursory interest in their arrival as they noted down the number plate of Barnard's car.

'Flash car,' one said. 'Oh, there was another bloke heading to Lane End Farm yesterday.'

'What was he driving?' Barnard asked.

'Some clapped-out old Ford,' the squaddie said. 'Didn't stay long.' And he waved them on their way.

'My goodness, it's bleak,' Kate said, staring out at the ranges cratered and rutted by military activity, after they'd crossed the rolling bridge over the navigable creek.

'It's like something out of science fiction,' she said.

'That's why the army chose it,' Barnard said. 'Way back. Hardly anyone lives here. The army's been messing about here since the First World War at least.'

'I'm not surprised,' Kate said. 'I don't suppose anyone out here's heard of the Beatles, let alone the Kinks.'

'Well, I looked at a map. There's a village and some farms further east, including the Dexters' farm. But it must be pretty noisy when they're firing on the ranges.' He accelerated down the relatively straight road until they could see a church steeple and drove through the village, past the pub and on to a rutted narrow track with a dilapidated sign pointing to Lane End Farm.

'It's the back of beyond,' Kate said.

'A good place to hide out maybe,' Barnard said. 'If you can avoid the checkpoint, and I dare say some of the locals know ways to do that. By boat, if nothing else.'

When they arrived at the farm gate, which was wide open, they could see no sign of life at the house or amongst the barns and outbuildings, so he turned the car slowly behind the largest of the barns and killed the engine.

'We can get away quickly if we have to,' he said. Kate shuddered slightly, wondering not for the first time whether this trip had been a good idea.

'Do you think Delia's got a phone?' she asked.

Barnard glanced around.

'That looks like a phone line,' he said pointing to a pole and wires leading back towards the village, which could still be seen behind them across the flat fields. 'You'd need one out here.'

He got out of the car and Kate followed.

'We'll just watch for a while,' he said. 'There are no other cars here, just the tractor in the barn over there. So maybe no one's here at all.' Kate could not help feeling a sense of relief, although she could see that Barnard was frustrated. In the end, he lost patience.

'Let's just make sure there's no one here,' he said and led the way slowly to the front door. As they approached, they could see it had been roughly secured with some nailed-on planks of wood after a recent assault that had forced it off its hinges.

'Something's been going on here,' Barnard said quietly. 'It doesn't look good. Someone was very anxious to get inside.' Kate shuddered and took hold of Barnard's arm.

'I think we should go,' she said.

'We need to make sure there's no one inside who needs help,' Barnard said. But before he could try the door to see if it could be pushed open, they were startled by a voice from behind them. A female voice, with no hint of welcome in it.

They turned quickly to find themselves facing a woman in dungarees and a thick sweater, her hair tied back and her face set in what was close to a snarl. She was holding a shotgun with a firm grip and pointing it unerringly in their direction.

'Who the hell are you?' she asked. 'And what the hell are you doing in my yard?'

Delia Dexter chivvied them round the back of the house and in through the kitchen door with the gun still menacing them from behind, much too close for comfort.

'I've had to nail up the bloody front door,' she said by way of explanation. 'Some beggar broke it down while I was out. Bastard.' She almost pushed them into an untidy farm kitchen and waved them into a sagging sofa close to the range where a fire burned a sulky red. 'It wasn't you was it?' The question sounded half-hearted. Barnard shook his head and showed her his warrant card.

'This is only an unofficial inquiry,' he said. 'This is my girlfriend and we were close by, so I thought it might be worth having a word. I'm from the Met, but I should think the Southend police won't be far behind us if they haven't been out here already. We want to know where your husband is and whether he's still with Sid Barrett. All this dates back to the post office robbery in Southend they were sent down for. And we think they might be connected with a case in Whitechapel, since they were let out. A man they knew has been found dead in suspicious circumstances.'

Delia loosened her grip on the shotgun slightly but didn't put it down. She was a well-built woman, her face pale without make-up and with dark circles under her eyes. She looked desperately tired.

'I've not seen Sid Barrett since the trial all those years ago,' she said. 'That man's a loony, believe me. A dangerous loony.'

'And your husband?' Barnard prompted. She shrugged and Barnard picked up a slight tightening of her hands on the gun.

'I used to visit him in jail for a bit,' she said. 'But I divorced him five years ago. He wasn't best pleased. I think he thought I would keep this place running on my own and he promised me we'd not go short again. We'd get out of here and live the life of Riley somewhere else.'

'That would be on the proceeds of the robberies?' Barnard asked.

'No one ever seemed to know where that money went, and I don't think Sam did either. It vanished into thin air, or so he said. In the end I stopped believing a word any of them said. So I finished with him long before he was due out of jail and I stayed on here on my own. I could just about make a living with a bit of help from hired hands. I felt safe enough while those two were locked up, but now they're out I'll not hang around. The police told me what happened to Bert—'

'Bert?'

'My brother. Bert Flanagan, Connie's husband.' Delia stared into space for a moment, her eyes blank.

'Of course,' Barnard said.

'And the boy's still missing. Did you know that?' Kate said quietly.

'Yes, no one seems to know where Luke is . . . And then someone comes here and smashes my door down. My ex and Barrett have to be involved somehow. So I'm off, I'm not staying around to see if I'm next.'

Kate and Barnard could see her grip tightening on the gun again. Barnard took Kate's hand and squeezed it slightly.

'Don't let us stand in your way,' he said. 'Did you know the Southend police are questioning Connie about your brother's death?'

'They think Connie might have killed Bert?' Delia asked with a mirthless laugh. 'They must be joking. All Connie Dowd was good for was producing kids. She was quite good at that.' There was an element of envy in Delia's tone.

'Did she know what your brother had got involved in?' Barnard asked.

'He wasn't involved, was he, according to the jury,' Delia snapped. 'They acquitted him. He was innocent, wasn't he? According to the law.'

'If you say so,' Barnard said sceptically. 'And what about Rod Miller, our man found murdered in Whitechapel? Was he their driver?' Barnard persisted.

'I wouldn't know,' Delia said sharply. 'Sam didn't confide much. But you can be sure he's involved somehow in all this mayhem – him and Barrett, looking for their cash, no doubt.'

'Did you always live here? Someone told us you lived on Canvey Island for a while.'

'You've been snooping about,' Delia said, her patience obviously wearing dangerously thin. 'We were there for a while. Had one of the small places, used to belong to my mother. But it got washed away in the flood. Sam was locked up by then, so I came back to live out here on the farm. It felt safer with all the troops around, and I can just about manage the place with a bit of help.' She gave a thin smile before breaking the shotgun and hooking it over her arm.

'Get out now,' she said. 'I need to finish packing and be away before dark.'

'And you won't tell us where you're going?' Barnard said.

'Not bloody likely,' Delia said.

Barnard led the way back to the car and sat for a moment in the driving seat looking thoughtful.

'That woman looks familiar,' he said. 'But there's no way I can have ever seen her before.' Kate gazed at the farmyard and the flat fields stretching away to the horizon.

'She's as tough as old boots,' she said. 'But then you'd have to be if you were running this place on your own.'

'And if you were married to Sam Dexter by the sound of it,' Barnard added as he started the engine.

They drove slowly back to Southend, still wrangling over the merits of the Beatles, the Stones and the Kinks, and parked on the seafront where a few intrepid strollers could be seen muffled in winter coats and scarves in spite of the supposed approach of spring. The fairground looked deserted but when they approached on foot it was obvious that they had been quickly spotted, as Jasper Dowd emerged from the caravans and headed in their direction with an extremely unfriendly look on his face.

'What the hell are you doing here again, girl?' he asked. 'And who's this?' As Dowd stared at Barnard, Kate could see his hands curling into fists and his colour rising. Not far behind him several other men had gathered, looking almost as menacing as their leader.

'I only wanted to know whether the police had let Connie go,' Kate said.

'No, they bloody haven't. Not as far as I know.'

'Has she been charged with anything?' Barnard asked.

'No one's told me anything.'

'There are time limits – well, supposed to be,' Barnard said.

'They do as they like,' Dowd snapped back, his anger rising. 'Now eff off! You're not wanted here. There's nothing you can do for Connie.'

'What about the children?' Kate persisted, in spite of the snarl that Dowd directed at her.

'The little ones are in care,' he said. 'Bloody social workers took them. Wouldn't let them stay here with me.'

'And Luke? Is there any sign of Luke?'

'No sign. The cops say they're looking for him, but I don't see any sign they're trying very hard. They're more interested in banging his mother up, as far as I can see. Now eff off, the pair of you! Didn't I say that already?'

Barnard took Kate's arm and pulled her away as Dowd's companions closed into a menacing circle around him.

'Come on,' he said. 'We'll get nowhere here.'

'Can we go to the police station to find out what's going on?' Kate asked as they walked away from the fairground, where a few punters were queuing for the big dipper and the dodgems although most of the smaller stalls were still closed. 'Or maybe her solicitor will still be around. She said she was working over the weekend.'

'As you know, I don't want to go to the nick,' Barnard said. 'But you can go in to ask about Connie if you like, or just ask where to find the solicitor. What did you say her name was?'

'Janet Driscoll,' Kate said as they headed back to the car.

But they were stopped by the sound of angry shouts from the fairground behind them. They turned, horrified, to see Jasper Dowd and his men running towards the dodgems where two men neither Barnard nor Kate recognized had suddenly appeared and were dodging between the cars, apparently trying to reach the far side. But the intruders were not fast enough to escape their pursuers, who circled round the ride and within seconds a mêlée had broken out and a running battle skittered across the floor of the rink as the assailants dodged between the now stationary cars to cut the two men off. The strangers were heavily outnumbered and both ended on the floor. Flinching, Kate saw heavy boots going in as the parents and children who had been innocently driving around rushed away from the violence, some in tears. As

she and Barnard watched, they heard a police siren quite close
by and saw the two men struggle to their feet and break away
to quickly thread their way between the stalls and rides and
disappear in the direction of the beach.

'Get in quick,' Barnard said. 'We don't want to get caught up
in that little lot.' And he pushed Kate into the car and pulled
away from the kerb almost before Kate had closed the passenger
door. Two police cars stopped behind them, but the officers who
jumped out took no apparent notice of the Capri as they pounded
down the slope on to the fairground.

'I don't know what Sam Dexter and Bomber Barrett look like,
though I can find out when I get back to the nick in London. But
my guess would be that that was them and they have unfinished
business with Jasper Dowd.'

He drove slowly through the town and parked close to the
police station.

'There you are,' he said. 'You can go in and ask the desk
sergeant if Connie Flanagan is still in there. She shouldn't be,
unless they've charged her and are keeping her in to go to court
tomorrow. But some cops bend the rules.' He glanced at her and
grinned. 'Not in the Met, of course.'

Kate walked slowly up the steps and found a lone sergeant
sitting at the front desk, seemingly more interested in a large mug
of tea than in any members of the public who happened to come
through the front door on a sleepy Saturday morning.

'What can I do for you, petal?' he asked after taking a hefty
swig of tea. But his eyes narrowed when she explained her mission.

'Friend of hers, are you?' he asked.

'Sort of,' Kate said. 'I just wanted to know if she and the
children were safe.'

'Well, as far as I know, they are. Social services are looking after
her kids – except the one who's gone missing, of course. And, as
far as I know, Mrs Flanagan's gone back home to the fairground.
But here's the man who can give you more details. This is DCI
Baker and I don't reckon he'll be best pleased to be pulled off the
golf course by those gyppos at the fair on a Saturday afternoon.'

Kate turned to find the DCI coming through the door, casually
dressed but red-faced and sweating and with an angry gleam in
his eye which turned to fury when he recognized Kate.

'What the hell are you doing here?' he demanded. 'I thought I'd told you to keep out of my hair.'

'She says she's a friend of Mrs Flanagan, guv,' the sergeant put in hastily. 'Wanted to know if she's still here.'

'No, she's not still here,' Baker said. 'She's on bail and if you want to know any more than that you'd better talk to her bloody solicitor, who managed to talk me into letting her go against my better judgement. They're slippery as eels those bloody gyppos from the fairground and I'll probably regret it. I told Mrs Flanagan to stay close to her uncle and not leave Southend again. Now bugger off, I've got work to do.'

Kate shrugged and headed for the door but as she passed Baker he grabbed her arm, digging his fingers in hard.

'How did you get here, anyway?' he asked. 'Are you with that beggar Barnard? Did he drive you down?' Still gripping Kate's arm, he pushed his way out through the swing doors beside her and glanced across the street to where Harry Barnard was lounging in the driver's seat with his radio audible through the open window. Baker marched across the road and as he pushed his face through the window Barnard turned the radio off with studied slowness.

'Sergeant,' he said, 'I thought I'd made it clear to the Met that I didn't want you trespassing on my patch for any bloody reason whatsoever. Didn't you get that message?'

'Loud and clear,' Barnard said quietly. 'But you can't dictate what my girlfriend wants to do in Southend, can you? I only gave her a lift down because the weekend trains are no good and she wanted to check up on Connie Flanagan. She's worried about her.'

'Connie Flanagan is fine and I'll be wanting to question her again next week,' Baker snapped. 'So now you can give your nosy girlfriend a lift back to London, and I don't want to hear about either of you interfering in my murder investigation again. Understood?'

'Understood,' Barnard said, adding with obvious reluctance 'Sir'.

FOURTEEN

Barnard set off back to London at a sober pace, not saying much, although Kate continued to fume about the unanswered questions they had left behind. As they approached the south-eastern suburbs, Barnard suddenly slowed.

'Of course!' he said.

'Of course what?' Kate asked without much enthusiasm.

'I've just thought where Ray Robertson might be holed up.'

'You're joking?' Kate said.

'No, I'm not,' Barnard said with a slight grin. 'Think about it. Ray's a Londoner through and through. He was brought up in the East End, took to crime long before his father died, moved into Soho and flourished after the war when there was everything to play for. He's been around a long time and is a well-known face. There's no way he could disappear like this in the Smoke. He'd be recognized within days if he was in any of his usual haunts. He could have gone abroad, I suppose, but I can't see Ray doing that. He'd be like a fish out of water.'

'So where might he go?' Kate asked, intrigued in spite of her reservations about Robertson and his relationship with Barnard.

'He might have gone to the one place outside London where he lived for any length of time,' Barnard said. 'He might have gone to Hertfordshire, where we were evacuated during the war. And I guess that Georgie and I are the only people who would remember that. If you don't mind a detour before we go home, we could have a quick look round.'

'It's a bit needle-in-haystack, isn't it?' Kate objected slightly wearily. 'And what are you going to do if you find him? Arrest him? Isn't that what DCI Jackson would expect?'

'If I'm right – and I agree it's a long shot – I'll play it by ear, try to persuade him to talk to the DCI. I don't believe he killed Rod Miller, but he may have information that would help nail the killer. After all, there are two reasons he could have disappeared. Either he actually killed him and is on the run. Or he didn't kill him but, for some reason we don't know about, thinks he might be next. If he's scared of someone, we need to know who and why. It's not like Ray to hide. He must have a very good reason.'

'I think you're taking a chance, la,' Kate said. Barnard pulled into a lay-by and turned to face Kate.

'If you don't want to come with me, I'll drop you at the end of the Tube line and you can go home. I don't want to get you into anything you don't want to get into.' She stared out of the car window for a long time and finally shrugged.

'All right,' she said. 'I'll come with you. But to be honest, I hope this is just a very long shot. I hope you don't find him.' Barnard shrugged.

'I need to give it a go,' he said.

They travelled largely in silence as Barnard worked his way round the North Circular and then headed north, following signs to Hertford.

'Where is it exactly?' Kate asked in the end, as they kept turning on to narrower and narrower lanes and passing signposts marked with village names that she could barely read as they passed.

'It's called Little Radford,' he said. 'It's only a hamlet really – a couple of farms, a church, a pub that lets rooms, and a tiny shop with a post office counter. There's a river where we used to muck about during the summer, trying to catch sticklebacks. And cows in the fields that came in for milking twice a day. The school was in the next village. We had to walk a few miles there and back.'

'Sounds like every boy's dream,' Kate said, as cottages began to appear at the side of the narrow lane. '*Just William* and all that.'

'It might have been, if the farmer hadn't been a bully and Georgie Robertson an evil little tearaway. Old man Green belted Georgie regularly until Ray stood up to him and made him stop. So he started on me instead. We were all glad to go home, in spite of the bombing and the V1 rockets.'

Kate could remember talk of the bombing of Liverpool, which had forced so many families out of their wrecked homes and set the docks ablaze, and knew that if Barnard was pleased to go home to something like that the country round here had been no idyll. Barnard pulled up outside the Green Man, which nestled close to an obviously ancient church with a low stone tower and an unkempt graveyard.

'Come on,' he said. 'We'll have a drink and see if they've seen any sign of a stranger. Ray's not a man you'd miss in a place like this.'

The bar turned out to be empty of customers. When they pushed open the door as they went in, it creaked on unoiled hinges, attracting the attention of a stocky man with a thatch of long grey hair slouching behind the bar. He looked up from the *Sunday Express* propped up against the beer pumps and raised one eyebrow in interrogation as Barnard surveyed the ales on offer. Barnard thought he looked vaguely familiar.

'I'll have a pint,' Barnard said, indicating his choice. 'And my friend will have a half of shandy. They waited in silence while the barman dealt with their request. After a thoughtful pull on his pint, Barnard glanced at the notice behind the bar offering rooms.

'We're a bit too far from home to get back tonight,' he said. 'Do you have a room free?'

''Fraid not. There's only the two and they're both taken. One by a weekender here for a wedding who's not leaving till the morning. The other's been booked for a week. Funny chap. Goes fishing a lot, though I've never heard of anyone catching much round here in twenty years. Makes long phone calls. Business, he says, though he never lets me get close enough to hear what he's on about. Trunk calls. Costing him a packet.'

'Pity you don't have a room,' Barnard said. 'I wanted to have a look round in the morning. I was evacuated down here during the war. Spent nearly two years on a farm.' The publican looked interested.

'You were one of the lads Tom Green took in, were you?' he asked. 'Some right little tearaways he ended up with. I'd have sent for the police if it had been me.'

'Is he still around?' Barnard asked.

'No, he died a good few years ago. Must have been '55, something like that. His wife moved away to live with her daughter, somewhere near Welwyn. There's a new man farming there now, full of modern ideas, he is.' The publican's view of modern ideas was clear enough on his face. Behind them the door creaked open.

'Here he is,' the publican said quietly. 'Did you have any luck today, Mr Roberts?' he asked as Kate and Barnard turned to face Ray Robertson, dressed in heavy tweeds and boots and a hat decorated with miscellaneous flies, pulled low over his eyes. He was carrying a rod and bait box with what looked like supreme confidence, although Barnard was sure he had never caught so much as a minnow since they were boys.

'Hello, Flash,' Robertson said with a smile, though his eyes were angry. 'I knew it must be you when I clocked the car. There's not many of those around here, are there?' He turned to the landlord. 'Can your missus do us some sandwiches? We'll have them in the snug. I don't suppose my friends will be staying long, but they'll need something to eat before they go.' Robertson led the way into a small room with just a couple of tables and a few stools and an old fireplace full of ash. He took off his coat and hat and flung them on to a stool and put his tackle on the floor with a clatter.

'I knew there were only two people in the world who could suss me out here,' he said as he sat down. 'You and Georgie. And as Georgie's safely behind bars, it had to be you. Come to take me in, have you? Though if you've got your dolly bird with you, I don't suppose you have.'

'I didn't seriously think you'd be here,' Barnard said. 'I thought you'd have melted away to Spain or South America by now, or somewhere else without an extradition treaty. Like some people we know.'

'They were train robbers,' Robertson said dismissively. 'I'm a legitimate businessman.'

'And a murder suspect,' Barnard said flatly. 'Don't kid yourself DCI Jackson's not serious about that.' He glanced away as a dumpy woman in an apron came in carrying a plate of doorstep sandwiches, which she dropped noisily on to the table without ceremony and with a sour look.

'I've only got cheese and a bit of ham,' she said. 'It's Sunday night. We don't cater on weekend nights.'

'That's fine, dear,' Robertson said expansively, slipping a pound note into the woman's hand. 'It's very good of you to take the trouble for my friends.' The three of them watched in silence as she went out and closed the door behind herself.

'Don't you worry about me, Flash,' Robertson said. 'If everything goes according to plan, I'll be out of here next week. This is only a temporary resting place, nice and quiet for a few days and well away from the Met.'

'I'd have thought you'd have found somewhere a bit more comfortable than this,' Barnard said, picking up a sandwich and examining it carefully.

'I suddenly had a yen to see what became of that old bastard at the farm,' Robertson said. 'If I did turn to murder, he might be at the top of my list. But apparently he died years ago, so the landlord tells me. Pity. I went down there but there's a young bloke running the place now. Looks a damn sight more business-like than old man Green ever was.'

'I didn't realize you disliked him so much,' Barnard said. 'It was always Georgie who got the back end of his tongue.'

'And his belt,' Robertson said. 'But I didn't find out until much later what else he'd been doing to Georgie while we were there.' The atmosphere suddenly froze and Kate shivered. They both waited for Ray Robertson to explain. He shrugged wearily.

'I've never had anything against queers myself,' he almost whispered. 'But when anyone interferes with kiddies that's different, isn't it? I guess that bugger Green knew he'd get nowhere with you or me, Flash, but Georgie was still too small to stand up for himself against a man like that. Good job he died, isn't it, or I might have been seriously tempted to help him on his way.'

'Georgie didn't give you a hint back then?' Barnard asked, taken by surprise at this revelation.

'He didn't tell me till years later. But you saw him go doolally while we were there. You remember the business with the cats? Now you know what was going on. The silly beggar never breathed a word.'

'No wonder he was such a pain in the bum while we were there. Sorry – not the best way of putting it,' Barnard said.

'And he's been doolally ever since,' Robertson said. 'Anyway, never mind all that. It's old history and there's no mending it. Now tell me the state of play at your nick. Haven't they found any other suspects for poor old Rod Miller's killing? As sure as hell I had nothing to do with it. As I told you, I was in Scotland on business. But I'm not going to waste my time with witnesses and alibis. They can whistle for that. I've got bigger fish to fry.'

'Well, DCI Jackson doesn't believe that. Nor do the Yard. And because the whole thing down in Southend is escalating, he's more convinced than ever that you're involved. There's been another killing and the Essex police are on the case now. When you took Rod on, did you know he'd been involved in armed robbery down there?'

'I never thought Rod was any sort of a choir boy, but I was hiring him as a trainer not a bloody Sunday school teacher. And he was a star at that.'

'He didn't have any sort of a record? Adult, juvenile, army? He must have been old enough to have been in the forces during the war.'

'Not that I was aware of,' Robertson said dismissively. 'Not that I'd have been bothered. You must remember what it was like after '45. No houses, rationing, no bread, no meat, no sweets, nothing for kids like us to do except pick over the bomb sites and try and flog whatever we could find. You wouldn't have thought we'd won the bloody war.'

'And you had no idea Rod might have been involved in the robberies?'

'The Essex police should have done a better job with those robberies in the first place,' Robertson said dismissively. 'I know one of the gang got off. What was his name? Flanagan? And if one of them got off, you can bet your life he'd be making sure he got his share of the loot if not all of it. And Dexter and that madman Barrett will be hopping mad if they can't lay hands on it now they're out. My guess is it was them who came looking for poor old Rod on the off-chance he'd been involved with Flanagan.'

'Flanagan's dead,' Barnard said flatly. 'They pulled him out of the mud on Maplin Sands. And his young son's disappeared.'

'Jesus wept!' Robertson said. 'Is your DCI talking to the Essex police? There's no way I've been anywhere near Maplin bloody sands. I don't even know where they are.'

'Off Foulness Island,' Barnard said.

'Ah,' Robertson said. 'Right down there with all the gunners?' He hesitated for a moment. 'If Barrett and Dexter have knocked Flanagan off, it stands to reason they might have come for poor old Rod Miller as well. Word is they stashed the money away and haven't seen a penny of it yet.'

'But there was no sign of Miller having cash to spare? I don't suppose you were paying him much.'

'If he had cash, he kept it very well hidden,' Robertson said. 'Rod was living in a council flat in Poplar for years once he came to the gym from Southend. He didn't smoke, hardly drank, and never had a bird that I knew of. He lived and breathed boxing and the lads he was training. You know that. You were there with him some of the time. Did he look like a man with money in his pocket? If anyone was divvying up the proceeds of those robberies, he wasn't getting a share.'

'You don't think Barrett and Dexter might come looking for you?' Barnard persisted. 'They might reckon Miller told you something about the state of play in Southend back then. You've been working together for a long time.'

Robertson hesitated for a moment and for the first time looked seriously worried.

'I told you. Only you and Georgie know about this place. I'm safe enough for a few more days.'

'But you won't be in the clear until you convince the Yard you weren't involved in Rod's murder,' Barnard urged. 'The *Daily Express* has you down as a wanted man and they don't pull their punches. And the rest of the papers will follow.' Barnard glanced at Kate, who was looking anxious. 'You need to clear this up once and for all. Come in with me and talk to the guv'nor. They won't call the hunt off without talking to you.'

'Nah,' Robertson said. 'It's a load of bollocks and I'll be out of here in a day or two. Go back to London and get your beauty sleep, Flash.' He glanced at Kate with something approaching a leer. 'If she'll let you.'

FIFTEEN

'So what are you going to do with your day off?' Harry Barnard asked Kate on Monday morning as they lay in bed taking in the pale sunshine filtering through the curtains. 'Can't you take a day off too?' Kate asked. She knew he had slept badly, feeling the tension as he lay beside her in the darkness. Both of them had slept fitfully at best. She glanced at the clock and realized that if Barnard was going in to work he was already late. But Harry kissed her and slid out of bed quickly.

'I'm in enough trouble with the brass already,' he said. 'I don't dare push my luck.' She sat up on the pillows and watched him dress, wondering how long their relationship could go on. Although her attempt to leave had been short-lived, since then there had been an uncertainty between them that she didn't seem able to forget. Nor, she thought, could Harry.

'I'll take the chance of doing some window shopping,' she said, hearing the lack of enthusiasm in her own voice and guessing that he would hear it too. When he came out of the bathroom, he sat on the bed beside her for a moment.

'Don't do anything silly,' he said. 'We'll go out for a meal tonight if you like. I'll get away as early as I can. Enjoy your day off. Don't forget you'll have to convince Ken that you've been in Liverpool when you get back to work.' In a second he was gone, and Kate lay back glad he had not stayed long enough to see the tears in her eyes. She knew he would not approve of the plan she'd already worked out at three in the morning to find out exactly what was happening to Connie Flanagan in the not very tender clutches of DCI Jack Baker. The only way to do that, she reckoned, was to take the train back to Southend and talk to Connie and her solicitor.

Barnard did not hurry to the nick. He parked the Capri in Soho Square and took a leisurely stroll down Frith Street, dropping into a few shops and restaurants and chatting to acquaintances,

legitimate and illegitimate, on the street corners before turning
west to cut through to Regent Street and head towards the nick.
He wondered how much longer this would remain his manor,
aware that he was trying to avoid the main issue. He should have
reported Ray Robertson's whereabouts the previous day, but
he had hesitated to call in the cavalry and have him arrested.
The old loyalties had kicked in and in all likelihood would cost
him his job, or worse. Kate, he thought, would probably never
forgive him.

As he walked into the CID room and hung up his coat, his
arrival seemed to attract some curious glances. But, he told
himself, he might have been imagining it. He flicked through
his case files without taking much in, then finally shrugged his
shoulders and set off down the corridor towards the DCI's office.
Jackson's secretary looked up in surprise when he approached
her.

'I was just about to come and find you,' she said. 'The DCI
wants to see you. You'd better go straight in, I think it's urgent.'
Barnard's mouth was dry as he knocked on Jackson's door and
responded to his instruction to come in. This time the DCI was
alone but his expression was no more friendly than when he had
been backed up by ACC Cathcart. Barnard took a deep breath
and prepared for the worst. Before he could speak Jackson himself
spoke, with a certain amount of grim pleasure on his face.

'I've just had a call from Hertfordshire,' he said. 'They've had
a tip-off from someone in a village called Lower Radford who
saw a picture of Ray Robertson in the *Daily Express* and reckons
he's seen him fishing round there. Does that sound at all likely
to you?' Barnard drew another deep breath, although this time
the anxiety accommodated just a glimmer of relief.

'Lower Radford was where we were evacuated during the
war,' he said warily. 'The three of us from our school, Ray and
Georgie Robertson and me. We lived on a farm. I went home
after about eighteen months to go to grammar school. The other
two stayed on a bit longer, but eventually they came back to
the East End. They lived just around the corner from my house.
I can't imagine Ray fishing, but I suppose he could have found
somewhere to hole up there well out of the way. He certainly
knows the area.'

'I'll ask Hertfordshire to have a closer look,' Jackson said. 'It sounds like a long shot but the Yard won't be pleased if we don't explore every possibility. As for you, I want you to keep up your inquiries. My own feeling is that Robertson is well out of the country by now. However, you say you've seen his wife. I want to know the moment either of them contacts you again. I've some questions for the ex-Mrs Robertson as well.'

'I've no idea where she might be, guv,' Barnard said. 'But I'll ask around. As far as I can remember, she had a sister somewhere in Essex when they got married but I've no idea what her married name might be. I suppose old Mrs Robertson might know, though the last time I mentioned Loretta to her she said she was a gypsy and that she wouldn't give her the time of day. I might be able to persuade her to get her daughter-in-law – ex-daughter-in-law – into trouble, I suppose. She's certainly someone who bears grudges. I'll see what I can do, though I must say Loretta Robertson looked as if she was doing all right for herself when I saw her, so my guess is that she's got a new man dancing attendance. She's still an attractive woman. One thing that's certain, she's not likely to go anywhere near her ex-mother-in-law. There's no love lost on either side.'

'And Sergeant,' Jackson snapped. 'Don't forget our last conversation with the Assistant Commissioner. If Hertfordshire don't pick Robertson up for any reason or if it isn't Robertson at all, I want you to redouble your own efforts. After all, he's contacted you once. If he does that again, I want to be the first to know about it. Understood?'

'Understood, guv,' Barnard said, hoping he was keeping the relief he felt under wraps. He felt like a man reprieved on the steps of the gallows. As he left Jackson's office, his hands were shaking and sweat was running down his back underneath his shirt. He walked past the CID office and out of the building without picking up his coat and hurried across Regent Street and through the swing doors of the Delilah Club. The young barman, Spike, was fiddling with the optics and looked surprised at Barnard's arrival in the deserted club.

'Give me a large Scotch with plenty of ice,' Barnard said. Spike looked as if he might demur but thought better of it and gave

Barnard a generous measure, which he drank down in one and pushed the glass back for a refill. He took a deep breath.

'I don't suppose you've heard from Ray?' he asked. Spike shook his head.

'No, he hasn't been in. The staff were getting stroppy again earlier in the week about not being paid. Mr Clarke said he hadn't heard anything from him, but then yesterday a registered letter came with enough cash in it to see everyone right. I couldn't believe it. I'd never seen so much cash at one time. So everything's hunky-dory again.'

'For the moment,' Barnard said sceptically. 'He didn't send a message with the cash, did he?'

'Just a scrap of paper saying "Keep calm and carry on". Didn't that come from the war or something?'

'It did,' Barnard said, as he sipped his second Scotch more slowly, feeling himself relax for the first time since he and Kate left Ray Robertson in the Green Man. 'And it's not a bad bit of advice at any time.' Barnard finished his drink and rang his own flat from the phone in the entrance lobby. Kate picked up quickly.

'Do me a favour, honey,' he said. 'Give the Green Man a quick call and see if Ray's still there. And if he is, tell him to move out quickly. Apparently the Hertfordshire police are heading in his direction. You'll get the number from directory inquiries. Make the call from a call box. I don't want anything traced back to the flat.'

'Are you really sure about this?' Kate said.

'It's the last thing I'll do for Ray,' Barnard said. 'I promise.'

Kate took the train to Southend with a sense of foreboding. The phone in Barnard's flat had shrilled again almost as soon as she hung up and she'd immediately identified the almost inaudible breathless voice at the other end as Connie Flanagan's. She'd been planning to go to Essex anyway, but what Connie told her convinced her the trip was more urgent than she had realized.

'I found Luke,' Connie said. 'He was locked up in one of the sheds under the pier. Uncle Jasper had been keeping him there, Luke said. I don't know what he thought he was doing. Luke's very frightened and I need to get away from here. But I've got no money and I don't know where to go. Can you help? I don't know who to trust here any more.' Kate could hear the fear in her voice and was not surprised when she broke down in tears.

'What about your solicitor?' Kate asked. 'Won't she help?'

'She'll just tell me to go back to the police station,' Connie sobbed. 'And Luke says he won't do that. He doesn't want to get Jasper into trouble. He says Jasper thought he was keeping him safe from some dangerous men.'

'The men who killed your husband, maybe?'

'Maybe,' Connie whispered.

'Can you keep out of sight until I get there? Meet me at the railway station at twelve o'clock and I'll come with you to talk to your lawyer.'

She stopped at a call box in Fenchurch Street station and made the call to the Green Man that Barnard had asked her to make, but the voice that answered was not the landlord's and she guessed from the tone that it might well be a police officer. She took no more than a second to decide to hang up without a word. Ray Robertson, as far as she was concerned, would have to look after himself.

The train pulled into Southend station after what seemed an interminable journey and she scanned the platform for a glimpse of Connie and her son before it finally ground to a juddering halt. She could not see them at first, but as she handed in her ticket at the barrier she caught a glimpse of a pale, anxious face peering through the window of the refreshment room.

She went in and saw that Connie had a tall skinny boy with her who looked even more distraught than his mother.

'This is Luke,' Connie said. The boy said nothing and continued to pick at the half-eaten sandwich in front of him. His mother drained her cup of tea.

'What do you think we should do?' she asked Kate, a look of desperation in her eyes. 'I don't know who I can trust now.'

'I really think you should talk to your solicitor,' Kate said. 'She'll go with you to the police station and sort this whole thing out. If you run away, DCI Baker will only be more convinced that you had something to do with your husband's death and he'll hunt you down. He's not just going to forget about you if you disappear. That's not the way they work.' Connie shrugged and looked at her son.

'I don't want to go to the police station,' he said sulkily. He ran his hands through a thatch of red hair. 'Why can't we go and stay with Auntie Delia? No one would ever find us out there.'

'Don't be silly,' Connie said. 'You know there's soldiers crawling all over Foulness.'

'I know a way in,' Luke said, his face mutinous. 'Dad showed me. He said it was useful sometimes.' Kate wondered exactly what it had been useful for, but left it at that.

'We'd better see what Miss Driscoll says first,' Connie said, finding some determination of her own at last. 'Someone needs to tell the police I've found you, Luke, else they'll carry on hunting and that won't help anyone. Auntie Delia was never much help to us when your dad was alive, so I shouldn't think she will be now.'

'Come on then, let's talk to your solicitor and get something sorted out,' Kate said. She paid for the drinks and Luke's sandwich and led the way out of the station towards Janet Driscoll's office, close to the police station. But as she went round the last corner ahead of the other two she stopped dead, her heart thumping. Three police cars and several uniformed officers could be seen outside the office block where Connie's solicitor worked.

Kate turned back and shepherded Connie and her son out of sight just as DCI Jack Baker got out of an unmarked car, red-faced and furious.

'I don't know what's going on there,' she said to Connie quietly, holding on to her arm tightly. 'But I think I'd better try to find out before we go barging in. You stay over there in that little park.' She gestured across the road to a playground where some mothers and small children were congregated. 'I'll come back in a minute and tell you what I find out.' She made sure Luke was close to his mother. 'Whatever you do, don't try to take off anywhere. That really wouldn't be a good idea. Do you understand that, Luke?'

The boy muttered something under his breath, but although he dodged Connie's outstretched hand he seemed to be following her willingly enough as Kate watched them go into the park – where in spite of the outraged glances of some of the mothers Luke, looking even taller than he was, began pushing himself on a swing intended for much smaller children. Connie slumped on to a bench not far away, watching him.

Kate turned away slowly and walked back round the corner, where even more police cars had assembled outside the office block and an ambulance, blue light flashing, had pulled up beside them. She crossed the road and went up to one of the uniformed constables who seemed to be in charge of the entrance, through which a number of people, who presumably worked there, were emerging. Most looked bewildered and a few were looking at their watches and complaining to each other.

'Hello,' Kate said. 'I was due to see Janet Driscoll this morning. Is there any chance of that?' The officer looked slightly startled. 'And your name, miss?' he asked. Reluctantly Kate told him and the PC immediately signalled to a sergeant who hurried over as she realized it was one of the officers she had spoken to on her last visit to the police station.

'You again,' the sergeant said. 'I think you'd better come with me. I reckon DCI Baker will want a word.' He led the way through the crowd of displaced workers and into the lobby, where she could see the DCI in animated conversation with the ambulance driver. When he spotted her with his sergeant, his face flushed and he waved the ambulance driver through into the building and hurried towards Kate.

'What the hell are you doing here again?' he asked. 'Is your boyfriend with you? I thought I made it clear I didn't want either of you on my patch.'

'He's not here,' Kate said. 'As far as I know, he's at work in London. But I was worried about Connie Flanagan and thought her solicitor would probably know where she is. She's desperate to get her kids back.'

'Well, her solicitor might know,' Baker said angrily. 'But she's not likely to be telling anyone anything for a while. The caretaker disturbed an intruder earlier this morning. Saved Miss Driscoll's life, he reckons. The bastards who were in her office were doing their best to kill her. She's on her way to hospital right now.' He glanced behind him to where the ambulance crew were manoeuvring a stretcher down the stairs. They were followed by a man in a formal suit carrying a doctor's bag.

'What do you reckon?' Baker asked. The doctor shrugged.

'Touch and go, I think,' he said and hurried out. Baker turned back to Kate.

'Your friend Connie Flanagan was due to see me back at the nick in about half an hour, no doubt with her solicitor in tow. Where she is now and whether she'll turn up is anyone's guess. But I'll find her, don't you worry, especially after this little lot. And if she thinks she's going to get her other kids back while her older boy's still missing and she's a witness – possibly even a suspect – in a murder case, she's got another think coming. If she doesn't turn up this morning, I'll take that bloody fairground apart. I'm damn sure that's where she's hiding.'

'You can't really imagine she killed her husband!' Kate protested.

'Perhaps not personally,' Baker said, 'but I reckon she knows who did. Now get out of my hair, Miss O'Donnell. I've got some sort of madman to track down, so stop getting in my way or I'll find something to charge you with as well. You'll know from your boyfriend that's not too difficult.'

SIXTEEN

Kate walked away slowly, knowing that if she hurried it might occur to Baker to send someone after her. But once round the corner she speeded up, anxious that Connie and Luke might have decided to disappear again. To her relief she found them both more or less where she had left them in the park, although Luke's acrobatic efforts on the swing had cooled to a desultory rocking, his head hanging on his chest in what looked like despair.

Connie got up quickly when she saw Kate, and listened in horror to what had happened to Janet Driscoll.

'I need to get away from here,' she whispered. 'I might be next.' Which seemed only too likely.

Kate seriously considered taking the two of them back to London, but realized that if she took them back to Harry's flat neither the Essex police nor the Met would believe Barnard had not been involved in the manoeuvre.

'Do you really think Luke could get you out to your sister-in-law's place on Foulness without anyone knowing?' she asked. 'I went out there with my boyfriend and we went through the checkpoints by car. But Delia said she was planning to move out. You might find the place empty.'

'Doesn't matter,' Connie said. 'I'm sure we could get inside. It's a dilapidated old place. It was damaged in the floods and no one's bothered to put it back together again really. But at least it would be safe for a while.' Kate thought for a moment, not believing for a moment that Connie and Luke would be safe on Foulness.

'I've got a better idea. I'll take you back to London with me,' she said tentatively, knowing that Harry Barnard would consider this a very bad idea indeed and not sure how many crimes she'd be committing if she went ahead with it or how many risks she might be taking.

'I thought your boyfriend said he was a copper,' Connie said doubtfully. 'Though that didn't seem to stop him being pulled over that night we went to Clacton. He won't go along with us running away from the coppers here, will he?'

'He's in the Met,' Kate said. 'But I won't take you to his place. I could take you to stay with a friend of mine for a few nights. There's a spare bed there and I'm sure Luke could sleep on the sofa. Then I'll talk to my boyfriend and work out the best thing to do. It's obvious that if someone's attacked your solicitor they're looking for you. They're not likely to find you in Shepherd's Bush.'

Connie looked dubious, but in the end she shrugged.

'I don't have much choice, do I?' she said. 'It's not safe here and the first place they'll look is my auntie's in Clacton, and you say Delia's done a bunk so maybe Foulness isn't such a good idea.' She turned to her son. 'Come on, Luke, we need to get out of Southend.'

'Can I see the Beatles in London?' Luke asked, his expression still mutinous. Kate laughed.

'You never know, la,' she said. 'They might be in America. But I'll find out for you and you might be lucky. I used to know John Lennon. We went to the same college in Liverpool.' That, she thought, as Luke gazed at her in something approaching awe, had got through to the boy like nothing else would. It was something to build on. She glanced at her watch. 'The next train back to Fenchurch Street goes in half an hour, so we'd better get to the station.' They strolled through the town, but as they approached the station forecourt Kate grabbed Connie's arm.

'There are two policemen in the booking hall,' she whispered. 'I wonder if they are looking for you – or for me, for that matter. DCI Baker was very keen to run me out of town.' She thought hard. 'Is there a bus to Benfleet? We could pick up the train there.'

'It stops by the pier,' Connie said.

'Come on then,' Kate said. 'Let's do it.' She was beginning to think like a fugitive herself and didn't like it, and she knew Harry would like it even less. Keeping to the back streets, they made their way back towards the pier and the fairground, where there were bus stops. But as they approached the seafront, Connie paused.

'If you keep an eye on Luke, I could go back to my van and pick up some stuff we might need,' she said.

Kate looked dubious.

'Are you sure?' she asked.

Connie put on a mutinous look.

'There's no one around now,' she said. 'It'll only take a minute and we can't go away in just what we're wearing, can we?'

Kate looked across the fairground. She could see a few paying customers on the rides and some milling around the ice cream van. There was no activity at all visible amongst the caravans close to the pier.

'We'll wait here,' she conceded, putting a hand on Luke's arm. 'But be quick. Your uncle must have noticed that Luke's not there any more.'

Connie nodded and slipped away, taking cover behind a family with three tall boys in tow before slipping away towards the living quarters. Kate waited for a good five minutes, with Luke becoming increasingly agitated beside her. Just as she spotted Connie making her way towards them lugging a heavy holdall, they were startled by the sound of a convoy of police cars heading in their direction along the seafront. They pulled up, brakes squealing and blue lights flashing, right across the main entrance to the fairground and at least a dozen uniformed officers spilled out and ran down the slope towards the rides and caravans. Close behind them, DCI Jack Baker got out of an unmarked car and stood watching events with his customary scowl.

'Mum!' Luke shouted and started running through the startled fairgoers towards Connie. Kate had little option but to follow.

'They can't all be looking for me,' Connie breathed as the three of them dodged behind the hoopla stall. Luke, Kate noticed, had gone very pale and had his hands clenched tightly in the pockets of his shorts.

'They've hardly had time to register that you haven't turned up for your interview,' Kate said, hoping to reassure Connie. 'They must be looking for someone else.'

'Hide, hide!' Luke said, clearly panicked.

'But where?' Kate said.

'The ghost train,' Luke said and, grabbing his mother's arm, pulled her and her luggage towards the sea wall. The entrance to the ghost train appeared to be firmly closed.

'It's not running today, there'll be no one there. This way, this way.' He led the two women down the side of the attraction to where he pulled apart two sections of thick canvas and slid between them into total darkness. Connie pushed her holdall inside and Kate followed. They were all gasping heavily and the clammy air inside did nothing to make breathing any easier. For a moment they stood still and Kate could hear her own heart beating fast, but they could hear very little of what was going on outside apart from an occasional shout.

'Where are the lights?' Connie asked her son. She was obviously as unfamiliar with their hiding place as Kate was.

'No lights,' Luke said. 'Only when the generator is running.'

'So how do we get out of here without being seen?' Kate asked. Luke pulled the edges of the canvas apart and peered out.

'Not this way,' he said as he pulled the fabric together again and plunged them back into darkness. 'There's coppers all over the shop.' Kate felt despair creeping up on her.

'We're trapped in here,' she said. But to her surprise Luke grabbed her arm.

'No we're not,' he said. 'Come on, this way, right round the edge of the ride. The rails and funny stuff's all in the middle. I nearly forgot, there's a door at the back, one of those emergency door things that you push. Me and my mates were always too scared to touch it, but we should be able to get out there. We'll come out just by the roller coaster and we can hide there too. Come on, quick.'

If they needed any more persuasion it came from the direction of the main entrance to the ghost train, where they could here shouts and demands that someone turn the electricity on. The police, it seemed, were going to instigate a search.

With Luke in the lead, they followed the canvas wall in total darkness for what seemed to Kate's frantic imagination like miles before they came, as Luke had promised, to the emergency exit at the back of the ride and pushed down on the bar to open it. The mechanism seemed stiff from disuse but eventually the double doors swung open and they found themselves in a narrow passageway where detritus from various rides and stalls had been dumped out of sight.

'We can go up on the roller coaster,' Luke said. 'If Fat Fred is taking the money, he'll let us on and we can go round as often as we like. You can see everything from up there. Me and my mates used to go up there to spy on my mum and dad – and Uncle Jasper.'

Connie noticed Luke's hesitation before bringing his uncle into the conversation and looked at him horrified.

'What did you do that for?' she asked. Luke shrugged and kicked at the tattered bumper of a discarded dodgem car.

'I just liked to see things,' he said.

'I suppose you're right,' Kate agreed, 'they're not likely to look up and see us.'

The three of them made their way cautiously to the terminus, where the stationary cars were filling up. After a brief negotiation with a heavily built teenager who she assumed was Fat Fred, Luke waved them into one of the rows of three seats and made sure they were secure.

'You don't throw up, do you?' he asked Kate uncertainly. It was strange, she thought, how easily the child had taken charge of their escape and how readily his mother accepted his lead. She supposed that boys who'd used the fairground as a playground for years had a knowledge of it that the adults, busy making a living, did not necessarily share.

'I don't usually,' she said, remembering her childhood rides at New Brighton and Blackpool, as the cars began moving and flung them up a gradient and then down a steep incline. It was true that once you got used to the motion the big dipper offered an unrivalled view of the fairground and what was going on there.

The police contingent seemed to be heading in the direction of the caravans parked directly underneath the highest point on the roller coaster's journey. They could hear shouting and the sound of knocking and banging on doors.

'If I'd still been there they'd have found me, anyway,' Luke said.

'I thought you said Jasper moved you around?' his mother said.

'He did, but only down there on the fairground,' Luke said.

'Why did he keep you there?' Kate asked. 'What on earth was

he doing that for when he knew your mother was going frantic?'
The boy hesitated before replying.

'He thought I knew too much,' Luke said at last in a small
voice.

'And did you?' Kate demanded. The boy shrugged and glanced
at his mother for help, but she seemed frozen by his plea.

'Not really,' he said. 'When I was up here, I saw Uncle Jasper
with some men I didn't know. I just asked him who they were
and he said I had to stay with him until he'd finished some
business.'

'You really didn't know the men? Know who they were, I
mean?' Kate persisted. 'You hadn't seen them before, with your
dad maybe?'

The boy looked at her and shook his head.

'But I might recognize them again, mightn't I? That's what
Uncle Jasper was afraid of, I think. He was frightened I might
recognize them and tell someone. He just wanted me to keep
quiet. He wasn't going to do anything bad to me.'

Kate looked at him incredulously. Uncle Jasper might not have
meant Luke any harm – but if the men he had seen were Dexter
and Barrett, who must have been in jail for most of Luke's life,
there was no doubt they could have harmed him.

'Look,' Connie said, pointing to where two men could be seen
running away from the caravans pursued by several police officers
and also by Jasper Dowd, who was shouting and gesticulating
furiously.

'That's Sam Dexter,' Connie whispered. 'Delia's ex. I haven't
seen him for years but I'd know him anywhere.'

Somehow Connie's Uncle Jasper managed to dodge through
the rides and stalls, taking a shortcut across the dodgem rink and
stumbling as he passed the hoopla, spilling a jumble of hoops
and cuddly toys across the floor in front of the following police,
who also dodged and stumbled in the mayhem and evidently lost
sight of their quarry close to the waltzer. It wasn't entirely clear
whether Jasper Dowd was chasing the other two men or running
with them, and it looked quite possible that the pursuing police
didn't know either.

'They went inside the ghost train,' Luke said. 'They'll never
find them in there in the dark.' Kate looked at the boy, whose

eyes were gleaming with excitement, and wondered whose side he was on.

'Were they the men you saw?' she asked quietly. Luke glanced at his mother again and then shrugged, his face closed and eyes blank as they watched the pursuing police officers scatter and pause as they lost sight of their quarry.

'Maybe,' he said. 'I don't know for sure. I don't know who they are.'

Kate looked at Connie but guessed this was not the time to pursue the fugitives' identities or their criminal records, with the boy listening in. She was just pleased that Luke was out of their reach, for the time being at least.

In the end, they did three circuits on the big dipper before the activity below calmed down and the police began to reassemble by their cars. Kate could see DCI Baker in apocalyptic mode berating his officers, who must have lost their quarry in the further reaches of the fairground, where bemused groups of visitors stood about not knowing what all the fuss was about.

'There's Uncle Jasper!' Luke said, pointing to the rear of the ghost train where they had successfully remained out of sight.

'So it is,' Kate said, recognizing Dowd's hat from above. She glanced at Connie, who was looking shell-shocked.

'We'll talk later,' she said, as some of the police cars pulled away and the remaining handful of officers fanned out among the rides again. 'As soon as we stop this time, we'll get off the fairground and I'll go and see if the bus to Benfleet is due while you two go up on the pier out of sight. We need to be out of here. No one will take any notice of us if it's Uncle Jasper and the other men they're looking for. But we need to keep out of their way.' She gave Connie a ten-bob note.

'Get yourselves an ice cream,' she said before making her way back to the road and the bus stops, feeling slightly desperate. The whole situation seemed to be spiralling out of control.

Kate walked slowly past the queues of people waiting for buses but before she reached the right stop she was surprised by a car suddenly pulling up beside her. She instinctively pulled back from the passenger door, but there was no one on her side and when she peered in at the driver she was surprised to see Delia Dexter behind the wheel.

Delia wound down the window. 'What on earth are you doing still here?' she asked. 'I thought you'd gone back to London.'

Kate inched closer. 'It's a long story,' she said. 'Anyway, I thought you were going as far away from here as you could get.'

'I am, but I thought maybe Connie had gone back to the fairground. I couldn't think of anywhere else she could have gone. My brother wasn't a very reliable husband as it goes, and she always relied on her Uncle Jasper for help.'

'Well, I don't think she'll be doing that any more,' Kate said. 'She found Jasper had Luke locked up down there to keep him quiet about something. She doesn't know whose side Jasper is on any more.'

'That explains why Jasper was so jumpy when I knocked on the door of his caravan a while ago. He had someone in there with him, though he made sure I couldn't see who it was. He said Connie was with the police, but he never mentioned Luke.'

'Well, Connie isn't with the police. She's with me, and so is Luke. We were going to London but the police are watching the railway station. They still want to question her about her husband's death and now her solicitor has been attacked as well. She needs to get well away until the police sort out what the devil's going on here. And she wants to get Luke well away from Jasper. She may have always thought he was a cuddly uncle, but not any more.'

'Where is she?' Delia asked, glancing at the bus queue. 'You won't get out of the town on the bus. It's much too slow. I'll take you as far as Canvey, if you like. You can pick up the train there.' Kate hesitated, looking back to where the police car lights were still flashing at the entrance to the fairground.

'Are you sure?' she said doubtfully. 'Stay here and I'll ask Connie if she's happy with that.'

'I am Luke's auntie,' Delia said tartly. 'I don't want him any more mixed up in this than he is already. His dad is dead, his mother's a police suspect and his brother and sister are in care, poor kid. The least I can do is get him out of here.' Kate nodded and glanced at the pier, where she had left Connie and Luke eating ice cream wafers well out of sight.

'I'll talk to Connie, anyway,' she said. 'See what she thinks.' But it did not take much effort to persuade Connie to accept

Delia's offer of a car ride in the right direction. They made their way back to the road and Kate helped Luke and then Connie through the passenger door into the back seats and prepared to get into the front. But as she pushed the seat back and picked up her bag Delia suddenly reached across and pulled the door shut in her face, then revved the engine and pulled away into the stream of traffic so suddenly that an approaching bus had to slam on its brakes, hooting loudly in protest.

Kate muttered all the expletives she could think of as she watched the car disappear along the seafront. But anger soon turned to a despair which threatened to overwhelm her. And her heart thudded in panic as she realized that the little drama on the road had been witnessed not only by an entire bus queue but also by two uniformed policemen who were now heading in her direction at a determined pace.

'What was all that about?' the leading PC asked, not hiding his suspicion.

'Wasn't that Connie Flanagan?' the other said. 'And the boy? Has she got her son back? We've been hunting for him for the best part of a week.'

'It was and it is,' she said. 'I think I'd better talk to DCI Baker.'

'I think you better had,' the older officer said grimly. 'As it happens he's still just round the corner on the fairground, so you'd better come along with me. I think you've got some explaining to do.' He took her arm in a vicelike grip and steered her firmly in the direction he wanted her to go.

Kate glanced at her watch and for the hundredth time tried to make herself comfortable on the bare bunk which was the only place to sit in the police cell where she had been confined on DCI Baker's orders.

'Take her to the nick and make sure she doesn't leave,' he had instructed the uniformed officers who'd escorted her to him at the entrance of the fairground. When they arrived at the police station, the desk sergeant interpreted that as an instruction to lock her up. So far she had been there for more than two hours and no one had so much as looked through the shuttered window in the very solid door. She had almost decided to bang on the door and demand to be taken to the lavatory when the hatch opened with a snap and she heard the welcome sound of keys outside.

'Come on,' the custody sergeant said. 'The DCI's back now and has time to talk to you.' She followed him upstairs away from the cells and down a corridor with doors to the left and right. Eventually he opened one and pointed her towards one of the four chairs set around a table firmly screwed to the floor. The room was not much more prepossessing than the cell below, with high windows of frosted glass that let in little light and walls and floor which looked filthy and stained, but at least it was a slight improvement on the previous two hours. She took a deep breath in preparation for facing DCI Jack Baker and his apparently permanent rage.

She had to wait a further quarter of an hour before she heard heavy footfalls outside in the corridor and the DCI and another plain-clothes officer came in and took two of the chairs opposite her.

'Right, Miss O'Donnell,' Baker said. 'I am interviewing you under caution on suspicion of aiding and abetting a fugitive, namely Constance Flanagan, who has failed to surrender to her bail. Do you know where she is?'

'No, I don't,' Kate said.

'Did you know where she was earlier in the day?' Baker snapped. Kate wriggled to get more comfortable in the unforgiving chair.

'I saw her earlier with her son coming away from the fairground,' she said. 'She said she was due to see you later and I went with her to her solicitor's office. But—'

'But what, Miss O'Donnell?'

'One of your officers told me that Janet Driscoll had been hurt. That was when Connie panicked.'

'What do you mean, panicked?' Baker barked. 'She could still have come in to surrender to her bail. Whatever had happened to Miss Driscoll, she was only a stone's throw away from the police station. Why didn't she come?'

'She was scared,' Kate said. 'Terrified, actually. What do you expect? You'd completely failed to find her boy. In the end she found him herself and I suppose she was afraid you'd whip him away again to put him into care, like you did Sally and Liam.

She might have come in with Janet Driscoll but she wasn't going to come on her own. And I was no substitute for her solicitor. Neither of us thought you would let me in with her, anyway.'

'So you encouraged her to abscond?'

'I didn't encourage her, Inspector. She made up her own mind. She's not a child.'

'You're not telling me you didn't have some influence on what she did?' Baker sneered. 'She's an ignorant little gyppo. You know that as well as I do. If you couldn't persuade her, you should have got some help from my officers. There were enough of them around. I hold you responsible. You've got in my way ever since you came to Essex. I told you to go home and stay home. Now you're in a barrel-load of trouble, facing charges yourself, and don't think for a moment I won't give your boyfriend's DCI chapter and verse.'

'This is nothing to do with my boyfriend,' Kate said angrily, though she knew she was spitting into the wind. 'He doesn't know I came to Southend today. There's no reason why he should. I was the one who met Connie Flanagan in the first place, when I came to take pictures, and I was the one who wanted to make sure she was safe. I was worried about her.'

'So where is she now?' Baker snapped. 'Is she safe now? Because if she's on her own in the town with the boy I can tell you she's taking a hell of a chance with those two maniacs on the loose. There have been two murders already and I wouldn't give much for Janet Driscoll's chances of surviving.' Kate looked at him, appalled.

'So where is Connie Flanagan?' Baker shouted, leaning across the table towards Kate, red-faced and spitting in fury. 'Where the hell is she?'

'I don't know,' Kate said very quietly. 'Her aunt, Delia Dexter, picked her up in her car and drove off. She said she would take me with her but then changed her mind. That's all I can tell you.'

'Her aunt!' Baker exploded again. 'You may believe these families look after each other, but most of the time they're at each other's throats. I tell you, we'll be lucky to see Connie Flanagan again. And that, Miss O'Donnell, is down to you. How do you know Delia Dexter isn't hand in glove with her husband? Why on earth did you think she was the right person to help Mrs

Flanagan? I've always thought she probably knew what was going on right from the beginning but, just like with her brother, I could never get enough evidence to pin her down.'

'She divorced him years ago when he was in jail,' Kate said, although she knew that could mean nothing at all. 'She says she's not seen him since he came out of jail and doesn't want to. I think she's as scared of him as everyone else seems to be.'

'And she didn't give you any indication of where she planned to take them?'

'No,' Kate said. 'She offered to take us all to Benfleet station so we could get a train to London. I'd thought of somewhere Connie and Luke could stay for a while. But she must have had a plan of her own, and it didn't include me. I don't think she drove off towards Benfleet, though. She drove off past the pier.'

'What sort of a car was it?'

Kate looked blank. 'Only two doors, so they had to clamber into the back. Once Connie and Luke were in they couldn't easily get out.'

'Colour?'

Kate gazed at the frustrated DCI and shrugged helplessly. 'Dark. Black, maybe, or dark blue.'

'And I don't suppose you've any idea of the make?'

'It wasn't a Mini or a red Capri,' she said. 'I don't know much about cars. We never had one at home.'

'So we'll have to see if she's a registered owner, and that can take for ever. And ask my officers to watch out for a dark-coloured car with two women and a boy in it. Wonderful!'

Baker sat looking at her for a long time before speaking again.

'I think you are the most infuriating young woman I have ever met,' he said. 'Right, I want a full statement from you. You'll have to wait until one of my officers is free to take it. And that could be a very long time.'

SEVENTEEN

H arry Barnard got home expecting to find Kate surrounded by shopping bags after her trip to Oxford Street. Instead he found the flat chilly and deserted, no sign of a shopping spree in sight, and the dirty breakfast dishes still in the kitchen sink. He flung his hat on to the sofa but kept his coat on as he suddenly felt very cold and slightly sick. Kate had not left any message he could see, and it struck him with complete certainty that she had done something impulsive that she knew he would not approve of and which might quite possibly compromise him as well.

He took a couple of deep breaths and made himself calm down and work logically through all the bases. He rang the Ken Fellows Agency, but there was no reply. Presumably all her colleagues had already gone home, and he guessed she would not have confided in them anyway. Next, trying to sound casual to hide the anxiety that threatened to overwhelm him, he rang Kate's friend Tess Farrell in Shepherds Bush to ask if she had seen her on-off flatmate.

'Of course I haven't seen her, I've only just got in from school,' Tess said, not sounding particularly friendly. 'Anyway, I thought she was back with you.'

'It was just a long shot,' Barnard said, his stomach tightening. 'She had the day off work and I expected her to be here when I got home.'

'It seems to me you expect far too much,' Tess said. 'But she's certainly not here and there's no sign that she has been. I thought you were looking after her, but obviously not.'

There was, Barnard thought, no answer to that and he heard Tess slam the phone down. He slumped in his favourite chair and spun round a couple of times, hugging his camel coat around himself although he knew that, while it might ward off the cold, it would not fend off the panic that was beginning to overwhelm him.

He guessed that Kate had gone back to Essex. She had become obsessed with the Flanagan woman and had obviously gone looking for her regardless of the fact that both the police and probably a couple of ruthless murderers wanted to find her too. He still bitterly regretted agreeing to drive Connie Flanagan to Clacton with her children. If it had not been for that mistake, neither Kate nor he would have got involved with the Essex police. And now DCI Jack Baker would be furious to discover that he might be involved again, even if at a distance, and would certainly carry out his threat to report Barnard to DCI Jackson if he hadn't already done so. But he had no choice but to contact him. If Kate was missing on his manor, then Baker had to know and had to help find her.

Barnard got to his feet reluctantly, sending the chair spinning, and picked up the phone to call Southend nick. Before he could dial, the doorbell began to ring persistently and he reluctantly put the receiver down. The urgency of the bell told him to expect the worst. But it was Ray Robertson who stood outside in the lobby and immediately pushed past him into the living room – a big man, looking smaller now he had abandoned his fishing gear, though puffed up by his obvious fury.

'Did you shop me?' he demanded angrily. 'Did you grass me up to save your own skin? Because someone bloody did, and if it wasn't you I can't imagine who it was.'

'Sit down, Ray, and have a drink,' Barnard said quietly, heading for his cocktail cabinet to avoid the clear possibility that Ray was about to hit him. He noticed that his hands were not quite steady as he poured two glasses of whisky and handed one to Robertson, who downed it in one.

'You and your dolly bird were the only people who knew where I was,' Robertson said only slightly more calmly. 'I only got away by the skin of my teeth because the landlord tipped me off. He remembered me from all those years ago when I used to try and get an illegal pint or two out of him. I reckon he was sorry for us when we were kids, stuck out on the farm with that bastard Green. Anyway, he was sympathetic enough to tell me to move on sharpish. I reckon I was only minutes ahead of the police, though that was enough. But what I want to know is who told the police I was there?'

'Well, it wasn't me,' Barnard said, sitting down again in his chair and pushing his coat back. 'I've got enough on my plate. I think my dolly bird, as you call her, went back to Essex today and seems to have disappeared. She's got herself involved in stuff down there that she should never have gone near.'

'Never mind her,' Robertson said. 'Are you telling me you never told anyone where I was holed up?'

'I didn't,' Barnard said again. 'Which isn't to say I didn't come close, on the grounds of self-preservation. But by the time I got to see him, the DCI had been told by the Hertfordshire police that you might be in Lower Radford. Someone had noticed your picture in the *Express* and thought they'd seen you fishing. Jackson asked them to check it out, which they must have done by now. But when I left the nick there was no sign they'd found you, so I guessed you must have got away in time. I'd have been told in no uncertain terms if they'd arrested you.'

'I got away by the skin of my bloody teeth,' Robertson said, holding out his glass to Barnard for a refill, which he drank more slowly.

'So if push'd come to shove with Jackson, you'd have told him where I was?' he asked eventually, his eyes hard. Barnard shrugged.

'Ray, we go back a long way, but this is a murder at your gym we're talking about. And another one, possibly related, down in Essex. I'm not going to risk my job and maybe end up in jail to cover for you. You should talk to Jackson. If you've really got an alibi for Rod Miller's killing, tell him and put yourself in the clear. If you haven't, you're on your own and I can't help you.'

'So you would have told him?' Robertson put his glass down on the coffee table with rather more force than was needed.

'I'd have told him this morning. But as it turned out I didn't have to, he already knew.'

'Very convenient, Harry,' Robertson snapped.

'Isn't it more likely the landlord tipped off the Hertfordshire police?' Barnard suggested. 'I saw him with his nose in the *Express* when Kate and I arrived.'

'I told you, he was OK with it. He seemed to think we were old mates. God knows why.'

'And you don't think he'll mention the fact that Kate and I tracked you down?'

'If he covered for me, I dare say he'll cover for you too,' Robertson sneered. 'You're right, your play-it-by-the-book DCI would have had you in a cell by now if he'd found out you'd been there. I reckon you're safe enough.'

'But you're not,' Barnard said flatly. 'Jackson will want to know whether you've contacted me again after your phone calls. I'll have to tell him in the morning. Why are you here, anyway? If they think you might have come back to London, the Yard will no doubt check me out as well. You're definitely not safe here.'

'Well, if the cops in Essex are bright enough to report back to the Met before morning, I dare say the Yard will check you out. But I have to say I'm not very impressed by the plods out in the sticks. And the Met's not covering itself in glory either. What I don't understand is why they're obsessed with fitting me up for Rod's death. It can't just be coincidence that all this business started when Dexter and Barrett got out. You think we've got evil bastards in London, but Essex has got them too. I remember them from when I did a bit of courting down there. It's obvious to anyone with half an eye that the killing had something to do with the robberies in Southend. Why the hell aren't they going after those two? And if they reckon they had help, it was much more likely to be someone on the fairground than me. They're all as thick as thieves, those gyppos. I should know. I married one of them. More fool me.'

Robertson glanced around the room until his eyes lighted on the phone.

'What I really want right now is your phone. I'm not planning a long visit. Don't you worry your head, Flash. I'm aiming to be well out of the country soon, but there are a few loose ends to tie up first. Obviously I couldn't go back to the Delilah or the gym, so I thought my old mate Harry Barnard might help – but clearly I was wrong. The first thing I need is a car. I dumped the one I had in a back street in Tottenham and came in on the Tube, just in case someone in that bloody village remembered the make and number. I'd borrow your motor but it would stand out like a sore thumb, so you just sit there quietly while I sort something out.' Barnard flung himself back in his chair knowing that Robertson was inexorably involving him in his escape plans and there was nothing he could do about it.

Robertson's couple of calls produced the promise of a car within ten minutes. Not for the first time, Barnard wondered at Robertson's apparently limitless network of contacts. But why on this occasion he was using them so cautiously? It made no sense unless he had something serious to hide, something as serious as murder.

'So now where?' he asked when Robertson finally hung up.

'A quick trip to see my sister-in-law to sort out some unfinished business,' he said.

'Your sister-in-law?'

'Don't you remember Loretta had a sister? You came to my wedding, didn't you?'

'It's all a long time ago,' Barnard said. 'Did I tell you I bumped into your ex-wife in Oxford Street? She was looking well. And she was looking for you.'

Robertson laughed. 'I bloody hope not,' he said.

'DCI Jackson wants words with her. He said so this morning. Wanted me to track her down, but I can't say I've had any luck. But they came from Essex, didn't they, those two girls?'

'What of it?' Robertson snapped. 'Anyway, it's her sister I've got some business with. Won't take long.' He stared silently at Barnard for a long time before getting to his feet.

'So now we know exactly where we are, don't we, Flash?' he said. 'Arrest me, why don't you? It would earn you brownie points, and your DCI Jackson will no doubt want to know why you didn't. Perhaps I need some other way to keep you out of my hair for a bit?'

As Robertson turned towards the door, Barnard followed him, eager by now to lock it behind him. What he didn't expect was the former boxer's quick spin round and the lightning upper cut that knocked him backwards, so he caught his head on the corner of the coffee table as he went down. Before he lost consciousness, Barnard heard Robertson's departing curse and the front door slam.

Kate O'Donnell guessed that DCI Jack Baker had deliberately kept her at the police station well into the evening before sending an officer to take down her statement, check it carefully and then get her to laboriously sign each page before allowing her to go. Once outside she glanced around the now quiet streets, found a phone box and dialled Harry Barnard's flat. She was surprised when there was no answer. She retrieved her coins and glanced at her watch. It was already gone eleven. She still had her return train ticket in her purse, but was not sure what time the last train to London was likely to leave or whether it might already have gone. She had never intended her visit to Southend to last so long. The more she thought about it, the more likely it seemed that DCI Baker had deliberately kept her hanging about until there was no way of getting home apart from persuading Barnard to come from London to collect her. But Barnard was not answering his phone.

She made her way to the station but, as she expected, found it closed for the night. She sat for a moment on a bench outside and counted the money in her purse. It might, she calculated, just about run to a night in a bed and breakfast but she doubted whether anyone would take in a lone woman without luggage as late as this. Landladies were notorious for thinking the worst. She spotted another phone box on the other side of the road, but there was still no reply from Barnard's flat. Surely, she thought with a flash of anger, he must have realized by now that she was missing? Surely he must have worked out that she might have come to Southend again and made some inquiries at the police station? But maybe he wouldn't do that for fear of annoying the Southend police even more than they were annoyed already. Maybe this time her interference really had gone over the top and fractured their precarious hold on their relationship. Maybe Harry Barnard had just abandoned her.

She counted her coins again and dialled her own place in Shepherd's Bush. The phone rang for a long time before the sleepy voice of Tess Farrell replied.

'Kate,' she said. 'Where are you? I was having an early night.'

'I'm stuck in Southend. I missed the last train back and I can't get hold of Harry to ask him to come and pick me up.'

'He called me earlier to ask if you'd been round here,' Tess said. 'I probably gave him a bit of a flea in his ear, la. Sorry – he was worried, I suppose.'

'He's not answering the phone,' Kate said and she could not

disguise the catch in her voice. 'I was with the police for hours and they wouldn't let me make a phone call before I left. It looks as if I'll have to sleep on a bench by the station till it opens in the morning.'

'You can't do that,' Tess said sharply. 'It's not safe. Go back to the police station and tell them they've left you stranded.'

'I don't want to do that,' Kate said, her voice breaking. 'They'll either send me away or put me in a cell again. And I couldn't bear that, it was horrible.' There was silence at the other end for a moment before Tess spoke again.

'Is there a directory in your phone box?' she asked eventually. Kate glanced at the bracket where one should have hung but it was empty and swung on a single screw.

'No,' she whispered. 'It should be here but it's not.'

'Look, I'll see if I can find some numbers for you from here. Bed and breakfast places, maybe, something like that. Even the Salvation Army. They have beds, don't they? We don't want you sleeping on the beach, do we? Ring me back in ten minutes, la. Have you got enough change to make more calls?' Kate looked in her purse.

'Yes,' she said. 'I'll try Harry's flat one more time and if he doesn't answer I'll call you back in ten minutes. Thanks Tess, you're a star.' But there was still no reply from Highgate and she felt a sense of dread threaten to overwhelm her that had been building up ever since she realized the station was closed and the last train gone. The cramped phone box was close and smelly and she needed to get out. Before pushing the heavy door open, she scanned the street outside but it still looked deserted. Southend, she thought, was not like London, where the streets seemed to be bustling for most of the night. With the holiday season still a distant prospect, Southend had clearly gone to bed early. She would walk down to the seafront, she decided, where at least the air off the sea would be fresher, and find another phone box. In the end, if Tess failed to come up with any answers, she might have to go back to the police station and take her chances that she would be able to find help there.

But looming ever larger was her concern for Harry. Where was he? And why wasn't he searching for her if he knew she hadn't got home by now? As she walked towards the seafront, she felt a rogue tear creeping down her cheek and dashed it away angrily. She would complain about DCI Jack Baker's tactics as soon as she got a chance. It might embarrass Harry Barnard, but she didn't see why the fat detective should get away with such blatant bullying.

That decision made, she walked more briskly towards the seafront, where there was much more activity. Most of the shops had put up their shutters and the pubs had closed, but there were still lights in a couple of cafés and several groups of young people milling around by the entrance to the fairground and the pier. But the stalls and attractions were in darkness and it was not until she got closer that she realized that the atmosphere amongst the groups of young men was restless, bordering on threatening. She hesitated on the opposite side of the road and watched for a moment, wondering if being here was a good idea. She could not see another phone box and was about to retrace her steps when one group of lads spotted her, all dressed in leather jackets and tight trousers which reminded her of John Lennon before he took to a suit.

'Hello, darling,' one of them shouted across the road, then began to move in her direction. The rest straggled behind him and almost before she could draw breath she found herself surrounded and up against the shutters of a darkened shop window where she could barely move, her heart thudding uncomfortably.

'Where are you going, sweetheart?' said the most aggressive of the young men, running a hand across his well-greased hair. 'We could give you a good time.'

'No thanks,' Kate said sharply, looking around for a way to slip out of the threatening mob. But there seemed to be no way through the wall of broad shoulders that surrounded her or to escape the boozy clouds of breath that turned her stomach. 'I'm looking for a phone box. My boyfriend's expecting me to call.'

'Well, he can have you back when we've finished with you,' the leader of the gang said with a laugh as he put a heavy arm on her shoulder and made as if to kiss her. Between the shoulders of her tormentors Kate could see a motor scooter approaching. In desperation, she screamed as loudly as she could. The scooter slowed and then turned into the crowd, pushing through the threatening circle, revving loudly and spinning round to face the road again.

'Get on the back,' the scooter rider said. 'Quick.'

Without thinking Kate flung her arms around the rider's waist and hung on as he accelerated away towards the pier, where he pulled up by the kerb and turned to face her. She realized that he was in army uniform and looked older than the boys who had been threatening to assault her. She took a deep breath and thanked him.

'I was only looking for a phone box,' she said, conscious that her voice was shaky and her knees felt weak. 'I've missed the last train home.'

'Where's home?' the soldier asked, but she didn't answer directly even though his accent was very close to her own. 'Not Fazakerly anyway, la, if you're right down here,' he said with a grin.

'Not any more,' she conceded. 'I was going to call my boyfriend and ask him to come to pick me up but he's not answering his phone. I need to try again.'

'Is he a Scouser too?'

'No, London born and bred, but he's all right,' Kate said.

'Do you want to go to the police and complain about those baby thugs?' her rescuer asked.

'No,' Kate said firmly. 'I don't want to go anywhere near the police.' The squaddie looked at her curiously but did not ask why.

'Well, there's a phone box a bit further along here, on the Shoeburyness road. I could take you there if you like. I'm going that way back to barracks.'

'That would help,' she said. 'I'll call Harry again, and my friend Tess. I'm sure we can somehow sort something out. I don't want to end up sleeping on the beach.'

'Not with that lot about, you don't,' he said. 'Hop on. I'll take you as far as the phone box and see if you get through. If not, I'm not sure what I can do with you.'

Kate hitched herself up behind her rescuer and they set off again, more slowly this time. The road became more built up as they travelled east and from what Kate could see, with the inter-mittent street lighting, some of the buildings looked distinctly military.

'Is this your barracks?' she shouted as they passed a well-lit and gated entrance with sentries on duty. The driver did not reply until she pressed a hand into his ribs. He looked over his shoulder.

'The phone box is round the back,' he shouted and turned left so sharply that Kate almost lost her balance.

'Steady!' she shouted into the wind and quite suddenly he stopped and pointed to a phone box almost hidden by thick vegetation at the side of the narrow road.

'There you are, darling,' he said. 'You'd better say thank you nicely.' Kate realized with a shudder that over the course of their short ride his tone had changed. She turned away abruptly and walked the short distance to the phone box and pulled open the heavy door. Which was enough to tell her that the place had been vandalized and she would not be calling anyone from there. Her heart began to thud uncomfortably as she realized that she might have jumped from the frying pan into something even worse. She cursed herself for a fool.

'You must have known this place was wrecked,' she said. 'Will you take me back to Southend now, please?'

'Not just yet, sweetheart,' the squaddie said, taking off his beret and tucking it into his epaulette.

'You owe me a thank-you for getting you away from those scallies. So give us a kiss, won't you?' He reached out a hand towards her but she quickly dodged round the corner of the wrecked box before he could get a grip. She glanced up and down the narrow lane, but although she could see lights in the distance there was no traffic in sight and no sound apart from the wind rustling the trees.

'You're no better than that gang back there,' she said angrily before she turned and ran. She had gained a slight advantage before she heard him start the scooter again and was conscious of him following close behind her.

'You won't get anywhere down here,' he said as he drew level. 'There's nothing here but the ranges and the road to Foulness Island. It's a bloody wilderness. I'll take you back if you're a good girl. I promise.'

Her heart pounding, Kate kept walking fast just ahead of the cruising scooter, aware that she could occasionally see the flash of headlights ahead, which might possibly mean salvation. Before they had gone far she was convinced that there was a busier road not far away and began to run in the middle of the lane, guessing that her tormentor would not run her down. But before she reached the junction he had skidded round her and stopped the bike broadside on, legs outstretched either side of the saddle, the engine ticking over, leaving her no room to squeeze past.

'Come on, darling, don't be shy. If you're out as late as this on your own, I'm sure you must be up for it.' Kate looked around frantically for a weapon of some kind, but all she could see in the light of the scooter's headlight was loose gravel at the side of the road. She scooped up a handful, threw it at his face, and as he cried out in fury dodged around the bike and ran for the main road as fast as she could. But it did not take him long to recover and as she reached the junction she felt a massive blow to her legs and back as the scooter hit her and she careered across the carriageway to land in the ditch on the other side of the road.

Cars were approaching in both directions. Her assailant spun his scooter around and accelerated back down the lane they had come along. Kate lay panting in the ditch for several minutes, cursing her own stupidity, before she gently tested all her limbs and found she could pull herself out of the ditch on to the edge of the road. The darkness was almost total. Feeling groggy and disoriented, she wondered if anyone would find her before morning.

EIGHTEEN

K ate O'Donnell woke with a start in a strange room that was almost completely dark. She seemed to be bundled under musty blankets on a sofa and was aching all over. She groaned but apparently no one heard and she tried shifting position to make her legs and hips more comfortable, but could not summon up the energy to shout. She could hear the low murmur of voices not far away, but could not tell who was speaking. She felt no inclination to move, her head aching almost as sharply as her legs, and eventually she dozed off again. The next time she woke, she was being shaken hard in a harsh light. She opened her eyes and to her astonishment found Ray Robertson leaning over her.

'Are you all right now?' he asked. 'You were lucky I found you when I did. You'd have frozen to death by morning. What happened for God's sake? How did you get to Shoeburyness and why were you sprawled across the road? I bloody nearly ran over you.' As he spoke, Kate's memory of her ordeal with an apparently helpful squaddie returned and she offered Robertson a few choice Scouse epithets as she told him everything that had happened after the police turned her out on to the streets of Southend.

'The police did it on purpose. I'm sure they did,' she said. 'DCI Baker told me to stay away from Southend and was obviously furious when I turned up again. To make matters worse, I'd tracked down Connie and her boy then lost them again and I had no idea where Delia was taking them. I was scared she was still in touch with her husband . . . I made a terrible mess of everything, and I couldn't get through to Harry. I would never have got on the back of a stranger's scooter if I hadn't been surrounded by a gang of scallies like that.' She felt a tear run down her cheek and dashed it away angrily. 'The lad on the scooter, the army lad, said he'd help. He seemed like a nice boy and I needed a phone box to get hold of Harry.'

'And?' Robertson said.

'Great mistake,' Kate said bitterly. 'I'd have been better off staying in the town centre and taking my chances with the scallies. There was no phone box that worked, just a pitch-dark road near the army barracks.'

'And then?'

'He wanted something in return,' Kate whispered. 'Don't they all? I should have known better after living all those years near the docks. So I ran.'

'Did he do anything to you?' Robertson asked and Kate could see the fury in his eyes.

'I didn't give him the chance,' Kate said. 'But he followed me and then rammed me with his scooter and knocked me over. But he took fright because I'd got to the main road and he went off the way we'd come, back down the lane.'

'Back to the barracks, I expect,' Robertson said. 'Try to remember everything that happened. When I did National Service, the military were pretty good at finding the bastards in their ranks. There's enough of them, especially when they've been boozing. And not the National Service boys either. It's generally the long-timers who end up in Colchester.'

'Colchester?'

'Military prison,' he said as if he knew it well.

'Can you take me back to London, please?' Kate asked. But Robertson shook his head slowly.

'That's the last place where I want to make an appearance right now,' he said.

'Where the hell am I?' Kate asked.

'You're at Delia Dexter's farmhouse on Foulness,' Robertson said. 'I needed to check something out with Delia before going on my way. Family stuff. She's my sister-in-law. What I said to Delia is that I'll take Connie Flanagan and the boy somewhere safe so she doesn't have to worry about them. I'll get hold of Flash Harry for you and tell him to come and pick you up. That's the best I can do. She's moving on herself, she says, but you'll be OK for tonight. I don't want to be nicked by some overenthusiastic copper at this stage in the game. I'm off out of it for a while, while the Met sort this mess out. Miller's killing was never anything to do with me and I'm not going to take the rap. Rod was a good bloke I'd known for years. I'd no more bump him off than I would my own ma.' Kate looked at him and almost believed him, but she felt deathly weary. The pain in her legs was jabbing intolerably and she didn't feel sure about anything.

'I couldn't get through to Harry,' Kate said. 'I don't know where the hell he can be at this time of night.'

'Looking for you I expect,' Robertson said. She wondered why he looked away so quickly and suspected he was lying, though she couldn't understand why. 'I'll keep trying his number. He'll be going frantic.'

'Will he?' Kate said doubtfully, wincing as she tried to sit upright. 'I'm never very sure about that.' Robertson stood up and helped her get her feet to the floor, but she couldn't move any further.

'Do you think you've broken anything? I had to carry you in here.' Kate shrugged and felt her knees.

'I don't know. The scooter pushed me sideways.'

'I'll get Delia to come and have a look at you now you're awake,' he said. 'Best if she does it, and I want to get on my way with Connie and the boy.'

'What are you doing here, anyway?' Kate asked.

'That's a very long story,' Robertson said. 'People kept telling me Loretta was looking for me and I knew that couldn't be right. I thought Delia could tell me what was going on.'

'And did she?' Kate asked. Robertson laughed, but there was no real mirth in it.

'Not entirely,' he said. 'I guess it was Delia looking for me in London. She's got some of Loretta's clothes here. They're twins, you know. And I knew damn well that it was unlikely to be Loretta toddling down Oxford Street. But what that was all about she wouldn't say – they always were a devious family, long before I met them – and I didn't hang around. I'll tell Harry where you are.'

'Look after Connie and the boy,' Kate whispered.

'Sounds as if somebody should,' Robertson said. 'Take more care now, will you?' Kate nodded and she watched him leave through the open door. He ushered Connie and Luke outside, then picked up what looked like a heavy suitcase that Delia

Dexter pushed in his direction. Within minutes she heard the sound of a car driving away, and then Delia came into the room with an unfriendly look on her face and shut the door behind her.

'I thought he was going to take you too,' she said. 'I suppose we'd better look at the state of you if you're staying. I can't get you to a doctor till the morning, so you'll have to manage with a bit of first aid until then. Where does it hurt?'

'Why the hell did you bring Connie and Luke out here and leave me in Southend?' Kate asked as Delia washed the cuts and bruises on her legs and applied some antiseptic.

'This seemed like the safest place and I'd left some of my stuff here,' Delia said. 'And you weren't needed any more. Those two are family. It was up to me to look after them now Bert's dead. I wasn't planning to keep them here except just overnight. I was going to move on in the morning. At least if I could get my car to start. It was supposed to be fixed the other day, but it was sounding a bit ropy by the time we got here.'

'You landed me in big trouble with the police,' Kate said, wincing as the antiseptic stung sharply. She glanced at her legs, which were badly cut and bruised, but as she flexed them experimentally it didn't feel as if anything was broken.

'And what's Ray Robertson doing here? He said he wanted to check something out with you?' she asked.

'He's family too, in a way, I suppose. Though I haven't seen him for years, not since the divorce,' Delia said. 'He wanted to know if I'd seen my sister. I thought she was in Spain, but he seemed to think she might be in England.'

'She was in London looking for him, according to my boyfriend in the Met,' Kate said cautiously, not sure which version of the story to believe. 'He saw her.'

'So I'm told,' Delia said sharply. 'She didn't bother to come and see me, did she? Stuck-up cow. There now.' She fastened a rough bandage with a safety pin and pulled Kate's trouser legs down. 'You'll survive till morning and then I'll drop you off at the hospital. Try to get some sleep.'

She turned the light out and closed the door behind her, leaving Kate to make the best of what would very likely be an uncomfortable night and quite sure that Robertson and his sister-in-law were not telling her anything like the truth.

The next time Kate woke, a pale grey light was filtering into the room through flimsy curtains and she was aware of loud shouting in the room next door. The voices were male, one relatively quiet but the other full of an anger that rose in intensity as the argument went on.

'I don't bloody believe you,' the more angry voice insisted. 'I don't believe that you and Bert and his wife didn't find the money and help yourselves to it. They were living on Canvey Island right up to the flood and no one else has even hinted that anyone else on that God-forsaken island found it. It must have been you and Bert and Connie. There's no one else. And Bert's your bloody brother. If he'd stumbled on a fortune you'd know about it. Don't tell me you wouldn't.'

'Is that why you killed him?' Kate heard Delia break in, sounding desperate. 'You've no idea what happened on this coast that night. You were safely tucked away in jail, well out of it. It wasn't just whatever you'd hidden that got washed away, you know. Whole houses were swept away, whole families and all they possessed. If you're still looking for your money you'd better start looking at the bottom of the North Sea, because that's where I guess it is. You've no idea what happened that night. We all had much more to think about than hidden loot. If you left it with Connie and Bert in that flimsy chalet, it was washed away and they were lucky not to have gone with it. Everyone was fighting for their lives that night with water up to the ceiling.'

'Which doesn't mean you or Bert wouldn't grab what you could,' the more angry voice broke in harshly. There was a sudden bang and a clatter and the quieter man seemed to gasp as the other gave a howl of rage.

'What's all this stuff here then, Delia?' he demanded. 'All this stuff in this cupboard. Silk dresses, a nice fox fur, hats . . . God knows what all this cost. Very nice for someone who's not supposed to have two pennies to rub together.'

'Leave that, Sam. They're mine.' Kate could hear the fear in Delia Dexter's voice as she pleaded with her former husband.

'Sure they don't belong to that sister of yours? Looks much more like her style. Fancy woman, Loretta. Is she back in the country? I thought she'd gone to live in Spain. Has she come over to get a cut too, you cheeky cow?'

'Not that I know of,' Delia said quickly. 'She left me some stuff to look after, that's all. It's been there years. It's not the sort of stuff I ever wear.'

'Wasn't she married to that boxing promoter Robertson? Always getting his picture in the papers in a poncey penguin suit with Lord This and Lady That?' the angrier voice broke in.

'She was,' Delia said. 'But they divorced years ago. Just like we did, Sam. I'm not your wife any more and she's not Ray Robertson's.'

'But that toerag Rod Miller worked for him, didn't he, after he left Southend? Who knows what Miller told Robertson about what was going on out here before we got nicked?' Kate guessed that this was the aptly named Bomber Barrett speaking, obviously consumed with fury. 'He worked for that puffed up ponce at his gym in Whitechapel all those years. I was sure that bastard Miller knew more than he was telling us. He had to, considering he was working for your bloody brother-in-law, who just happens to think he's Mister Big in Soho.'

'Not any more,' Delia said. 'As I hear it, Ray's disappeared and that poor beggar Miller's dead.'

'We made sure of that,' Barrett said and Kate hoped that the sharp breath she drew could not be heard by the group on the other side of the door.

'Never mind all that, Bomber.' The other voice – which Kate now realized belonged to Delia's ex-husband Sam – was obviously on the edge of panic. 'You never know when to keep your mouth shut, do you? They haven't done away with the noose yet, you know, in spite of all the chatter. They're probably saving a special rope for you.'

'What does it matter?' Barrett said. 'I thought you said it was all family here. Who's going to grass us up for murder?'

'You never had anything to do with Robertson, did you petal, after Loretta divorced him?' Dexter asked. 'I always thought you said she'd moved away. Spain was what I heard.'

'I never saw either of them after the divorce,' Delia said and Kate could hear the fear in her voice.

'You're a lying cow,' Barrett screamed. 'How come she left you all that stuff to look after if you haven't seen her for years?'

Kate froze as there were sounds of a scuffle in the outer room. She heard Delia cry out in pain or fear, or both, and Sam Dexter shout almost as angrily as Barrett.

'Leave her alone, Bomber!' he yelled. 'There's nothing to be had here. We've searched the place. The bloody money's gone. There's no point in more violence. How many people are you planning to kill anyway? Let's go. Now!'

Kate stood with her back to the door breathing heavily, knowing that if she was discovered eavesdropping by Barrett it would be the end of her. But Barrett seemed to be persuaded by Dexter's argument.

'We'll take this cow with us,' he said in more reasonable tones. 'Where's your car, Delia? There's no way I'm going back over those bloody sands.'

'You came over the Broomway?' Delia sounded surprised. 'I didn't know Sam knew the way.'

'Sam here persuaded me it would be best not to go through the checkpoints,' Barrett said. 'But I nearly ended up in the mud more than once. And there was fog coming down. We'll go back out on four wheels. Give me your keys, woman, and let's get going.' There was a moment of silence before Delia spoke again.

'It was giving me trouble when I got here,' she said tentatively. 'I'm not sure it'll start.'

'If it doesn't start, I'll take you across the sands and pitch you into the bloody mud.' Barrett screamed. The door banged and Kate could hear him trying to start the engine, until the battery finally died and he came back in beside himself with rage. She heard Delia cry out again and Dexter protest.

'Bloody leave her alone, Bomber!' he shouted. 'So we'll have to take the Broomway again. It'll be all right if you don't try to rush it. It won't be so dark now, so it'll be easier. You just have to keep calm and move carefully.'

'It's treacherous out there,' Delia said. 'And it's quite likely they'll start firing on the ranges as soon as it's light. If the red flags are flying, you shouldn't go near. You need to wait for daylight before it's safe, anyway, and for the tide. You'd be better off walking down the road and over the bridges.'

'And be clocked by the army,' Barrett snarled. 'Not likely. Anyway, you're coming with us. I'm not leaving you here to talk to the bloody cops. Where's your phone?' Delia didn't reply, but Kate could hear something being torn from the wall closest to her door. That was another link with the outside world severed, she thought, and she wondered again if she would get out of this situation alive. She didn't give much for Delia's chances or her own if she was discovered. As she stood with her back to the door praying that no one would be tempted to open it, to her surprise she heard the sound of a car outside. Then a new voice broke in, deep and slightly husky, which sounded familiar though she could not place it exactly. The front door slammed shut hard.

'Stop that or I'll blow you away,' the newcomer said. 'I came to see you, Delia. I didn't expect to find these two toerags here. It's a good job I came prepared, isn't it? Now let's be quick about this. You two get over there, and keep your hands where I can see them while Delia tells me where Connie Flanagan and her boy are hiding. I reckoned you might be stupid enough to give them shelter out here.'

'They're not here,' Kate heard Delia whisper. 'I've no idea where they are, Jasper. No idea at all.'

Of course, Kate thought, the voice belonged to Connie's uncle. And judging by the ease with which he had reduced Dexter and Barrett to silence, he had come armed.

'Come on, Jasper,' Dexter said with a note of desperate appeasement in his voice now. 'You know what we're looking for. And we think Delia knows the answer. You don't need to be waving that bloody shotgun at us. We're all in this together, aren't we? We were back then, and we're still looking for what we're owed. If you know who's got that money, we can find it and share it out.'

'There was a time that was true, but it's long gone,' Dowd said. 'I'm not interested in where your bloody money's gone any more, but if you start interfering with my family you'll live to regret it. Flanagan's dead, Connie's disappeared, and her kids are God knows where. And now you're threatening Delia. Get out of here before I blow you away. My finger's itchy. You can be back in Southend before the shops open if you start walking now.'

But Bomber Barrett's reaction was probably not what Dowd or anyone else expected. The sight of a firearm might reduce most people to fear, but from Barrett there was a shriek of pure rage. Then Kate heard the sounds of a sudden scuffle and an explosion echoed round the stone walls of the farmhouse, followed closely by a second one before Delia began to scream hysterically.

'Shut up woman,' Dowd said, sounding unperturbed. 'Now tell me where Connie and Luke are. Did they come here? Are they still here?'

'No. No, they're not,' Delia said through her sobs. But Dowd didn't appear to believe her.

'Let's just make sure, shall we?' he said. And before Kate could move away from the door, it was flung open and she found herself facing the tall tattooed showman, who held a still smoking shotgun in his hands.

'You!' he said. 'What the hell are you doing here?' He pulled her roughly into the living room, where the bodies of Dexter and Barrett lay sprawled across the floor in pools of blood and shredded flesh, and pushed her on to a chair. 'Sit very still while I think,' he said. Kate met Delia's eyes for a moment but could see nothing but shock there, which she guessed mirrored her own. Completely frozen by fear, she could not think of any way out of the situation they found themselves in and reckoned only that now Dowd had killed two people he would hardly hesitate to kill two more if he felt he needed to. But Dowd came up with a more complicated plan.

'Right,' he said. 'I need to get out of here and those two need to disappear. We'll put them into my car and shove the whole lot into the quicksands. It was nicked, anyway, so it can't be traced back to me, and it won't take long to disappear. Then we'll walk out. I need you, Delia, to navigate. It's years since I used that pathway. What do you call it, the Broomway? We'll have to wait until it gets properly light. No one's going to find that route in the dark. And you, miss, will have to come with us,' he said to Kate. 'You may come in useful if we're spotted. And when anyone comes out here, all they'll find is a patch of blood on the carpet and an empty house.' Kate looked at him appalled. Delia might make it back to dry land with Dowd, but she doubted very much that she would. She would die on Maplin Sands, just as Bert Flanagan had done, and no one she knew would be any the wiser.

NINETEEN

Harry Barnard woke up realizing that the loud banging was not just the thumping in his head but was also shaking his front door. He rolled off the sofa, which was where he found himself, but he had no idea why he had slept there rather than in his bed, although he had a vague and uneasy memory that Kate had not come home last night. He staggered to the door and opened it, and to his surprise found a uniformed sergeant and a constable he did not know standing outside in the hallway with unfriendly expressions on their faces.

'DS Harry Barnard?' the sergeant asked. Barnard nodded, his stomach clenched tight as a dim memory of the previous evening's events filtered back into his mind through what seemed like chunks of cotton wool.

'Is it Kate?' he whispered, but the officers looked puzzled and didn't bother to ask who Kate might be.

'We're local, from Highgate, but your DCI wants you at your nick now,' the sergeant said. 'We're to take you in to see him.'

'Are you arresting me?' Barnard asked, mouth dry and hands clenched.

'Not necessarily,' the sergeant said. 'Let's just say he didn't give you the option to say no and he wants to be sure you get there.'

'Jesus wept!' Barnard exclaimed, panic threatening him as his head cleared enough to recall quite clearly that he had not heard anything from Kate for twenty-four hours and he had no idea where she was. But it was obvious that his colleagues from Highgate were not interested in any of that, and clearly the sooner he got away from them the better.

'We'd better go then,' he said, picking up his coat and hat from the chair where he had evidently dropped them the previous evening and trying to conceal the raw fear he felt. 'I need to talk to DCI Jackson just as much as he needs to talk to me.'

The journey into the West End passed in silence and Barnard spent the time trying to put his thoughts into some sort of order.

He remembered getting home and he remembered his fear when he discovered that Kate could not be found. He also remembered Ray Robertson's unexpected arrival and what must have developed into a blazing row which ended with Ray hitting him hard. After that, he had no recollection of anything until he woke on the sofa to the thunderous banging in his head and on the door.

Walking ahead of his escort, he went straight to DCI Jackson's office and found his boss on the phone. He glanced at Barnard with open hostility.

'I'll tell him that,' he said to whoever was at the other end of the line and, although he waved the two uniformed officers from Highgate out of the door, he did not wave Barnard into a chair.

'Give me one good reason why I shouldn't have you arrested and charged with assisting a fugitive to escape,' he said.

'Because that never happened, guv,' Barnard said flatly.

'Pull the other one, Sergeant,' Jackson scoffed. 'Robertson was spotted last night close to your flat by a beat officer who didn't have the sense to report it until he came off duty this morning. He was heading to see you, I suppose?'

'He turned up unannounced, guv,' Barnard said, his mouth like sandpaper and his head still feeling as if it was being assaulted by a cannon.

'And you didn't call in? You let him walk away?'

'Not quite. As far as I can remember, it developed into a brawl. He hit me hard and I didn't come round till this morning. He was a contender once, a handy man with his fists in and out of the ring. I wasn't expecting it. I was about to come in to talk to you when our friends from Highgate nick turned up.'

'So you say,' Jackson snapped. 'And what caused this alleged brawl?'

'I told him I wouldn't cover for him,' Barnard said, almost sure that since he ended up unconscious that must have been what he had said. 'I said I couldn't and I wouldn't. I told him to come in and talk to you about the alibi he claims he has for Rod Miller's murder.'

'Did he tell you where he was going next?'

Barnard shrugged. 'I don't think so, but it's all a bit fuzzy.' He fingered his head and realized that not only was there a large bruise at the base of his skull but that his hair was matted with

dried blood still oozing enough to stain his fingers red, which
suggested that he had hit something pretty solid on the way down.
'I was out cold. I didn't wake up until I heard the local plods
trying to bash my door down.'

'You expect me to believe all this?' Jackson asked. 'After your
history with Robertson? Did he arrive by car?'

'Yes,' Barnard said. 'Well, I think so. Or maybe he said he'd
left his car and come in on the Northern Line.'

'Did you see a car? Make and number?'

'No, I didn't see one,' he said, still unable to recall what
Robertson had said about his plans. 'He wanted to use my
phone—'

He broke off, suddenly feeling dizzy, and put a bloodied hand
out to steady himself on the back of a chair. Jackson harrumphed
angrily.

'Sit down, Sergeant,' he said. 'If you're as bad as that, you'd
better see the doctor. You don't look fit for duty.' Barnard took
a deep breath to steady himself.

'You're probably right,' he said. 'But there's something else,
guv. My girlfriend, Kate O'Donnell, is missing. I think she went
to Southend yesterday, and she hasn't come home. I was about
to ring Southend nick last night when Ray Robertson turned up
and I never got the chance. It's been twenty-four hours since I've
heard from her.'

Jackson sat and looked at Barnard intently for a moment.

'The Yard want you suspended now, this minute,' he said.
'That's who I was talking to when you came in. But I want a
medical report before we go any further. See the doctor and make
sure he lets me have an assessment immediately. In the meantime,
I'll mention Miss O'Donnell's disappearance to Southend.
Twenty-four hours isn't very long for a missing person, but she
seems to have a remarkable ability to push her nose in where
it's not wanted, so I suppose we'd better make sure she's safe.
We'll continue our conversation when the doctor says you're fit
to answer more questions. But don't take that as any indication
I believe a word you've told me about what happened last night
between you and Robertson. You are skating on very thin ice,
Sergeant. Very thin. Now get out before I change my mind.'

*   *   *

The police doctor probed Barnard's head wound with what he thought were unnecessarily heavy fingers, cleaned it up and inserted two stitches which he protected with a bandage.

'The DCI tells me you're having trouble remembering what happened,' the doctor said. 'That's not unusual after concussion. I'll report back and advise him to leave it twenty-four hours before he talks to you again. In the meantime, go home and rest and ring your own doctor if it gets any worse. Don't drink alcohol, that won't help. And don't drive.'

'Aspirins?' Barnard asked.

'Aspirins are fine,' the doctor said. Barnard picked up his coat and hat and made his way unsteadily to the door. In the corridor outside he was stopped by DC Peter Stansfield, who looked slightly embarrassed by Barnard's unusually dishevelled state – shirt crumpled, tie askew and coat pulled on over the rest with the collar tucked inside at the neck. Flash Harry knew he was not looking flash this morning.

'You OK, Sarge?' he asked. 'The guv'nor told me to try to catch you with a message before you went off sick.'

'Right . . .' Barnard said cautiously.

'He said to tell you that Southend took a statement off Miss O'Donnell and let her go yesterday evening. They haven't seen her since. He's asked them to keep an eye out for her. Is that OK?'

Barnard groaned.

'I very much doubt it,' he said. 'Thanks, anyway.'

'You're welcome, Harry,' Stansfield said and turned on his heel leaving Barnard in near despair, his head banging and his stomach churning. How, he wondered wearily, had he allowed himself to get into this state over Kate? But he knew the answer.

After taking a cab home, Barnard stripped off and had a shower before brewing coffee with his usual care. Having swallowed two cups and three aspirins, he slumped in his revolving chair wondering wearily where to start looking for Kate. As the drugs kicked in and the headache receded, he felt his brain move slowly back into gear and his memory of last night's events improving. He got up and looked at the coffee table, which was standing unusually askew. On one corner he could discern a trace of dried blood and a few dark hairs – his own, he assumed – and beneath the table a small brownish stain. He smiled slightly. He was used to looking at forensic traces, but generally not his own. When he looked back to the previous night's events, he realized that Ray had probably not hit him hard enough to knock him out. It was the table that had done the damage, a thought which he found oddly comforting.

He sat down again and tried to work out what Ray had told him before his explosion of temper. He had, he realized, talked of going abroad but needing to see someone before he went. And one word became insistent. Gyppos. Ray had talked about gyppos. And so, he recalled with greater clarity, had Ray's mother the last time he spoke to her. Ray's ex-wife, Loretta, was a gyppo, she had said. And his ex-wife had been looking for him at the club, and probably at the gym as well. And she had a sister called Delia at the farm on Foulness who had been married for years to Sam Dexter, the Southend post office robber just out of jail. If Robertson was going to see Delia, Barnard concluded, there had to be a much closer relationship between him and the Southend criminal fraternity than anyone had ever suspected. And he began to wonder how completely he had been conned by Ray and for how long. He pulled his car keys out of his pocket and dangled them over a third cup of coffee. Kate had last been seen in Southend, and Ray Robertson he was certain had been on his way there last night. Concussion or no concussion, he needed to get there fast.

Later Barnard could remember very little about his drive to Southend except the mist rolling in from the estuary and that his safe arrival outside the nick had been achieved more by luck than judgement. He walked into the police station and, waving his warrant card, pushed past everyone waiting to speak to the desk sergeant.

'Is DCI Baker in?' he asked. The sergeant looked as though he was about to protest but took a second look at Barnard's expression and changed his mind.

'First floor, beyond the CID office, if it's urgent.'

'It's urgent,' Barnard snapped. He followed the desk sergeant's directions to Baker's office, knocked cursorily on the door and went in. Baker was at his desk, head down over a pile of paperwork. His face reddened when he recognized Barnard and took in his dishevelled state and the bandage across his head.

'What the hell are you doing here?' he asked. 'I thought I told you to stay well out of my way.'

'My girlfriend is missing and I reckon you or someone in this nick must have been the last person to see her,' Barnard said, knowing that his voice was slurred. 'Sir,' he added as an afterthought.

Baker looked for a moment as if he were about to explode, but thought better of it as Barnard swayed and sat down abruptly and uninvited.

'Sorry,' he said. 'I got hit on the head last night.'

'Your guv'nor told me,' Baker conceded. 'And the rest. And I told him that Miss O'Donnell left here safe and well last night after giving us a statement.'

'In time to catch the last train?'

'How should I know? I'm not her bloody nanny. Didn't she phone you?' Baker asked.

'I wasn't in a fit state to answer the phone,' Barnard said. 'I was out cold.' The two men stared at each other, Baker in exasperation and Barnard in increasing fear.

'Did she tell you in her statement what she'd been doing yesterday? Who she talked to?' he asked eventually.

'She'd been poking her nose in again,' Baker said. 'She'd been in touch with Connie Flanagan again and with Delia Dexter, Sam Dexter's ex, who was a Flanagan before she married. And she claimed that Delia had driven off with Connie and her son, though she didn't know where they were going. I told her she was a bloody pain in the neck and should go home.'

'Well, she never made it,' Barnard said, close to despair. Baker looked at him for a long moment then sighed.

'Mrs Dexter might have gone to the farm on Foulness Island,' he conceded. 'Maybe your Miss O'Donnell followed them there.'

'How would she do that?' Barnard asked. 'It's miles away.'

'All right, all right,' Baker said. 'It's not as if I don't want to track Connie Flanagan down myself. She's still on bail. I'll get one of my DCs to make some inquiries. The military keep a check on who goes in and out. We'll ask them if there's been any movement overnight. In fact, I might ask them to send one of their sentries down to take a look at the farm. It would be quicker than driving to Foulness from here in this fog.'

Barnard swallowed hard.

'Thank you,' he said. 'Can I get some coffee in your canteen?'

In the end, though, the police had to drive through the fog to Lane End Farm. A military police officer had come back to Baker quite quickly to report that the farmhouse was empty but the doors had been left unlocked and there was blood spattered around the living room and shotgun pellets embedded in two of the walls. A car with a flat battery had been abandoned outside, and nowhere was there any sign of life.

Baker had put Harry Barnard in the back seat of his car for the painfully slow journey through the fog. They stopped at the checkpoint to confirm who had come and gone through it the previous day. The log confirmed that the abandoned car had gone through, with two women in the front. Later, a man and woman had gone in and come out again after about an hour. There had been nothing suspicious about the coming and going – in fact the sentry had recognized Delia Dexter as a regular who lived on the island, although he had never seen the other driver before. The only other visitor was a solitary driver who, in spite of the deteriorating visibility as the mist began to roll in from the river, claimed to be heading to the pub in the village. There was no record of his having gone back, but that might have been just because of the weather.

Barnard absorbed this information and found little comfort in it. It appeared that Delia Dexter had not taken Kate to the farm, and he had no idea whether the other cars had any connection with Delia or not. Baker's enquiries, he became convinced, could have little to do with Kate's disappearance and as he gazed out of the car window at the mist swirling across the bleak fields and ranges he wondered if time had already run out.

When the car finally pulled up at Lane End Farm, Barnard insisted on getting out and following Baker into the building after his driver, DS Reg Hamilton, a tall taciturn man with the shoulders of a prizefighter and an expression to match. Outside the temperature felt Arctic and it was just as bitterly cold inside the farmhouse, the fog that seeped in through the open door forming a haze around the underpowered lights. And it smelt like a butcher's shop. After a quick look at two distinct areas of clotted blood on the floor and walls inside the house, Barnard quickly stepped into the fresh air again as nausea threatened to overcome him. He knew that Delia Dexter had a shotgun – after all, he and Kate had been threatened with it. But he had never imagined she could use it on a human being, even less on two. More likely, he thought, she had been one of the victims and Connie Flanagan the other. His mind flinched at the possibility that one of those pools of blood might be all that was left of Kate.

Taking gulps of cold air, he went back inside. Wandering around the blood-stained room, he idly pushed open the door into an adjoining space where the curtains were still closed. He pulled them back, which only marginally improved the illumination, but found nothing of interest until he moved back towards the door and felt something crunch beneath his feet. He bent down to see what he had stepped on and drew a sharp breath as he picked up a gold chain with a pendant with a single stone at the centre. The setting was crushed, the gold chain snapped and grimy. He gripped the necklace tight and swayed slightly, before staggering back into the farmhouse kitchen only to find it deserted.

Out of the window he could see DCI Baker bustling out of the house and making his way back to the car. He rested against the door jamb for a moment before stepping outside and then, as his sick headache almost overcame him, had to lean against the outer stone wall. He lit a cigarette with shaking hands and took several drags before he was able to summon the strength to follow the DCI across the yard.

'Oh, there you are,' Baker said irritably. 'As I see it, we've two possibilities. We need to trace the man and woman who came over the bridge by car and left again after about an hour, and the man who claimed to be going to the pub and appears not to have gone back through the checkpoint at all. We can easily check that out. I've put someone back at the nick on to that. The other possibility is to assume that someone came in by one of the illicit routes over the sands and went back the same way. You're not supposed to go near the sands without the military's permission, but they won't be firing today in this fog.'

'You reckon they could take bodies with them?' Barnard asked incredulously.

'There's one sure way to get rid of bodies not far from here,' Baker said bluntly. 'And that's on the sands.'

'Jesus wept!' Barnard said, shivering violently. He held his hand out to Baker.

'I found this,' he said, handing him the crumpled necklace. 'It's Kate O'Donnell's. She must have been here.'

'How do you know that?' Baker snapped.

'Because I gave it to her for her birthday. She's been here, and either she dropped it deliberately so we would know or someone wrenched it off her neck.'

The thought that if the second of these possibilities was true then one of the clotted puddles of blood on the farmhouse floor was hers hit him like a punch in the stomach. He turned away and walked back across the yard hardly able to breathe. As he stood by the door waiting for his heart to stop thumping against his ribs, the fog lifted slightly revealing a second farm gate opposite the one they had come in by. Looking harder, he could see ruts leading to the gate that were obviously fresh, as there was no sign of their having been disturbed since they were made.

'Guv!' he shouted across the yard. 'Do we know where this track goes? There are fresh tyre marks here.'

The Essex officers hurried over.

'It goes down to the river,' DS Hamilton said. 'I think it leads to the track across the sands. To the Broomway. But I don't see how anyone could have gone that way in the dark and fog. It's difficult enough in daylight, and you need to know the tides.'

'Can we have a look, guv?' Barnard asked and hoped his voice did not sound too desperate. Baker looked at him and nodded.

'Maybe we'd better,' he said.

They drove in silence across foggy tracts of flat sodden land. The track occasionally seemed to almost disappear, only to appear again through a muddy landscape of pools and waterlogged grass. Eventually Sergeant Hamilton pulled up at a point where even in the poor visibility it was clear that the narrow road headed down a slope and into the estuary.

'There's the car,' Baker said. Ahead of them the roof of a car could be seen just visible above the waterline. 'If they thought it would sink, they misjudged it in the fog. Reg, get on to the army again and see if they can help pull it out.'

'You think whoever pushed it in will have gone across the sands?' Barnard asked.

'There's no other reason to drive down here, is there?' Baker said. 'We know no one's gone out over the bridges.'

They got out of the car and walked along the start of the muddy Broomway until they were only feet from the submerged vehicle. 'It could be an accident, I suppose. A misjudgement in the fog, and all the occupants were trapped inside.'

'I don't think so,' Barnard said quietly as he stared at the ground. 'There are footprints on the track here. As well whoever was inside, there were people outside the car too.'

'Another murder then?' Baker asked himself as much as the two sergeants. 'Or disposal of the bodies? Either way, we've got an evil bastard here. Have you made contact with the army?' His sergeant nodded.

'They'll bring a winch,' Hamilton said.

'Right, you stay here and wait for the troops,' Baker said. 'I'll take Sergeant Barnard back to civilization and see if we can arrange to cut them off before they get away.'

'Where will they come ashore?' Barnard asked as the DCI accelerated down the muddy track back to the village, swinging wildly in his hurry.

'Wakering Steps,' Baker said. 'There are various places where you can get back to the shore, but if you want to avoid the checkpoint you have to go beyond the bridges. Unless they set off in the dark, I doubt they'll have got that far by now in this fog. They'd have to wait for something approaching daylight and probably for the tide. Anything else would be suicide. The only thing in their favour is that no one will be firing today, but the place is littered with unexploded ordnance. It's not a place you go for a Sunday stroll.'

Barnard lit another cigarette and drew deeply. If I was a religious man, he thought, I would say a prayer. Failing that, he cursed steadily as Baker flung the car through Delia Dexter's farmyard gate, past her own car with the dead battery, and then down the track through the village and along the military road back to civilization. He put his hand in his coat pocket where he had put Kate's pendant and clutched it so tightly that the sharp edges cut into his palm. But he hardly noticed. He knew with no doubt at all that if she was dead he might as well be dead himself.

TWENTY

For the fifth or sixth time Kate slipped on the mud and clutched Delia Dexter's shoulder to keep herself upright. She was bitterly cold and she was terrified as Dowd, who was walking last in their column of three, prodded her in the back with his shotgun, making her wonder how long he would have the patience to continue at her slow pace. The fog was still thick and Delia, who reckoned she knew the way across the Broomway even in this weather, occasionally moved so far ahead she could barely see her. But with her bruised and cut legs, from which Delia's makeshift bandages had long since disappeared into the mud, she struggled to keep up. Her feet and legs stung and jabbed intolerably. And after more than an hour of struggling through the sticky black dirt she did not think she could go on much longer, though Dowd continued to poke her in the ribs with his gun to hurry her up.

Delia had driven the three of them to the sands at Asplins Head, where the Broomway came back to dry land. Dowd had sat in the back with the shotgun close to Kate's neck. Nobody spoke, but there was a sense of menace coming from the big muscular man behind them and Kate guessed that he had found no difficulty in heaving the two bodies into the boot, which he had left ajar. She wondered if her fate was to be heaved into the car with them when they reached their destination. Delia followed a slow and erratic course through a landscape where none of them could see further than a couple of feet ahead, but she never hesitated. It was obviously a route she knew well. She finally stopped where the track began to drop through a gap in some sort of dimly visible embankment following the coast on either side. As she followed Dowd's order to get out of the car, she guessed that there was nothing but the sands stretching out to sea for miles. The silence was almost unbroken, with not even the cry of a gull to be heard.

Dowd stood for a moment looking around and in particular at Kate.

'Can you really not get a vehicle across?' he asked Delia.

'No chance,' she said. 'A few fools have tried, but the track won't take the weight. The cars have got bogged down and the drivers have had to be rescued – or sometimes not. We're not even supposed to use it without permission from the army, but that's not going to matter in this.' She glanced around at the enveloping fog and shrugged.

'Right, the car goes in,' Dowd said. 'You can help me push, and if you don't behave you'll go in with it. We need to get down the slope on to the soggy stuff. I'm guessing that once we've got it into the mud it'll sink under it's own weight.' And the weight of two bodies – or maybe three – Kate thought. Delia maintained a brooding silence.

Reluctantly the two women did as Dowd instructed and put their weight behind the two front doors, while Dowd pushed strongly from behind. Eventually the car gained some momentum and toppled from the causeway into the mud, where it immediately began to founder, sending only an occasional murky bubble up to the surface.

Kate was aware of Delia gazing at Jasper Dowd. 'Don't even think about it,' she said at length. 'If I go, she goes too. She might be useful in the end, anyway.'

The three of them waited for what seemed like hours beside the gradually sinking car. Eventually Delia said it was light enough, in spite of the fog, to make a start across the sands. She had assured them there were markers along the Broomway to guide them. But although the tide had now noticeably begun to ebb away down the track sloping into the estuary, Kate had not seen many of those so far. Meanwhile the surface squelched beneath them and their feet were occasionally sucked into the mud, so that they had to pause to extricate themselves before the three of them could set off in single file again across the black stuff that the tide had left behind. Kate, on the edge of panic, began to wonder whether Delia had decided not to lead them to dry land, as she had promised, but was deliberately taking them out to sea – where they would be unseen from the shore in the swirling fog and would undoubtedly drown as the tide quietly rose and engulfed them. Dowd was deadly dangerous, but Delia too was unpredictable and hardly someone who could be relied on. But with Dowd's shotgun at her back, Delia Dexter was her only hope. She had to trust her to take them safely across the sands. The alternative was despair. There was no way and no place to run.

The fog was still thick when DCI Baker and DS Harry Barnard arrived at Wakering Steps, where the Broomway climbed gently up from the sands on to the mainland close to Great Wakering village and the army base at Shoeburyness. When Barnard got out of the car, he realized how busy Baker and Hamilton had been on the phone. They found half a dozen police officers and the same number of soldiers waiting for them where a reasonably firm causeway could be seen heading off into the waterlogged sands before disappearing into the fog. A military police officer with sergeant's stripes detached himself from the huddle of troops – all carrying regulation rifles, Barnard noticed with surprise – and hurried over to make himself known to the DCI.

'Normally we'd have the red flags flying by now, sir,' he said curtly. 'No one should be out there on the ranges today, whatever the visibility. When your officer reported that they'd started from Asplins Head, which is three miles away, we knew it would take them a couple of hours to cross – more, probably, in this fog. If they make it, that is. You couldn't have conditions more conducive to getting lost out there, I hope you realize that.' Baker nodded but did not argue, and Barnard groaned. These people knew the area and would not be exaggerating the risks. Out here he was a rank amateur.

For more than half an hour the welcome party, which would be only too unwelcome to Jasper Dowd if he and his companions made it, peered into the fog but saw nothing.

'Couldn't you go out to meet them?' Barnard asked the MP, who glanced at him with contempt.

'From what I've been told, your man is armed and not shy of using his shotgun,' he said. 'The sands are treacherous. If anyone panics for any reason and leaves the Broomway, we might never see them again in this weather. It's not just the mud. There's stray ordnance out there. You need to be able to see where you're going, and today you can't.' He glanced at his watch. 'It'll be high tide again at 13.50. We need them all out of there long before that.'

Barnard's shoulders slumped, and he sat down on a concrete barrier sited to prevent vehicles reaching the sands and lit another cigarette. He wondered how his life had imploded so comprehensively and whether there was anything he could have done differently to save Kate from this. Even the police and the army troops seemed to be infected by the same pessimism and gathered in silent huddles, while DCI Baker and the MP sergeant stood with binoculars focused on the spot where the Broomway faded into the deep grey haze but apparently seeing nothing.

Barnard kept looking at his watch, realizing that the tide would have begun to flow towards the land again. He didn't think it would surge in – there was no wind although the fog banks appeared to swirl around, but that would make no difference to the incoming water. It would slowly and steadily rise and eventually sweep across the track and continue inexorably, so that anyone out there would drown. He had seen what water could do on Canvey Island all those years ago, and knew there was no way of stopping it. At high tide no doubt boats could get out on to the sands, but that would be too late.

Another half hour inched by and Barnard smoked his last cigarette. As he ground it out, the whole waiting group was galvanized by the sound of a shot.

'Shotgun,' the army sergeant said. 'And not far out either.' He raised his binoculars again and peered into the gloom. 'I can see something, but not how many people it is.' He turned to DCI Baker. 'If we can all get out of sight, sir, they may just walk out. If we can't see them, they won't see us. It's worth a try.' The two men waved the whole group back, away from the last few yards of the track behind the sea wall. Baker gripped Barnard's arm tightly.

'Don't do anything stupid, Sergeant,' he said. Barnard did not reply but crouched down with the rest, out of sight of the Broomway's end. In the event it was Jasper Dowd, still holding his shotgun, who emerged from the sands first, boots and trousers caked with thick mud and half-dragging, half-carrying a woman, exhausted and staggering, behind him. He had neither time nor energy to raise his gun before he was surrounded by troops with their rifles at the ready. Barnard realized instantly that Dowd's companion was not Kate – it was Delia Dexter, and there was no sign of anyone else emerging from the fog. He grabbed Delia's arm so hard she cried out.

'Where's Kate?' he demanded. 'Has that bastard killed her?' Delia looked at him with tears in her eyes.

'She couldn't walk any further,' she said. 'He shot at her, but I think she dodged him and disappeared into the fog. I was in front, so I didn't see it clearly. She's somewhere out there still.'

Barnard let go, and before anyone could stop him ran down the slipway and on to the sands. The MP officer gestured to two of his men and they followed more slowly.

'Wait!' he shouted at Barnard. 'You don't know where it's safe.' Barnard slowed slightly and allowed the men following him to catch up.

'She must be close to the track,' he said, his breath catching in his throat.

'Try shouting,' the MP said. 'She may hear you before she can see you.' The four men shouted in unison and then listened, but there was no sound except the slight gurgling of the water as the tide began to move in. They walked cautiously along the track and as they went the fog began imperceptibly to thin, drifting in white clouds above the emerging miles of sodden sands. Barnard swallowed hard.

'I heard something,' he said. 'Listen.' It was the faintest of cries, clearly seeking help. Treading carefully off the Broomway towards the shore, they eventually saw Kate lying in the mud, which had sucked her far enough in for her to be unable to gain enough purchase to stand up again.

'One each side,' the MP said sharply. 'Under her arms. She'll be all right if we're careful.' He and Barnard took hold of Kate and gradually eased her out of what had been so close to becoming a greedy sodden grave, then the other two soldiers helped carry her back to the relative safety of the track.

Barnard doubled over, then took Kate's limp hand and squeezed it hard.

'Jesus wept!' he whispered close to Kate's ear. 'Don't do that again, sweetheart. I can't lose you now.'

*   *   *

The next morning Harry Barnard sat by Kate's hospital bed in Southend, where she was recovering from her ordeal on Maplin Sands. Once she had been patched up as an emergency, the doctors had recommended that she stay in overnight for observation and she had thankfully let sleep overwhelm her.

Barnard had gone home looking shell-shocked. He arrived back bringing clean clothes to replace the outfit, now mud-sodden, she had gone to Southend in the day before. 'I chucked your other stuff in the bin,' he said, putting a carrier bag on the bed. 'We're ready to go as soon as the doctors are happy with you.'

His explanatory phone call to DCI Jackson had been met by a chilly acknowledgement. Clearly there would be an unpredictable and possibly terminal reckoning back at the nick when he finally reported in, with the Yard no doubt still breathing down the DCI's neck. In the meantime he quietly celebrated the fact that when Kate had woken from what looked like a profound sleep her eyes had met his and she'd summoned a wan smile which he reckoned was much better than no smile at all.

'Are you feeling any better?' he asked. 'Really?'

She nodded almost imperceptibly. 'Where were you?' she whispered. 'I couldn't get hold of you when I needed you, la, and then the whole thing got out of hand.' She shut her eyes to try to escape the kaleidoscope of appalling images that the long night and early morning had left behind. Worst of all was the constriction in her chest as she remembered how the quicksands had clutched her tight as she slipped into their grasp. 'I thought I was going to die,' she said. 'But if I hadn't run, he'd have shot me.'

Barnard took her hand, feeling helpless.

'Did they get Jasper?' she persisted. 'He was obviously in on the robberies.'

'Remanded in custody this morning, with a charge sheet as long as your arm. And they're holding Delia Dexter. Whose side was she on, for God's sake?'

'She was all right, la,' Kate insisted. 'She did her best to help. Is she all right? She tried to help me. I think Dowd would have shot me back on Foulness and dumped me with the others if it hadn't been for her. He'd nothing much to lose by then, and I knew too much. She convinced him I might be more use as a hostage.'

'I can't think what they might charge her with. She was obviously acting under duress.'

'But what I don't understand is what Ray Robertson was doing out there. He kept saying he was going away but then he did that long trip out to the farm. He said he wanted to know if Delia was pretending to be her sister, but why did it matter? It didn't make sense. He picked me up off the road and then ended up taking Connie and Luke away but refused to take me. Somewhere safe for them, he said.' Barnard gave her a curious look.

'Do you know where he took them?' he asked. 'Or why?'

'I've no idea,' Kate said.

'There was I thinking that it must be Delia who had got hold of the money and had probably spent it, but maybe it wasn't,' Barnard said. 'She didn't look as if she had two pennies to spare, did she? Maybe Connie and Bert somehow managed to hang on to it through the flood, keeping it safe for the other two in jail. And then when Bert was murdered, Connie decided to hang on to it herself.'

'Connie took a bag with her to Foulness,' Kate said. 'I saw her put it into Delia's car. But I guess Delia would have searched that. She gave it to Ray willingly enough when they left. I saw her. But I think mainly she was just relieved to get out of there. She must have guessed her husband and Barrett would eventually turn up.'

'We didn't go through the bags Connie carried to Clacton, did we?' Barnard whispered. 'But you can bet your life Ray did when he got her there and made himself at home with her Auntie Vi. He wouldn't miss a trick like that. He can be very persuasive when he tries.'

'I never fathomed why Ray went out to Foulness, anyway,' Kate said.

'Ray has an unerring instinct for the main chance,' Barnard said. 'He must have known for years that the cash from those robberies had never been recovered. Rod Miller could have told him easily enough. And once Dexter and Barrett were on the loose again, it got urgent. With his connections to the Flanagan family from way back, he must have reckoned he stood as good a chance as anybody of getting hold of it.'

'Right,' Kate said.

'Your friend DCI Baker will want statements from you about what happened, but I've told him he'll have to wait until you've recovered. Jackson even allowed me that much when I stupidly knocked myself out.' He hadn't told Kate yet about Ray Robertson's involvement in that episode. He would wait to see what the Yard made of it before giving her something else to worry about.

'Baker won't like waiting,' Kate said.

'He turned out OK in the end,' Barnard said. 'He got hold of the cavalry when it was needed. Armed to the teeth, too. Dowd took one look at those six rifles and gave up.'

'Baker's a bully,' Kate said with a spark of anger. 'He nearly got me raped.'

Barnard's expression hardened.

'We'll talk to the military police about that,' he said. 'Would you recognize the bastard again?'

'You bet,' Kate said. 'And his scooter.'

'We'll pass that bit of information on to Jack Baker before we head home,' he said. 'Are you ready to go?'

'Oh yes,' Kate said. 'Good and ready.'

'Let's face the music then, shall we?'

Lightning Source UK Ltd.
Milton Keynes UK
UKOW03f1628080217
293940UK00001B/8/P